COLD JUSTICE

Rayven T. Hill

Ray of Joy Publishing

Ray of Joy Publishing
Toronto

Books by Rayven T. Hill

Blood and Justice
Cold Justice
Justice for Hire
Captive Justice
Justice Overdue
Justice Returns
Personal Justice
Silent Justice
Web of Justice
Fugitive Justice

Visit rayventhill.com for more information on these and future releases.

This book is a work of fiction. Names, characters, places, businesses, organizations, events and incidents either are the product of the author's imagination or are used fictitiously. Any resemblance to actual persons, living or dead, events or locales is entirely coincidental.

Published by Ray of Joy Publishing
Toronto

Second Edition

ISBN-13: 978-0-9938625-1-9

COLD JUSTICE

PROLOGUE

Monday, August 15th, 1:12 a.m.

ABIGAIL MACY'S pain ran deep. Her once beautiful life had been shattered.

She had never considered herself to be a strong woman, and the shrink she was seeing twice weekly had concluded she was suffering from anxiety disorder brought on by her recent tragedy.

She was filled with overwhelming feelings of panic and fear, uncontrollable obsessive thoughts, and recurring nightmares.

Her job performance had suffered. Personal relationships were falling apart, and now, she half-staggered the four blocks home, disappointed that the pain she had been feeling earlier had not been successfully smothered this time by her evening at Eddie's.

They had seen her there often lately, as a recent but now frequent customer. She hated herself for it, but the reprieve helped to dull her senses.

Usually.

This time, her effort to gain relief made her pain more overwhelming, and tonight she sobbed quietly to herself as she walked down the dark street, toward her home and her faithful husband.

As she went, she began to feel ill. Physically ill. Nauseous.

At first she thought it was another panic attack, but soon realized the consumption of one too many glasses of cheap house wine at Eddie's had been the cause.

She stopped and took a deep breath. Her queasy stomach was rebelling. She looked around. The street was quiet, so she stepped off the sidewalk and leaned over beside a hedge dividing two properties. There she deposited the contents of her stomach.

She looked up and hoped she hadn't been seen. There was a light on in the front room of the house directly in front of her, but no one was around.

As she turned away, the sound of running footsteps came to her from the side of the house. She heard a cry for help. A woman's voice.

She crouched in the shadows, frozen, watching. She saw as the helpless woman came into view, scrambling and stumbling. She stood rigid and motionless as the half-naked woman was overtaken, grabbed from behind, and brought to the ground. She saw her attacker kneel beside her, saw his hands go about her throat and cut short her final scream.

His victim struggled and clawed feebly. Soon all was still and quiet.

Abigail Macy saw the killer rise to his feet, then lean over and grab the woman's hands. He began dragging her across the grass toward the darkness at the edge of the home.

She felt numb and lightheaded. The branches beside her rustled and crunched as she rose to her feet. As she stared open-mouthed, he stopped and looked up from the shadows, staring into her frightened eyes.

She turned and ran.

She heard him behind her now, and she chanced a glance over her shoulder. He was close and getting closer with each step.

Home was just ahead. Home and safety. She forced herself on, terrified and exhausted.

She stumbled the last few feet and fell onto the brightly lit steps of her home. She was unable to move, but was relieved to see her would-be attacker was gone.

After a while, she rose to her feet. She fumbled in her handbag for her key and opened the door. She fell inside and lay there for a few minutes before finally slipping quietly upstairs, careful not to wake her sleeping husband as she tiptoed past their room and fell exhausted into the safe double bed in the guest room.

CHAPTER 1

Monday, August 15th, 3:32 p.m.

JAKE LINCOLN sauntered into the home office and plunked his six-foot-four-inch body into the guest chair in front of the desk just as Annie dropped the phone back into its cradle.

"Who was that?" he asked.

"CNN."

"What did they want this time?"

"More of the same. Seems like the whole world wants a piece now." Annie leaned back in her chair and looked at her husband.

"Yeah, but we've already been on CNN. And FOX, and ABC, and all the rest of the alphabet."

"It's a big story," Annie said. "Small-town private investigators nab serial killer!"

"Not exactly a small town, but it makes a good headline."

"I'm sure it'll die down once the trial's over. Meanwhile, the publicity has been great for business."

Their office, formerly an unused bedroom, contained only the bare necessities. A couple of bookcases on one wall were filled with novels as well as a few law journals. Other books that looked like manuals of some sort sat below a row of obsolete encyclopedias. A few prints hanging on the wall completed the look.

"Hi, Mom! Hi, Dad!" An eight-year-old boy shot into the room and skidded to a stop.

"Hey, Matty, how was school?"

"It was good, Dad. All the kids think you're a hero now. Of course, I had to tell them I knew it all the time."

Jake laughed. "Your mom's a hero too."

Matty frowned. "No, she's not," he said. "Women can't be heroes."

"Of course they can, Matty."

"Nope. She's a heroine." Matty laughed and darted from the room.

"My son, the linguist," Annie said.

Lincoln Investigations had been a struggling young enterprise, employed mainly to obtain evidence for cases of divorce, child custody matters, missing persons, and research into the character or financial status of individuals, as well as some security work. Until recently, it had barely been enough to keep them both busy and keep things afloat. But when they had been engaged to find a missing child, it had turned into much more than they'd expected. Catching a serial killer had led to all the publicity they were now receiving.

Prior to their venture into private investigation, Annie had been a part-time research assistant, while Jake had been a construction engineer for Cramer Developers. When Jake had lost his job due to downsizing, Annie had had to carry the family financially for a while. Her research experience had led naturally into their current undertaking.

Annie leaned forward in the swivel chair and dropped her elbows on the timeworn desk. She picked up a sheet of paper and scanned it briefly. "All these missing children," she said with a sigh. "It's sad. Everybody's calling now, hoping we can find their missing child. All across the nation, suddenly they think we're the experts."

"I wish we could help them all," Jake said, "but there're too many, and they're too far away. Anyway, we have a lot of steady local clients now, so it keeps us busy."

"Speaking of clients, Edward Franklin from Franklin & Franklin called." Annie leafed through a small stack of papers and pulled one from the pile. "They have some papers to serve. Their regular process server is on vacation, and they want us to serve a notice to appear in court. I believe it's a child custody case." She handed the paper to Jake.

Jake leaned forward, took the paper, scanned it, and looked at his watch. "I can probably do this today, or maybe in the morning." He folded the paper and tucked it into his shirt pocket. He rubbed his hand through his short dark hair, stretched, yawned, and then rose to his feet. "But right now, I need to do a little workout. Matty'll be down there waiting for me."

As Annie stood and walked around the desk, Jake watched her. He had never stopped admiring the trim figure she kept all the years since he'd known her. She stood five feet four inches tall, and Jake leaned down so she could give him a quick kiss. Married for seventeen years, he never grew tired of that. He looked into her beautiful blue eyes and grinned down at her.

She kissed his grin and said, "I have a few things to clean up here, so go ahead, lift your weights, or whatever it is you two guys do down there." As he let her go and turned to leave, Annie frowned and said, "Make sure Matty's careful."

Monday, August 15th, 6:05 p.m.

PHILIP MACY was a patient husband. After the tragic death of their child, which had hit them so hard a few weeks ago, he was able to struggle on, but Abigail just seemed to be getting worse every day. As she grew more withdrawn, he became increasingly concerned. He was doing his best and didn't know how to do anything else for her other than to be patient and pray she would improve.

He sighed deeply as he tucked a paper napkin onto the tray beside the tuna sandwich, small salad, and glass of orange juice. He took a last look at the meal to be sure he had everything prepared, then carried the tray from the kitchen and up the steps to the guest bedroom.

Balancing the tray with one hand, he tapped lightly on the door and pushed it open. Abigail was sitting on the bed, propped up by a couple of pillows. She stared at the wall in front of her, taking no notice of him.

The curtains were drawn to hold back the evening sun, allowing only a peep of light in, painting a slash of white across the floor. The overhead light was off. The only thing illuminating the otherwise gloomy room was a small lamp on the night table. He stood still a moment, watching her, before he finally approached the bed.

He slid the tray onto the nightstand beside her and sat down gently on the edge of the bed. "Abby," he said softly, "I brought you something to eat."

She stared at the tray a moment, and then slowly turned her face toward him. Her eyes were vacant. Her pretty face was haggard, and she seemed much older than her twenty-five years.

He reached out and gently caressed her long dark hair, once so beautiful, now unbrushed and uncared for.

"Thank you, Phil," she whispered hoarsely. "I'm not hungry." She put her head back and closed her eyes, breathing slowly and carefully as though each breath was an effort.

"You should eat something."

She opened her eyes, looked at him, and managed a weak smile. "Maybe later."

"Honey, you seem to have gotten worse, sadder, the last couple of days. It's more than just Timmy. What's troubling you?" he asked.

She shook her head and looked down, rubbing her fingers together as though nervous.

"I love you, Abby. You know that. I want to help you any way I can. You know you can talk to me about anything." His voice was gentle, but pleading.

She reached for a bottle of pills on the night table and popped the top. She took the glass of orange juice he offered her and, taking a big drink, she swallowed a couple of pills and set the glass back.

He continued to study her, watching, waiting, and feeling helpless, useless, and weak.

A tear fell from her eye. She ignored it. Then another, and another.

He leaned forward and held her, soothing her as she began to sob, quietly at first, and then uncontrollably. She clung to him. Her tears soaked his collar, her sobs in his ears, his gentle heart breaking.

She wept for a while, then finally managed to speak, her voice weak, low, and husky. "He killed her."

He thought he'd misunderstood her. He pushed her gently back so he could see into her eyes, a puzzled look on his face.

"He killed her," she repeated.

He cocked his head. "Killed who?"

"I saw him kill her."

Philip studied his wife thoughtfully, frowning slightly. She appeared to be frightened, and she still clung to his arm. "Whom did you see?" he asked.

"Last night. On the way home. I felt sick so I stopped for a minute. I saw a man kill somebody."

Philip frowned deeply. "Are you sure, honey?" he asked.

She looked intently at him and nodded slowly. "I'm sure," she said.

"Did you see who it was?"

She shook her head.

"Did you see who did it?"

She shook her head again. "I saw him, but I don't know who it was."

Philip sat up straight and looked at her carefully. She was motionless, her moist blue eyes telling him the truth. "Why didn't you tell me before?" he asked.

"I was afraid."

Philip could see she was still afraid, hesitant, and reluctant to say more. "We have to call the police," he said.

She nodded and whispered, "Okay."

CHAPTER 2

Tuesday, August 16th, 6:55 p.m.

ANNIE TRIED TO avoid going out on business in the evenings. That was family time, and Jake and Annie liked to spend time with Matty. But sometimes it was unavoidable.

They had gotten a call from Philip Macy. It sounded urgent, so Annie promised to come right away. She called her friend next door, Chrissy Pascual, who watched Matty occasionally if they had to go out.

"Sure, Annie, bring him right over. Glad to help."

Chrissy was a single mom, and her seven-year-old son, Kyle, and Matty were good friends. When Annie told Matty that Chrissy would watch him, he was out the front door and gone before Annie made it outside. He ran into the neighbor's house without knocking and was through the house and into the backyard with Kyle before Annie got there.

Chrissy was at the front door when she arrived. "You guys go on and do whatever you have to do. He'll be fine here."

Jake was already waiting, revving up the Firebird when Annie got back. She jumped in the front seat and they roared from the driveway.

Silverpine Street was about five minutes' drive away. Jake made it in three and squealed to a stop under the shade of a towering maple. They climbed from the vehicle and surveyed the house in front of them.

Number 88 was a typical middle-class house in a typical middle-class neighborhood. A well-manicured lawn. Hedges on both sides of the property. A flowerbed ran under the front window and down the edge of the driveway. It seemed to be somewhat overgrown with weeds. A single-car garage jutted out in front. They skirted around the Lexus in the driveway and approached the front door.

The door swung open on the first buzz by a man whose face revealed a heavy weariness. He looked to be in his late twenties, but had a dangerously thin spot on the top of his head, framed by shaggy dark hair caressing his ears.

Jake spoke first. "We're Jake and Annie Lincoln."

"Hello, I'm Philip Macy. Come in, please." He had a gentle, quiet voice, soft-spoken and calm.

They followed him into the front room. He motioned toward a couch snuggled up against the window and waited for them to sit before taking a seat on the edge of a loveseat opposite them.

Jake sat back, crossed his legs guy style, and looked around. The room had a bit of an uncared-for appearance. Not careless, just dust on the furniture. A few things lying around. Perhaps the room could do with a vacuuming. It seemed to be missing a woman's touch.

Annie snapped open her handbag and pulled out a notepad and pen.

"Thanks for coming so soon," Macy said.

Annie encouraged him with a smile. "How may we help you, Mr. Macy?"

"Please, call me Philip."

Annie nodded. Jake smiled. Philip sighed. "I hope you can help me … us. It's my wife, really. I don't know exactly where to begin."

"Tell us about your wife," Annie suggested.

Philip looked at the ceiling and rubbed his hands slowly together. "My wife," he began. "Abby is the kindest soul I ever met. And always so sensible and levelheaded. Until recently." He paused.

They waited for him to continue.

He sighed again before speaking. "We have a son … had a son. Timmy. He was three years old." He glanced down for a moment, and then back up with a faraway look in his eyes. He continued with a hoarse voice. "He was killed just over a month ago. Abby blames herself, but it was just an accident." He stopped speaking abruptly, looking down at his hands as he fidgeted with them.

"Wow," Jake whispered.

Annie wrote something in her note pad and looked at Jake, and then back at Philip. Her face was sympathetic while she waited for him to continue.

"It was very hard. For both of us, but Abby has slipped into a deep depression. She's been seeing a psychiatrist, and he diagnosed her with anxiety disorder. She's been on some medication, but I don't know how much it's helping her. She doesn't want to see anyone and barely speaks even to me."

"I can't imagine how both of you are feeling," Annie said, "but you have our deepest sympathy."

"Do you have any children?" Philip asked.

Annie nodded. "We have an eight-year-old boy."

Philip nodded slowly. "Then I'm sure you can imagine what losing a child would do to you."

Jake looked at Annie and shuddered at the thought before turning back to Philip. "That must be about the worst thing any parent could experience."

Philip nodded again and cleared his throat before continuing. "However, she seems to have taken a turn for the worse in the last couple of days, but I was finally able to get something out of her."

"Is your wife here now?" Annie interrupted.

"Yes, she's upstairs. She knows I called you, but she doesn't want to see anyone."

"That's fine," Annie said. They waited.

"Like I said, my wife, Abby, hasn't been taking Timmy's death well at all. She has been drinking often lately. She says it helps her, but I think we both know it's just a temporary remedy."

Jake nodded.

Annie agreed, "Yes."

"She finally told me last night … she was on the way home from Eddie's. That's a bar a couple of streets over. She was walking home, and she claims to have seen someone get killed. Murdered."

Annie caught her breath.

Jake leaned forward.

"I called the police as soon as she told me," Philip said. "They came here right away. She talked to them briefly and told them where she had seen the murder. They called me back this morning. Apparently, they investigated right away. They went to the house where she had seen it. They talked to the owner, checked out the lawn, etcetera, and filled out a report. They found no evidence of a crime."

Jake gave a low whistle.

Philip said, "They talked to her psychiatrist. He was reluctant to say anything at first. Patient confidentiality and all that. But I talked to him, and he was willing to give some information. He said he had diagnosed her as having anxiety disorder. I already knew that much, but he also stated it has been making her delusional and paranoid, as evidenced by the sessions he has had with her. Also, the fact she had been drinking that evening—well, the police agreed with the psychiatrist's report."

"But you don't agree with that, do you," Jake said. "You believe she really saw what she said she saw. Is that right?"

Philip nodded his head vigorously. "Oh, yes. I do think she saw something. I've spent a lot of time with her lately. Even though she doesn't want to talk much, she still needs my support. And I haven't seen any evidence of delusional thinking at all."

"So, you want us to do what?" Annie asked.

"I want you to get to the bottom of this if you can. She seems to be afraid. Not just paranoid for no reason, but genuinely afraid. She may think the killer knows who she is. I'm sure if this is straightened out, if you can find out if she saw a murder, and hopefully find the person responsible, then she will recover a lot quicker."

Annie poised her pen over the notepad and asked, "Do you have the address of the house?"

"It's just a few doors down. At number 76. Apparently it's a Mr. Kevin Rand."

Annie wrote the information on her pad. "Is there anything else you can think of?" she asked.

"Unfortunately, that's all I have. She didn't seem to know any more details."

"Where do you work, Philip?"

"My wife and I have a small accounting firm. Macy & Macy. Abby worked there part-time as a receptionist, or just helping out in a variety of areas. Until recently, that is. She hasn't been in since … Timmy."

Annie consulted her pad and thought a moment before looking up. "I guess that's about all for now," she said.

"If your wife happens to think of anything else, please be sure to let us know right away," Jake said. "In the meantime, we'll come up with a plan of action, and we'll let you know how we proceed."

Annie tucked her notepad away and stood up. Jake stood

and Philip followed them to the door. Jake dug a business card from his top pocket and handed it to Philip.

"We'll be in touch," Annie said as they left.

Philip thanked them and shut the door.

Jake whistled. "Not much to go on here," he said.

Annie agreed.

CHAPTER 3

Tuesday, August 16th, 11:55 p.m.

THE DARK FIGURE waited in the shadows while a car drifted by. He watched it drive out of sight, and then rose to his feet. He glanced up and down the street. It was empty. All clear.

Adjusting his ski mask, he stepped out of the shadows, then crept cautiously to the side of the house, keeping low. He stopped to listen a moment before continuing along the side of the house toward the back, rounding the corner.

He saw a basement window a few feet away. Silently, he stole across the grass and knelt down in front of it, avoiding a row of blooming rosebushes. He tested it. Locked.

Reaching in the side pocket of his jacket, he retrieved a knife. He snapped it open and forced the blade between the upper and lower panels of the window. After working at it awhile, he heard a satisfying snap. He grunted softly and withdrew the knife, folded it carefully, and tucked it away.

Cautiously and slowly, he inched up the lower window. It slid easily, making only a soft squeak as he pushed it open.

He stopped to listen again and heard nothing. Finding a penlight in his other pocket, he switched it on and flashed it briefly inside, then carefully eased through the window feet first, finally landing with a faint thud on the basement floor.

Switching the flashlight back on, he looked around and

saw the steps to the main floor on the other side of the room. He stepped around a pile of boxes and weaved his way around furniture and chairs, cursing to himself when his foot connected with something lying on the floor. It sounded like a soda can, or a beer can maybe. It skittered away and rattled for a moment, then became silent. He stood frozen for several minutes, listening, waiting, and hoping he hadn't been heard.

Finally, he was convinced he was safe. Moving more cautiously now, he crept across the room to the stairs ascending to the main floor of the house.

He tested the steps for squeaks, seemed satisfied, and slowly made his way up. The door at the top swung smoothly as he turned the knob and pushed it open. He switched the flashlight off and stopped again to listen.

The kitchen was straight ahead, the living room to the left, and a small bathroom to the right. There were no lights burning. Only the bright moonlight broke through the darkness of the house, allowing enough light to see as he made his way down a short hall to the stairs leading up to the bedrooms.

He removed a pistol from an inside pocket of his jacket and, holding it ready in his right hand, he took the stairs two at a time to lessen the odds of hitting one that squeaked. None did. He took the last step and stood quietly at the top, listening, pistol poised.

He glanced to the right. The door to the master bedroom was closed. A smaller bedroom was dead ahead, and to the left was the guest room. He went left, creeping, the soft carpet deadening the sound of his footsteps. Just a few feet more.

He reached the door and twisted the knob with his gloved hand, swinging it gently open a few inches. He could see the bed at the side wall and smiled grimly when he saw Abigail.

Her face was toward him, and her shallow breathing told him she was in a deep sleep.

He cautiously moved across the carpeted floor until he stood by the side of the bed. She hadn't moved. Satisfied, he reached into his side pocket and removed a small bottle. He twisted the top off and slowly poured its contents into the drinking glass, half-full of water, sitting on the nightstand.

As Abigail continued to breathe, sound asleep and unaware, he reached for the bottle of pills on the nightstand, tucking the bottle under his jacket to reduce the sound as he popped it open. Then he poured several pills into his hand, counting as he went, and dumped them into his side pocket. Again, using his coat, he muffled the sound as he snapped the top back on and returned the bottle to the nightstand.

He took one last look at his sleeping victim and stole quietly from the room. Holding the pistol ready, just in case, he listened. All was quiet. He made it to the top of the stairs, then down, carefully closing the door behind him before descending to the basement.

He stole across the basement floor, avoiding obstacles, and hoisted himself out of the window. After sliding it closed, he turned and made his way across the back of the house, down the side, and then he was gone, blending into the shadows and out of sight.

Wednesday, August 17th, 8:05 a.m.

THE EARLY DAWN threatened to brighten up Abigail Macy's room even through the drawn curtains.

She had slept soundly. The extra sleeping pill she had taken the night before had done the trick. She felt wide awake and refreshed.

Suddenly the events of the last days crashed back into her memory.

She sighed and sat up, reaching for the bottle of pills. She dumped two into her hand and picked up the glass of water. It felt warm, so she dropped the pills on the nightstand and went into the washroom in the hallway outside of her room.

She dumped the lukewarm water down the drain and turned on the tap, looking at herself in the mirror while waiting for the water to run cold. She looked a mess. Reaching for a hairbrush that sat in a basket beside the sink, she gave her hair a few strokes. Just enough to loosen some knots. Then she frowned at herself and tossed the brush back into the basket.

Rinsing out the glass, she filled it with cold water, then carried it back into her bedroom and swallowed the two pills.

Abigail looked at her watch. Philip would be gone to work by now. She picked up her housecoat, which had been tossed over the end of the bed, and put it on wearily, then knotted the belt, drawing it snugly.

Her slippers were peeking out from under the bed. She kicked them out and slipped into them, wandered from the room, and went downstairs to the kitchen.

After making a pot of coffee, she poured a cup and sat sipping it silently.

She wondered if the murder she had seen was real. She hoped it wasn't but couldn't convince herself. She had seen his face, and she was afraid to tell anyone who it was. He would come after her if she said anything.

Abigail sat alone in the kitchen, fearful, and thinking.

CHAPTER 4

Wednesday, August 17th, 9:30 a.m.

DETECTIVE HANK CORNING was slouched at his desk in the precinct. The desk, like the rest of the building, was well worn and had seen better days. The ancient hardwood floor was popping in places, the paint beginning to peel on the walls, and chairs squeaked and rumbled as officers moved about. All around were the low sounds of chatter, interrupted by a louder voice now and then, and the incessant ringing of phones, all mixed with the hum of the naked fluorescent lighting overhead.

Hank was sucking on a pencil and staring at the monitor of his outdated computer. As head detective of Richmond Hill's small robbery/homicide division, he was trying to unravel a series of break-ins that had been taking place in the south end of this small Canadian city he called home.

He ran his hand through his short-cropped, slightly graying hair before massaging the back of his stiffening neck. Too much desk time.

The phone on his desk jangled. He scooped it up.

"Detective Hank Corning."

"Hank, it's Jake."

Hank sat forward and put his elbows on the desk. "Hey Jake, what can I do for you?"

Jake and Hank had known each other a long time. They'd

met as teammates on their high school football team and had been good friends ever since. Hank had gone on to the police academy after that. No amount of convincing would get Jake to become a cop. He had already met Annie at the time, and as she was going to the University of Toronto, Jake had decided to go there as well.

"We've been hired by Philip Macy to look into a murder his wife claims to have witnessed," Jake said. "I'm hoping you have some info for me."

"The Macys? There's nothing much to it."

"You may be right, Hank, but we need to look at it anyway. If you can help us?"

"Sure, okay. That was a couple of days ago as I recall. I was at the scene. Let me grab the police report and I'll drop over and see you guys. Just give me a half hour or so."

"Sounds good. See you soon."

Hank was eager to get out. He was more comfortable on the streets than sitting behind a desk.

The Macy case was already closed, so he ran to the file room, made a photocopy of the report, returned to his desk, tucked it into his briefcase, and strode out the door.

His old brown 2008 Chevy was waiting for him in the parking lot. It coughed a couple of times as he turned the key, then it sputtered into life. He popped it into gear, and ten minutes later, he turned onto Carver Street and squeaked to a stop at the curb in front of the Lincolns'.

Jake answered the buzz at the door with a wide grin. "Come on in."

Hank followed him into the office, where Annie was parked at the desk. She looked up and smiled when they came into the room.

Jake pushed the guest chair toward Hank. "Have a seat," he said as he grabbed a fold-up chair, flipped it open, and dropped into it. It groaned gently under his two hundred and ten pounds of muscle and bone, but held.

Hank sat down, snapped open his briefcase, and pulled out the report. He handed it to Annie. She browsed it.

"It's rather strange," Hank said. "We talked to Philip and Abigail Macy. Abigail is very convincing. Her husband certainly believes she saw something, and I'm not so sure she didn't either."

Annie was consulting the notes she had made during the interview. She frowned and said, "Apparently she had been drinking that night. And she was on some kind of medication …"

"And," Hank broke in, "we went to see her psychiatrist, a Dr. Hoffman, who seems to be of the opinion she was delusional."

"The booze, the drugs, and her anxiety disorder," Jake said. "That's quite a combination."

"Yes, it is, and the fact that we saw no indication of what she claims to have seen … well, we had to close the case."

"And you talked to the owner of the house?" Annie glanced at the notes. "Kevin Rand?"

Hank pointed toward the papers Annie was holding. "Last page of the report. We talked to him. If he killed someone, we saw no evidence of that except for the lack of a woman in the house."

Annie frowned. "Do you think maybe he killed his wife?"

"We checked into that as well. He claims they're divorced and she moved out west. He gave us her contact number, so we checked it out. Unless this is an elaborate cover-up, the woman I talked to certainly seemed to be his ex-wife."

"Maybe he had a girlfriend?" Jake suggested. "And he killed her?"

Hank looked at Jake and shrugged. "Anything's possible, but unless we have a body, or at least some evidence of a crime, we have nothing to go on."

"And Abby didn't want to talk to us," Annie said.

"She didn't say a lot to us either," Hank said. "Philip did most of the talking, and she nodded a lot. She seemed to agree with everything he told us."

Annie sighed and leaned back in her chair. "Where do we start?" It was a rhetorical question.

Hank shrugged. "Beats me."

Jake looked at Annie. "Any point in our talking to Rand?"

"That's about all we have."

CHAPTER 5

Wednesday, August 17th, 11:30 a.m.

"ACCORDING TO THE police report," Annie said, "Kevin Rand runs a sporting goods store, called Game Time, in Midtown Plaza."

"We'll take the Pontiac," Jake said.

Annie grabbed her handbag from the small table in the hallway. She checked to be sure it contained her cell phone and notepad, along with the police report and other necessary items, and then headed for the front door. Jake was right behind her, slipping his keys from a ring by the door on the way out.

The Hurst mufflers rumbled when Jake turned the key. The motor purred like a contented kitten, and they swung from the driveway onto the street. The wide tires squealed as they sped away. Annie frowned and rolled her eyes. She was used to it.

The sun glinted off the hood of the bright red Firebird as they rounded the corner, heading for Main Street. Jake squinted, grabbed his sunglasses, and poked them on his face.

Another left and they were on Main, and in two minutes, they pulled into Midtown Plaza.

The plaza was the home of the local Walmart store along with a long row of other shops and businesses. Game Time was a large corner store at the far end of the plaza.

Jake was able to find a parking space in front. He pulled in slowly, careful to keep a distance from other vehicles so a careless driver wouldn't open their door and ding his beloved machine.

The engine roared as Jake revved it a couple of times, then died down to silence as he switched off the key. They climbed from the vehicle and went into the store.

"Is Mr. Rand here?" Jake asked the cashier inside the front doors.

She motioned vaguely toward the back. "In his office, I think."

Jake led the way, wandering down aisles of jerseys and t-shirts, skateboards, hockey sticks and pucks, baseball bats, gloves, and caps. A big-screen TV hung from the ceiling replaying yesterday's baseball game. Jake stopped to try on a Blue Jays cap, then tossed it back on the rack and turned away. Annie put the hat back in its proper spot and followed him.

A sign on the door along the back wall said, "Office, Employees Only." Jake tapped.

"Come in."

Jake pushed the door open. Kevin Rand was sitting, crouched over a desk, writing in a ledger of some sort. He looked up as the door swung open. He was fairly short, maybe late thirties, with a dab of gray already invading his temples. Thin, but not muscular. To Jake, he didn't look like the type to own a sporting goods store.

"May I help you?" Rand asked.

Jake offered his hand. "I'm Jake Lincoln, and this is my wife Annie. We're from Lincoln Investigations. May we ask you a few questions?"

Rand frowned and shook Jake's hand, nodding at Annie. He motioned toward a single empty chair. Jake moved aside and let Annie sit down, and he stood and tucked one hand in his pocket, waiting for an answer.

Rand was still frowning as he looked up at Jake. "What's this about?"

Annie cleared her throat. Jake took the hint and shut his mouth. He should let her ask the questions. She was always a little more calm and patient than him.

"On behalf of Philip Macy, we're looking into his wife's claim she saw somebody killed on your property."

Rand leaned back. "I don't know anything about that." He sounded impatient. "I already talked to the police and told them everything I know. Nothing."

"Yes," Annie said, "we saw the police report."

"I have nothing more to tell you."

"Mr. Rand, are you divorced?"

"Yes."

"And your wife moved out west?"

"Yes, but what does that have to do with anything?"

"Probably nothing. Are you seeing anyone now? A woman?"

"None of your business."

"I'm sorry, Mr. Rand," Annie said. "I don't mean to pry. It's just if there was anyone in the house other than you, perhaps she heard or saw something after midnight Sunday evening."

Rand rolled his eyes in exasperation. "I'm too busy for a girlfriend, and I start work early in the mornings. I was home alone. And asleep. I heard nothing. I saw nothing." He raised his voice. "In fact, I don't think there was anything to see. That woman made it all up." He stood up. "Now, if there's nothing else, I'd like to get back to work."

"Thank you for your time, Mr. Rand," Annie said as she stood.

Jake smiled slightly and nodded. "Thanks," he said as he turned to leave.

Back in the car, Annie turned to Jake. "He wasn't very receptive, was he?"

Jake shrugged as he turned the key. "Maybe he was just annoyed with answering the same questions twice."

"Maybe," Annie said. "Maybe not." She dug her notepad out of her handbag and consulted it. "Rand lives at 76 Silverpine Street. Just down from the Macys' house. I want to go there."

Jake shrugged, backed the car out of the slot, and sped away, heading for Silverpine.

"What do you expect to see there?" he asked.

"Maybe nothing. I just want to get a feel for the place."

Annie studied the report a little more as they drove. She looked up as they pulled onto Silverpine Street. She watched the numbers on the houses. "There it is."

Jake pulled up to the curb in front of number 76 and Annie climbed out. She stood on the sidewalk for a moment, surveying the house, and then crossed the lawn and stopped at the front of the house underneath a picture window. She studied the grass for a minute. It appeared normal. Nothing scuffed up or any obvious signs of a struggle.

She went to the side of the house and looked toward the rear. It was open all the way through. She kept her eyes on the ground, walking slowly toward the rear of the house. Reaching the back, she could see the yard was well kept, the lawn manicured, with a couple of large maple trees bordering the far side. The back of the large lot joined the neighbor's property behind, and she could see through to the street beyond.

There was a small wooden deck attached to the back of the house. She climbed up the three stairs and peeked inside the sliding door, into the kitchen. Dirty dishes were piled on the counter. The floor could do with a sweeping.

She went back around to the front of the house. The street

was deserted except for Jake watching her, so she stepped up to the picture window. She had to stand on her tiptoes to see in. There was no one inside, and everything appeared normal.

She stepped back and went to the front door. She rang the doorbell, waited, then rang again. No answer. It seemed Rand was telling the truth, that he did indeed live alone.

She went back to the car and climbed in. Jake looked at her. "Well?"

She shrugged and shook her head. "Nothing much to see. He appears to live alone."

"What next?" Jake asked as he started the car.

"I have no idea. Home for now."

CHAPTER 6

Wednesday, August 17th, 12:05 p.m.

SAMANTHA RIGGS knocked on the door of the Macy home.

In a few moments, Abigail Macy opened the door as far as the security chain would allow and peeked out. She was still dressed in her housecoat and looked exhausted and physically drained, but she brightened somewhat when she saw the visitor. She closed the door again and removed the chain.

"Sam," she said as she smiled feebly and swung the door open. "Come in."

Sam smiled and stepped inside. "I'm taking an extended lunch break today. I just wanted to see how you're doing, Abby. It's been a while."

Sam followed as Abby walked wearily into the living room, her slippers scratching along the floor, and dropped into an armchair. Sam sat on the couch opposite and leaned forward. "Is everything okay?" she asked.

"Not really."

"We really miss you at work," Sam said, looking concerned. She worked for Philip Macy's firm as an assistant accountant, and she and Abby had been friends for some time.

Abby nodded. "I miss you too, but I just haven't felt like

doing much of anything lately." She sighed and looked at the table beside her, at a photo of her husband holding a small child. She was lost in thought for a moment, and then looked back at Sam.

Sam said, "Philip doesn't talk much about what's going on with you, but you know me—I have a way of getting information." She laughed, and then continued, "He says you have been feeling more down in the last couple of days. What's going on?"

Abby sighed and studied Sam before saying, "I saw a terrible thing."

Sam cocked her head.

"But nobody believes me."

"Yes?"

Abby hesitated.

"I'll believe you, Abby. We've known each other for a long time."

Abby looked down. She rubbed her hands and twisted her fingers into a knot. Finally, she looked up and spoke. "Sunday night I was coming home … I was just out for a walk, and I saw … just a few houses down … I saw somebody … a woman … killed."

Sam sat frozen, her mouth and eyes wide open.

Abby continued, "I told Philip. He believes me but the police don't."

Sam was finally able to speak, but all she could say was, "Wow."

"The police looked into it, but they found nothing."

"Do you know … did you see who it was?"

Abby shrugged. "I didn't see the woman's face."

"But the killer. Did you see him?"

Abby hesitated. "Yes," she said finally.

"Didn't you tell the police?"

"No. I have been afraid to say anything. If they can't find any evidence it happened … well, if I say anything, I'm afraid he may come after me. He saw me. He knows who I am. He chased me home, but then left when I got to the door."

"But you saw his face?"

Abby nodded.

"Do you know him?"

Abby nodded again.

"So, are you going to tell me who it was?"

Sam sat still, shocked, and unable to speak, as Abby told her whom she had seen that night murdering a woman on the front lawn of her neighbor's house.

Wednesday, August 17th, 12:15 p.m.

JAKE HAD INTENDED to serve the legal papers yesterday, but his schedule just hadn't allowed it. He dug the paper containing the address for Franklin & Franklin from his wallet and poked his head into the kitchen where Annie was cleaning up after their quick lunch.

"I'm going to serve those papers now," he said. "I shouldn't be too long."

Annie threw the dishcloth into the sink and turned around. "Your timing is impeccable."

"Huh?"

"Mom is coming over. I know how much you'd love to see her."

"Yeah, like a bad cold."

Annie laughed. "I'll tell her you had to go out for a while. I don't expect she'll be here long." She looked at her watch. "You can probably come home safely by two o'clock or so."

"Then I'd better get moving," he said as he walked over and leaned down, giving her a quick kiss. Annie held on, her arms wrapped around his neck, enjoying his smiling brown eyes for a few moments before letting him go.

He grabbed his keys from their spot by the door and was gone, the Firebird roaring down the street and out of sight.

Franklin & Franklin was on the third floor of a high-rise office building in the downtown core of the city. He made it there in a few minutes and swooped into the taxi waiting area. He strode through the revolving door and into the lobby of the building. People were hustling about, suits with briefcases scurrying to and from the elevators, the clicking and clacking of heels echoing off the Italian marble floor. Urgent business of all kind was being done in a never-ending frenzy.

Jake slid into the elevator behind two professionals in thousand-dollar suits and pressed 3 on the panel. They ignored him, talking urgently about an impending court case and the hanging judge it had been their luck to draw. The elevator dinged and the doors swung open on the second floor. Two chatty women bustled in and touched the 12 button. The elevator rose again and stopped, the door slid, and Jake stepped out onto the third floor.

Franklin & Franklin took up the entire floor of the building. Jake regretted not doing this yesterday. This was a great firm to get in good with, and he would like to see more of their business come his way.

He gave his name to the receptionist. She was expecting him, and she withdrew a manila envelope from a cubbyhole in front of her and handed it to him with a warm smile. "His addresses are here," she said, pointing to a paper attached to the front of the envelope.

Jake looked at it briefly, smiled, and thanked her. "I'll get this done right away."

She beamed back at him, sighed dreamily, and went back to work as he turned to leave.

Jake squeezed back into the elevator as it dinged open. It dropped to the lobby, where another swarm was desperate to get on as the doors clanked open. He swung out and crossed the expansive space, and then exited back onto the sidewalk, breathing in the fresh air, glad to be out of the hive of incessant activity.

Back in his vehicle, he looked at his watch, and then at the information attached to the envelope. His target should be at work now. He memorized the address and tossed the envelope onto the passenger seat.

He had lived in Richmond Hill all of his life and knew every street and alley in the city. He dropped the shifter into reverse and backed out. He squealed away, roaring past a cop who was giving a parking ticket to some unfortunate citizen. The cop looked up and frowned, watching the Firebird speed out of sight, taking a left at the next lights.

In a few minutes, Jake turned onto Branson Street. He watched for Jackson Auto and saw it just ahead on the right. He rumbled into the lot and parked behind a banged-up Tercel. He grabbed the envelope and swung from his vehicle.

The huge garage door at the front of the decaying building was wide open. A car was up on the hoist, and a mechanic was changing the oil. Jake saw a steady drip, drip, drip from the transmission and knew the owner would be in for a wallet-breaking job very soon.

Two guys were on the side wall, one standing with his hands tucked firmly in his pockets, the other leaning against a work bench, puffing on a cigarette hanging from the corner of his mouth. Jake couldn't hear what they were saying, and as he walked toward them, they stopped their chatting and looked at him.

Smoker raised his brows at Jake. "Can I help you?" Tiny puffs of smoke shot from his mouth as he talked.

"I'm looking for Fred Thornbury?"

The other guy said, "I'm Fred."

Fred took the envelope as Jake handed it to him.

"You've been served," Jake said as he turned and walked away. He grinned as he listened to Fred cursing and sputtering, until he jumped in the Firebird, shutting out the angry sounds.

CHAPTER 7

Wednesday, August 17th, 12:37 p.m.

ANNIE WAS IN the office doing some invoicing and looking after a few bills when the doorbell rang. That would be her mother. She hurried to the door and opened it.

Alma Roderick was approaching sixty years old and, despite her often-sour disposition, had kept a youthful appearance. She was still an attractive woman with a good figure. She could be considered beautiful on the occasions when she allowed her tight lips to unfurl into a smile. It was obvious where Annie had gotten her good looks.

She smiled thinly and came in as Annie stepped back. She bustled straight into the kitchen and sat at the table. She crossed her legs and looked at Annie, who had followed and sat across from her.

"Hello, Mom," Annie said.

"Hello, darling. I don't get to see my daughter enough."

Annie faked a smile. "It's good to see you."

"How is Matthew?"

"Matty is fine, Mom. We're all doing well."

"I am still hoping you will accept my offer and get him out of that infernal school. You know, Richmond Academy is where he should be."

Annie sighed. "Thank you, Mom, but he's doing well where he is. He's at the top of his class in most subjects."

"We're willing to help you with that. Financially, I mean."

"Thanks, but no thanks," Annie said firmly.

Alma sniffed and looked around the kitchen as if looking for a dirty dish on the counter, or a buildup of dust, or anything other than perfection. She seemed satisfied and turned her nose back toward Annie. "I was worried about you getting involved in that murderous affair. You could have been killed yourself."

"It turned out fine, Mom."

"Still, with a serial killer on the loose, you never know what's going to happen."

"He's behind bars. He won't be hurting anyone ever again."

"And they have you to thank for that. I can't imagine, Jake getting you involved with that." She shook her head.

"It wasn't Jake, Mother. It was my decision as well."

Alma leaned forward, her voice lower. "I seriously hope you will consider getting out of that dangerous business and getting back into something safe."

Annie stood up. "Would you like a cup of coffee, Mom?"

"Yes, I have time for a quick cup." She sighed.

There was nearly a full pot left, so Annie poured two mugs, setting them on the table along with cream and sugar.

Alma put half a spoonful of sugar in her cup and poured in a drop or two of cream. She stirred her coffee thoughtfully and then said, "Your father could probably use a bookkeeper if you would consider that."

Annie knew her father's small local trucking and delivery business had no need of a full-time bookkeeper, so she said, "We're fine, Mom. We're doing well. We've had a lot of publicity lately and we can pick and choose what we do. You don't have to worry about us."

"I still worry. Please stay away from dangerous people. Let the police deal with them. That's what they get paid for, and they get paid well, I might add."

Annie wondered if the modest paycheck the police actually

received was worth risking their lives for, especially for ungrateful people like her mother, but she said nothing. It was hopeless to argue with her, especially over such a pointless claim.

They sipped their coffee silently for a moment. Finally, Alma asked, "Where's Jake? Out looking for a job, I hope?"

"He has a job, and right now he's delivering some court papers for a legal firm." Annie smiled. "It's quite safe, I assure you."

Alma sniffed again and looked at her watch. "I must go," she said as she stood up. "I have to be at work by two. I have a regular coming in, and she likes her hair done just so. They'd be lost without me there." Alma Roderick worked part-time at a hair salon, and she considered herself indispensable.

Annie stood and followed her mother to the foyer. She smiled as she shut the door, then sighed deeply and went back to the office, irritated and frustrated.

Wednesday, August 17th, 12:55 p.m.

ABIGAIL MACY had been pacing the floor for some time. What she was considering doing could be dangerous, but then on the other hand, perhaps it might help her out of a frightening situation. At any rate, she assumed it couldn't make things worse.

She made a decision, strode quickly into the kitchen, and picked up the phone before she could change her mind.

She consulted a pad on the counter and dialed a number. She was shivering a bit as she spoke his name, and gave hers, asking to speak to him.

"Yes, Abigail, what is it?" she heard him ask.

"I want to assure you I won't tell anyone what I saw."

"Whatever do you mean?"

"I know you saw me," she whispered hoarsely, "but I won't say anything."

Silence on the line for a minute, then, "What did you see?"

"I saw you … saw you … and that woman."

More silence.

Abby was wondering if she had made the right decision in calling, but continued, "I didn't tell the police, or my husband, and I never will."

Silence, then, "I really don't know what you're talking about, Abigail."

Abby hesitated. Did he not know it had been her? But no, he had chased her home, and he knew where she lived. *He surely knows I saw him.*

"Please," she said, "I will do whatever you ask."

"Anything?" he asked.

"Yes," she said eagerly.

"Then please don't call me again." She heard a click on the line. He was gone.

Abby had hoped he would at least admit it, but then realized he couldn't say he had murdered someone over the phone. The line might be bugged, or tapped, or whatever it was called. He had to play it safe and pretend he didn't know what she was talking about. She hoped he would accept her promise not to say anything, but she was still fearful.

She didn't know what else to do. Perhaps she should have told the police. She still could, but then they hadn't believed her when she'd told them what she saw, so why would they believe her now?

Suddenly she had an idea. Not to save herself, but if anything happened to her …

She went to her writing table in the den, got a piece of paper, and composed a note. She signed it, folded it neatly, and then tucked it into an envelope, addressed it, and pasted on a stamp.

Abby hurried outside. Just down the street, two or three

houses away, she stopped at a mailbox. She hesitated a moment and then dropped the envelope in. It would be picked up that afternoon and probably delivered tomorrow.

The police would be sure to see it, if …

Wednesday, August 17th, 1:11 p.m.

ANNIE WAS THINKING about Abigail and Philip Macy and the death of their child. She hadn't asked them what the cause had been, but was curious to know.

She leaned forward to her keyboard and googled, "Abigail Macy."

There were several hits. They appeared to be women with the same name who lived in other cities and towns.

She tried, "Abigail Macy Richmond Hill."

She saw it. The first result. "Tragic Death Claims Toddler."

She clicked on the link. It was from the Richmond Hill Daily Times. When the page loaded, she saw a photo of a happy and proud Abigail holding a small child. A boy. He was grinning and waving at the camera.

She read the news story under the picture, dated July 3rd.

Tragic Death Claims Toddler

Richmond Hill was shocked today to hear of the untimely death of a toddler, three-year-old Timmy Macy, the victim of a tragic accident.

According to his mother, Abigail Macy, the two of them were outside on the front lawn when Timmy wandered into the open garage. He pushed the button that closed the automatic door, and then tried to make it through, but was pinned by the door as it closed.

The cause of his death was listed as asphyxiation when the heavy door crushed down onto his back, shutting off his air supply so he couldn't breathe.

Despite his mother's efforts to save the boy after hearing the door close, the child was found dead when police and paramedics arrived.

Investigators said there was no garage door sensor installed and are warning the public that sensors are important and should be installed on all garage doors to prevent such an accident.

The death was ruled accidental and not due to the negligence of his mother. There are no charges pending.

It was not hard to understand now why Abigail had been so depressed. She probably felt fully responsible.

Annie was saddened to hear of such a tragic death. She closed the browser window and sat back, pondering the senseless death of one so young, realizing it could have been Matty, and thankful it wasn't.

CHAPTER 8

Wednesday, August 17th, 2:30 p.m.

THE MAN WALKED slowly and warily down the sidewalk toward the Macy home.

Each time a car passed, he would turn his back, pretend he was talking on a cell phone, and then continue on when the way was clear.

Once he had to duck behind the wide trunk of a maple tree and wait until a pair of women walked by. One was pushing a baby carriage, while the other talked incessantly. He waited until they were safely past before stepping back onto the sidewalk and continuing.

At the edge of the Macy property, he stopped and looked around. All clear. He walked along the hedge to the side of the house and peeked in a window. He could see Abigail sitting in the living room. She appeared to be reading. No one else was in the room.

He dropped down and continued to the back of the house, being careful not to be seen by any of the neighbors. He climbed the deck quietly and looked into the window. It led to the kitchen. No one there. He smiled grimly.

At the other side of the house he peeked in another window. Same result, no one else around. He continued to the front of the house, watching carefully for cars or pedestrians, then boldly approached the front door.

He rang the bell.

Abigail removed the chain and opened the door. She gasped and stepped back, her hand to her mouth.

"Don't worry," he said. "I just want to talk to you."

She hesitated, so he smiled the gentlest smile he could and stepped inside.

She backed up a few more steps and stopped with a jolt as she hit the bannister of the stairs leading up.

"May I come in and sit down?" he asked.

She seemed frightened as she kept her eyes on him and motioned toward the living room.

He went in and she followed.

He turned to face her. "Please, sit down."

She tightened the belt on her housecoat and sat gingerly on the edge of the padded chair, wringing her hands nervously.

He sat on the couch and leaned back, relaxed. "Please," he said in a kind, gentle voice, "I can see you're afraid. There's no need to be. You must understand, I couldn't say anything to you when you called me, but it's okay now. I believe you when you say you won't tell anyone." He smiled tenderly.

She relaxed a bit.

He spread his hands out, palms up, to appear nonthreatening. "I trust you," he said. "Can we talk?"

She nodded.

"That woman you saw. I didn't hurt her. She was just a crazy I met on the street. She was being rude, and when I tried to walk away, she began to be violent toward me, so I chased her. I just wanted to scare her a bit. I let her go and she ran away. She wasn't harmed, just afraid. I haven't seen her since."

Abigail stared at him and appeared to be thinking. She relaxed a little more. Did she believe he was telling the truth?

He smiled at her. "Would you have any coffee?"

She got up carefully and headed to the kitchen. He followed her in case she thought about running out the back door, or maybe calling 9-1-1. She turned and saw him standing in the doorway watching her.

She made a pot of coffee and, in a few minutes, carried a tray containing two steaming cups along with cream and sugar into the front room. He sat back down, and she set the tray on the coffee table between them and dropped into her chair.

"Sorry to bother you again," he said, "but would you have just a couple of cookies or a cracker or two?" He grinned. "I missed lunch today and my tummy needs something small. I would appreciate if you could be so kind."

She nodded and headed back to the kitchen.

He had but a few seconds to get this done. Slipping his hand quickly into his jacket pocket, he removed a small bottle. He twisted off the lid and poured its contents into her cup. Then he stood up, dropped the bottle back into his pocket, and went to the doorway. Abigail was on her way back with a plate. She handed it to him and they sat down.

"Ah. Chocolate chip. My favorite," he said with another forced smile. He took a bite and munched it slowly, then leaned forward and prepared his coffee. He took a sip and set the cup back down.

He looked up at her. "How do you take your coffee?" he asked.

"Just a bit of cream."

"That's smart. I should cut back on sugar too." He rubbed his belly and laughed as he dumped a few drops of cream into her cup. He stirred it and leaned forward, handing it to her.

She took it from him and sipped at it, watching him.

"Now, Abigail … Abby, I hope you know now you have no reason to fear me." He took another bite of his cookie. "Mmm. Very nice."

He sipped his coffee and watched as she sipped hers.

There was silence for a few minutes. Then he talked on softly. She looked tired, her head drooped, and she appeared to be unaware of what he was saying.

She slumped.

He got up quickly and dug a pair of surgical gloves from his side pocket. He put them on, and then going to her limp body, he pushed back her eyelids, checking her eyes. They were hazed over, unseeing.

He smiled and removed a sixteen-ounce bottle of vodka from an inner pocket. He twisted the top off and put it carefully on the stand beside her. Lifting her by the back of the neck, he forced her head back, her throat open. He slowly poured the alcohol down her throat. She choked on occasion, but he covered her mouth, let it pass, and then poured a little more, patiently continuing the process until the bottle was half gone. Then, satisfied, he wrapped her right hand around the bottle, being sure her fingerprints were on it, then set it on the stand beside her.

He took the tray with the coffee cups and plate of cookies to the kitchen and carefully washed and dried each item, finding where they belonged and putting them away.

Looking through the cupboards, he found a small glass. He brought it into the living room, poured a few drops of vodka into it, swished it around, and put that into her hand as well. He raised it up and looked at it. Her fingerprints were clearly visible on the glass. He set the glass on the stand.

Next, he hurried up the steps to the second floor. He knew where her room was. Her bottle of pills was on the stand. He grabbed the bottle and looked at the label. Lorazepam. He hurried downstairs and popped the top off, placing the cap on the stand, then counted out some pills and dumped them into his pocket. He put the now nearly empty bottle of Lorazepam on the stand beside the glass.

Reaching into another inner pocket, he withdrew a cash register receipt. The receipt was for a bottle of vodka he had purchased that morning from a nearby store. He hurried to the kitchen. Her handbag was in a basket on the kitchen counter, and he snapped it open, dropped the receipt in, snapped it shut again, and carefully put the handbag back into the basket.

He stopped and thought for a minute, looking around. Everything seemed to be fine. He went and checked her pulse. It was getting weaker. Satisfied, he moved quickly to the door. He opened it a bit and looked out. All clear.

He turned the lock on the doorknob so it would lock when closed, and being extra careful now, he stole out the door, shutting it firmly behind him. He strode quickly to the street. Again, he avoided passing traffic once or twice, and before long, he was safely gone.

CHAPTER 9

Wednesday, August 17th, 5:15 p.m.

PHILIP MACY closed the ledger and gathered up the loose papers on his desk, stuffing them into a file folder. He dropped them into a drawer and pushed back from his desk.

He had tried to reach Abby a couple of times that afternoon but she wasn't picking up the phone. He tried once more but got the same result. No answer. He dropped the phone back into its cradle.

Samantha had already gone home for the evening, and the office was empty except for him. He sighed wearily as he stood up, grabbed his briefcase, and left the suite of offices, locking up behind him. He hurried down the two flights of stairs to the underground parking.

He tossed his briefcase into the backseat of his Lexus and headed for home. He tried again to call her from his cell phone. Still no answer. This wasn't like her. She always answered the phone if the caller ID showed it was him.

He spun into the driveway and threw the gearshift in park. Forgetting his briefcase, he jumped from the car and sprinted up the steps to the front door.

As he pushed the key into the lock and swung it open, he knew something was wrong. The door wasn't chained the way Abby always left it lately when she was there alone. Perhaps she had gone out for a walk.

"Abby?" he called. "Are you here?"

No answer.

He stepped inside the foyer and walked into the kitchen.

"Abby, are you here?"

No answer. Probably up in her room.

He ran up the steps and into the guest room, calling her name. He was sure he would find her there, but the room was empty. He walked back down the stairs.

It was when he went into the living room that he saw her. She was slouched back in the stuffed chair in an unnatural position.

He dashed over to her. Something didn't seem right. Frightened now, he shook her gently, trying to wake her. There was no response.

"Abby. Honey. Wake up!" He shook her more, almost violently now.

Her eyes were closed. She looked to be sleeping peacefully, but there was still no response to his pleading.

He checked her pulse. On her arm, then her neck. Nothing. She didn't appear to be breathing. Her skin felt cool.

Panicking now, he dug furiously into his pocket. Found his cell phone. He dialed quickly, his hand shaking. His whole body shaking.

Two rings, then, "9-1-1. What is your emergency?"

He spoke rapidly. "It's my wife. She's unconscious. I can't revive her. I'm afraid she might be dead."

"I'll send an ambulance right away. What's your address, sir?" The operator spoke calmly.

"It's 88 Silverpine Street. Please hurry."

"It's on its way now. Sir, is she breathing?"

"No, she doesn't seem to be."

"Do you know how to perform CPR?"

"Yes. Yes, I'll try."

He dropped the phone onto the coffee table, leaving the speaker on, and carefully lifting Abby from the chair, he laid her on the floor. He forced her head back and her mouth open, blowing his own air into her lungs over and over again.

He tried to get her heart pumping. Working furiously. Her heart didn't respond. She didn't breathe. He wasn't getting any sign of life.

Again, he forced air into her mouth. Into her lungs. He begged her to answer him as he pumped furiously at her heart again and again.

The awful truth finally crashed into him and he stopped. He rose from his knees and sat on the edge of the chair, his face in his hands, sobbing uncontrollably.

"Abby." He wept. "My Abby."

Finally, he sat back, trying to gain some control of himself. He wanted desperately to make some sense of this. It was then he noticed the half-full bottle of vodka and the nearly empty bottle of pills on the stand beside the chair.

He was bewildered. Had she done this herself? Had she overdosed? He blamed himself. He should never have left her alone. He dropped his head and wept again in shock and disbelief. "It can't be. It can't be," he said again and again.

He fell to the floor, holding her in his arms. "Abby," he moaned. "Oh, Abby. My Abby."

He could hear the sirens in the distance now. He looked up and listened. The ambulance was coming. He prayed they would know what to do. Maybe she wasn't dead. Maybe just sleeping. Unconscious.

He laid her back down gently, then stood and ran to the door. He had locked it again when he came in, so he unlocked it and swung it open, begging for them to hurry.

The ambulance screeched to a stop in his driveway. The doors opened and two paramedics climbed out carrying some equipment. As they hurried up the steps and through the open door, he motioned toward the living room.

"In here," he said.

They rushed in, one paramedic kneeling down beside her. He checked her pulse and looked for signs of breathing, then sat back. He looked at Philip and shook his head slowly.

"I'm sorry, sir," he said. "She's gone. There's nothing we can do."

"She can't be." Philip's voice was frenzied. "She can't be. Try again."

"I'm sorry, sir. There's no pulse. She's gone."

Philip dropped to the couch and wept in despair as the paramedics went back outside, returning in a moment with a gurney. He watched as they lifted his wife's body onto the gurney, covering her face with a snow-white sheet.

One at each end, they carried her out the door and loaded her into the vehicle.

Philip stumbled into the back of the ambulance and it sped away. The lights flashed and the sirens screamed, drowning out the sound of Phil's own wailing as he knelt on the floor of the vehicle holding his wife's cold dead hand.

CHAPTER 10

Wednesday, August 17th, 5:32 p.m.

THE DOOR LEADING from the garage to the kitchen slammed. Jake walked in. Annie slouched sideways at the kitchen table reading a book on police procedure. Her feet were propped up onto a chair beside her, a half-finished cup of coffee at her elbow. She looked up as he came in.

"Did you get the oil changed?" she asked as he went to the sink to wash his hands.

"Yup," he said, and then, "Where's the grease remover?"

"Under the sink," she said, gulping down the rest of her coffee.

"How was the visit with your mother?" Jake asked, scrubbing at the grime on his fingers.

Annie dropped her feet and sat up. She tucked the bookmark into the book and closed it, sliding it away. "The usual."

Jake grinned over his shoulder at her. "Any gossip?" he asked.

Annie laughed. "No. Thankfully, she had to get to work and didn't stay too long."

"Hey, Mom. Hey, Dad." Matty gave the usual greeting. He had been next door playing with Kyle since he'd come home from school.

Annie caught him as he went by and gave him a hug. Jake turned and said, "Hey, Matt."

Matty went out the back door onto the deck. They could hear him kicking around a soccer ball.

"I checked out Timmy, the Macys' little boy," Annie said. She told Jake about the news story she had found online and the tragic accident that had taken the boy's life.

Jake whistled. "Wow. That's a nasty thing to have happen."

Annie nodded and sighed, thinking of Matty, and then asked, "Did you get those papers served okay?"

"Yeah, no problem." Jake grinned. "I could hear him cursing all the way back to the car. He wasn't too happy about it."

Annie laughed. "They never are."

"Franklin & Franklin is a pretty large firm. I hope they can send some more work our way."

The jangling of the phone on the kitchen wall interrupted them. Annie scooped it up. "Hello?"

"Mrs. Lincoln, it's Matty's teacher, Beth Cobblestone."

Annie covered the mouthpiece with her hand and whispered to Jake, "It's Matty's teacher." Then into the phone, she said, "How are you, Miss Cobblestone?"

"I am well, thank you," Annie heard, then, "I was hoping you could come to the school and see me this evening. It's about Matty. He's been in an altercation with another student, and I'm quite concerned."

Annie frowned, "What kind of altercation?"

"I'm afraid he's been in a bit of a fight with another student."

Annie looked at Jake, an anxious look in her eyes. "We'll talk to him, Miss Cobblestone," she said.

"Can you come at six thirty, please? The other boy's parents will be there as well."

"I'm very sorry. Yes, yes, we'll come at six thirty."

She hung up the receiver and studied it for a moment

before turning around. "Matty's been in a fight," she said as she went to the back door and opened it. "Matty," she called, "will you come in here, please?"

Matty could tell by the tone of his mother's voice he had better hurry. He gave the ball a good kick. It jumped and tumbled across the deck and rolled onto the lawn. He came inside and sat at the kitchen table. He looked meekly at his parents. He knew what was up.

His father finished drying his hands on a paper towel and tossed it into the flip-top garbage can. He came over and sat across from him.

Annie stood beside Matty and put her hand gently on his shoulder. She leaned over and looked him in the eyes. "Matty, your teacher called. What's this about a fight?"

He looked up. "It wasn't my fault, Mom."

Annie waited. Jake asked, "What happened, son?"

Matty played nervously with his fingers. "It was Kevin. Kevin Jordan. He was pushing Kyle around. I told him to stop, but he didn't."

"And?"

"And so I pushed him away."

"And that's all?"

Matty looked at the table, now playing with a placemat. "He wouldn't stop," he said.

They waited for Matty to continue.

He looked up at his dad. "He tried to punch me."

"And?" his mother asked.

"He missed. But I didn't."

"You punched him?"

Matty gave his mother an uncertain frown, shrugged his shoulders, and then nodded.

Annie and Jake looked at each other and then back at Matty.

"Is that the whole truth, Matty?" she asked.

"Yes, Mom. That's all that happened. I just hit him once and he ran away. He ran into the school and told the teacher. He's just a mean kid and he's always bullying the little kids there. He started it." He paused for a minute, and then looked bravely at his mother. "I'm sorry Mom, but he really deserved it, and I would do it again if I had to. There were a lot of other kids there and they all saw what happened. Maybe he'll stop bullying now and leave them alone." He looked down and continued, "I feel sorry for him, though. He has no real friends, except for one kid who lets him boss him around all the time."

Annie studied him thoughtfully for a minute, then stood and said, "Okay, Matty. You can go back outside now. But stay close by. We have to go and see your teacher this evening."

"Yes, Mom," Matty said as he dropped from the chair and sauntered back outside.

Annie sat down and leaned into the table, looking at Jake. "What do you think?" she asked.

"I think he's telling the truth," Jake said. "We'll see what this Kevin brat has to say."

CHAPTER 11

Wednesday, August 17th, 6:02 p.m.

ABIGAIL MACY had been pronounced DOA at Richmond Hill General Hospital. Hank had been watching a distraught Philip Macy trying to control his emotions. He seemed to be well past the denial stage and was flip-flopping now between despair and anger. At times, he was pacing up and down the long sterilized corridors and then back to the waiting room.

Hank spoke briefly with the doctor. He had pronounced Abigail dead, a necessary formality, and her body had been taken down to the hospital morgue located somewhere in the bowels of the massive building. An autopsy would be performed if the coroner thought it necessary; generally they were mandatory if a death occurred outside of the hospital.

Philip had stopped pacing now and was sitting slouched forward, his head in his hands. Hank sat down beside him. "I can take you home," he said gently, putting his arm around his shoulder. "There's nothing more we can do here. I expect they will release your wife's body tomorrow."

Philip looked up and nodded. "Okay," he managed.

Hank would have to wait for the autopsy report, but he knew Mrs. Macy's death was likely going to be labeled a suicide. But he wasn't so sure. Something just didn't add up. It was too convenient. She claimed to be a witness to a murder and now she was dead. Coincidence? Maybe. He also knew it was important to get statements as soon as possible, but Philip was as yet unable or unwilling to speak.

Philip followed Hank to his car, which was parked out in the emergency area's parking lot, and they drove away. He stared quietly out the side window as Hank weaved through the north end traffic, his faltering old Chevy finally making it to the Macy home on Silverpine Street.

There was a cruiser, lights still flashing, parked by the curb alongside a couple of unmarked vehicles belonging to investigators. He saw curious neighbors across the street, gathered to see what was going on in this usually quiet neighborhood. One guy was sitting comfortably in a lawn chair as if waiting for a big event. Three or four more were standing on the sidewalk or on their front lawns.

As he pulled in the drive and squeaked to a stop behind Philip's Lexus, he saw a uniformed cop at the front door. The cop watched as they climbed from the vehicle and approached the house. He nodded at them and mumbled something as he opened the door for them.

As they stepped inside the foyer, Hank turned to Philip. "They're still processing the scene, Mr. Macy. If you could wait here until they're done." He motioned toward a bench in the foyer, and Philip nodded and slouched down, closing his eyes.

Crime scene investigators were there, making notes, taking prints, and snapping photos. Lead crime scene investigator Rod Jameson was directing operations. Hank had asked them to do a thorough job and treat the scene as if it were a crime scene.

As Hank stepped into the living room, he approached Jameson. "How's it going here?" he asked.

Jameson looked up from his clipboard and glanced around. "Just about done here, Hank. We're waiting for you to take a walk-through and then they'll bag the evidence and we'll be out of here."

"Did you find a suicide note?"

Jameson shook his head.

"Thanks, Rod."

Jameson grunted and went back to his clipboard.

Hank looked around the room. He unfolded a paper from his pocket, the report from the responding paramedics. Apparently when they'd arrived, Mrs. Macy had been on the floor, where her husband had laid her before trying to revive her. He saw the chair where she had been slouched over and noticed the stand containing the bottle of vodka, the glass, and the pills. Lorazepam and vodka. Not a good combination. He picked up the glass and smelled it. Alcohol.

He spent several minutes taking in everything in the room, and then went into the kitchen, looking for anything out of place. He looked in the fridge and in the garbage bin, then checked the door to the backyard. It was locked and bolted from the inside. He noticed the nearly full pot of coffee. He scrutinized everything, absorbing all he saw.

He went upstairs and took a look around the guest room, checking in drawers, in the closet, under the bed, and on the floor. The room had already been checked for fingerprints, leaving traces of dust on the stand and the doorknob.

The upstairs bathroom got the same inspection. In the medicine cabinet. In the bathtub. Towels were dry, the window closed and locked.

Back downstairs, Hank examined the rest of the main floor, checking windows, doors, studying the floor, even the walls and ceiling.

There was a small office off the living room. He peeked inside and saw a desk, a few bookcases half-full of books, a printer, a computer, a couple of chairs, and some other office furniture. He rummaged through the desk looking for a note.

Nothing. The computer was off. He left it.

Finally, he approached Jameson. "You can clean up here now," he said.

They bagged and tagged, and in a few minutes, the investigators were gone.

Hank found Philip still waiting. They went into the living room and sat on the couch. Hank had a notepad in his hand, his pen ready. Philip slouched back and closed his eyes.

Hank turned sideways and looked at Philip. "I realize how hard this is, Mr. Macy, but I need to ask you some questions if you're up to it." Hank hated this part. Hated questioning someone who was obviously grieving so much. They just wanted someone to share their pain, or perhaps just to be left alone, not to be interrogated. He had seen so much grief in his almost twenty years as a cop, and it never got any easier for him, or for them.

"Mr. Macy, I'm sorry, but I must ask, did your wife ever talk about ending her life?"

Philip opened his eyes and looked at the ceiling. "No, no. Never." He seemed to be pleading. "She never would. She may have had problems lately, but she wasn't suicidal." He turned and looked earnestly at Hank. "I know she didn't kill herself. She just wouldn't." His voice shook, his hands working nervously.

Hank nodded. He didn't know what to say to that. He was thinking about the murder Abigail had stated she witnessed. "Did your wife ever tell you if she had any idea who was involved in the murder she saw? Who the killer was, or the victim?"

Philip shook his head. "No, I don't think she saw them clearly. She didn't like to talk about it, but she was obviously fearful."

"Mr. Macy, when you came home and first found your wife, did you touch anything? Or move anything?"

"Nothing. I just tried to revive her and then called 9-1-1." He glanced over to the chair where he had found his wife's body and looked away quickly.

"Had you been in any contact with her throughout the day? On the phone, or otherwise?"

"I had called and talked with her briefly this morning. She appeared to be fine. I tried again a few times this afternoon but got no answer."

"When was the last time you spoke to her?"

Philip looked up and thought a minute before answering. "Probably around noon. Maybe twelve thirty."

Hank scribbled in the notepad. He needed to ask for an alibi but wanted to be careful how he framed the question. "And you were in the office all day?"

Philip nodded. "Yes, all day. My assistant, Samantha, was there. She left for lunch about twelve and came back a few minutes after one. Other than that, she was there all day."

"And until recently, your wife worked at the office with you?"

"Yes."

"So, I take it she knew Samantha?"

"Yes, very well. They didn't socialize outside the office, but they went to lunch together a lot. Things like that."

Hank nodded, scribbled, and then asked, "What's Samantha's last name?"

"Riggs. Samantha Riggs. I can get you her address and phone number if you'd like."

"Yes, I would appreciate that. I need to talk to anyone who knows Abigail."

"I'll make you a list as soon as I can and get it to you," Philip said.

Hank consulted his pad, made a couple of quick notes, and then stood. "I think that's all for now, Mr. Macy, but I may have more questions later."

Philip stood, and they shook hands. As he showed Hank to the door, he stopped and looked earnestly at him. "Detective, my wife would never kill herself. I know she's been murdered. Please find out who did this," he asked, pleading.

"I'll do everything I can," Hank said as he left and made his way down the steps to his vehicle. He climbed in and sat there for a moment. He would have to wait for the autopsy report, but it sure looked like suicide.

CHAPTER 12

Wednesday, August 17th, 6:28 p.m.

JAKE SWUNG the Firebird into the guests' parking lot of North Richmond Public School. In the three years Matty had been attending, they had been here several times for parent/teacher meetings and special occasions, but never before had they been called in because of a problem with Matty.

As they crawled from the vehicle, Jake looked up at the sprawling school. When he had been a student here uncountable years ago, it was just a small square cube of ugly red brick, but now had wormed its way around the lot with three additions jutting out at awkward angles, threatening to devour the entire property.

Jake and Annie followed Matty down the weathered concrete walkway to the front of the building and through the doorway of the latest wing. The drab green walls were covered with posters and announcements. Except for the odd teacher, or perhaps a parent or two hurrying to appointments, the place was deserted and quiet.

Around the next corner, a pair of teachers overloaded with books and teaching manuals were huddled in urgent conversation. A student scurried by, a violin case tucked under his arm. As he slid through a door at the end of the hallway, the uncertain sound of a student orchestra wafted out.

Matty stopped in front of room 104 and looked at his father. Jake opened the door and went in first. The far wall of windows let the early evening sun in, flashing off the rows of deserted desks. The square room was colorfully decorated with student masterpieces. A+ test results of accomplished students were tacked proudly onto a corkboard.

Miss Cobblestone looked up from her overloaded desk at the front of the room. She appeared to be in her late thirties, nice enough looking, but more dedicated to her students than to a social life, and by choice, destined to be called Miss Cobblestone forever. Her tight black hair culminated in a stern bun at the back of her head, her reading glasses slouched on her nose, contrasting with her smiling eyes that peeked out above the black frames.

She stood and smiled as they approached, motioning to a group of three hardback chairs to the right of her desk, strategically placed a safe distance away from the three to her left.

"The Jordans should be here momentarily," she said.

They sat down and waited, discussing the weather and exchanging mandatory pleasantries. Matty fidgeted with his hands. He didn't appear to be nervous, maybe just bored.

The schoolroom door opened again and Jake looked up. Mr. Jordan was in his early thirties, short scruffy hair, with a round face and a body that had consumed a few too many calories. He held a smaller carbon copy of himself firmly by the wrist as he blustered into the room. They were followed by a more sedate Mrs. Jordan. The teacher greeted them and motioned toward the remaining chairs.

"Let's get on with this," Jordan said. The feet of his chair squealed on the tile floor as he pulled it a few inches closer, dropping his bulk into the seat. He leaned forward as Kevin and his mother took a seat beside him. He stared at Matty, his eyes small, and then at Jake, sizing him up.

Jake stared back.

Annie crossed her legs and looked at Miss Cobblestone.

Mrs. Jordan sat timidly, her hands quietly in her lap.

"Thank you all for coming." The teacher spread her smile around. She seemed at ease. Probably done this many times before.

Jake and Annie acknowledged her with a smile and a nod. Jordan grunted.

"We'll keep this short," the teacher said. "As you know, we have a no fighting policy in this school. We like to encourage our students to get along together and to understand each other's differences. We also realize at times things can get out of hand. Tempers flare, and children argue on occasion …"

"This was more than an argument," Jordan interrupted. "Look at Kevin's face." The side of his face had a dark spot, a welt forming below his left eye. Jordan waved a finger at Matty. "That little brat over there did that."

Jake moved forward in his seat. He glared at Jordan and opened his mouth. Annie cleared her throat. Jake leaned back again and crossed his arms.

Annie spoke, "Mr. Jordan, apparently your son started the fight." Her voice was calm, polite. "Matty was protecting a friend your son was bullying."

"He punched my boy!"

"Yes, after your boy tried to punch my son."

Jordan pointed at Matty again. "It's hard to believe that. Look at him. Not a mark on him."

Jake had to speak. "Look Jordan, just because your son

can't land a punch doesn't mean he didn't try. It just means he's a lousy fighter."

Jordan's eyes narrowed.

Kevin looked at his father. "Dad, you can't let him say that to you."

Jordan waved him off. "Hush," he said. Kevin sat back and folded his arms, a hostile look on his face.

"We're not here to cast any blame," Miss Cobblestone said, "but rather to ensure this doesn't happen again in the future."

Jordan's finger waggled again. "It wouldn't happen if that boy would stay away from my son."

"Mr. Jordan," the teacher spoke sharply. "Can we please keep this civil?"

Jake held back a smile as Jordan sat back and grunted, folding his arms.

"Miss Cobblestone," Annie said. "We have had a talk with Matty about this, and you can be sure we will talk to him again. If Mr. Jordan would do the same with his son, I'm sure this can be prevented in the future."

The teacher looked at Jordan and raised her brows, waiting for his response.

"I'll talk with him," he said reluctantly.

Jake doubted it would be much of a talk.

Miss Cobblestone looked back and forth from the two boys. "From now on, if there's any bullying or fighting, you must tell one of the teachers and let them handle it. No more fighting, understood?"

"Yes, Miss Cobblestone," Matty said.

Kevin glared at Matty. "Yeah, okay."

"Will the two of you shake hands, please?"

Matty slid off his chair and approached Kevin, offering his

hand. Kevin reluctantly shook hands, and crossed his arms again.

Jake stood and offered his hand to Jordan, who ignored him and stood and turned toward the door. As the three of them bustled out, Mrs. Jordan looked back at Annie, a faint smile of apology on her face, and then turned and followed her husband.

"I think that went well," Jake said.

CHAPTER 13

Wednesday, August 17th, 7:22 p.m.

WHEN THE LINCOLNS arrived home, there was a message waiting on the answering machine. Annie sat in the swivel chair and touched the "Play" button. It was Philip Macy. Could they please call him? He would like to speak to them urgently.

Jake dropped into the guest chair. Annie returned the call and put it on speaker.

"It's my wife," Philip said. He sounded broken. "She's dead."

Annie's mouth dropped open. She stared at the phone, not knowing what to say. She said, "Ohhh."

Jake looked at Annie and then at the phone. "What happened?" he asked.

"I … I don't really know … they say suicide, but I don't think so. Can you drop over here this evening?"

"We can come right now," Jake said.

Annie ran from the office and called Matty. She would ask Chrissy to watch him for a while. She ran next door, Matty following. Chrissy was home and eager to help.

"We shouldn't be long," Annie said.

"Any time. We love having him here."

Annie hurried back. Jake tossed her handbag to her and they jumped into the already running car.

The tires smoked a bit as Jake swung from the driveway and roared down Carver Street.

Annie found a brush in her purse and touched up her hair, freshened her light pink lipstick, and then sat back as Jake steered onto Silverpine and approached the Macy home.

They spun into the driveway, stopped behind Philip's Lexus, and stepped out, hurrying up the steps to the front door. As Jake reached for the doorbell, the door swung open.

Philip greeted them and showed them to the living room. He motioned toward the couch by the front window. They sat as Philip pulled up a chair that seemed to have been brought from the kitchen. The overstuffed armchair remained conspicuously empty.

Annie crossed her legs and studied Philip. His young face was haggard and appeared ten years older. She could see he had been crying.

His voice was hoarse. "Thanks for coming so quickly."

Jake nodded and forced a polite smile.

"We're very sorry to hear about Mrs. Macy," Annie said.

Philip sighed. "I realize you didn't have a chance to talk to my wife," he said. "But she would never have … done this to herself."

"Can you tell us what happened?" Jake asked.

"I came home after work today, maybe around five thirty or so. My wife was lying there … not moving." He motioned toward the stuffed armchair and continued. "I tried to revive her, but she was … already gone. I called 9-1-1 immediately, but she … it was too late."

"How did it happen?" Annie asked.

Philip looked at the stand by the chair. "There was a bottle of alcohol on the table. Half-full. And her bottle of pills was there too. Almost empty. It appears she had been drinking and took an overdose of pills." He looked back at Annie and shook his head. "But she would never do that."

Annie reached into her handbag for her notepad and pen. She flipped it open and asked, "What pills was she taking?"

"Lorazepam."

She wrote in her notepad. "What kind of alcohol was it?"

"Vodka. But the police took it. They took the pills as well."

"Was there a note of any kind?"

"No." Philip shook his head.

"Had you talked to your wife today at any time before that?" Jake asked.

"I talked to her this morning. She appeared fine and in a much better mood than she was in the last couple of days."

Annie consulted her notes and frowned. "You mentioned before she would occasionally go out for a drink. A place called Eddie's. Did she drink at home as well?"

"I have never known her to. And the last time she went to Eddie's was on Sunday night. The night she saw the murder."

"When was the last time she had been to see her psychiatrist …" She flipped through her notes. "Dr. Hoffman?"

"I believe the last time she saw him was last Friday afternoon. She may have had an appointment today as well, but I don't know if she went. Perhaps she did. I was unable to reach her by phone this afternoon."

"Did she keep a schedule here anywhere?" Jake asked.

"I believe so," Philip said as he stood up. He went into the adjoining office and returned in a moment with a calendar. He was studying it. "She had an appointment today at one o'clock. She may have gone."

"We'll check with Dr. Hoffman," Annie said. "At this point, we don't know the time of death, but after we know that, and then talk to Dr. Hoffman, we may be able to piece together her day."

"Please find who did this."

"We'll make it our top priority," Annie said.

"We'll get the police report as soon as possible," Jake said. "And that will help us. We will approach this with the assumption this was … not of her own doing. We'll get him."

Annie looked at Jake and back at Philip. "We can't actually promise we will succeed, only that we will do our absolute best."

Philip nodded.

Annie stood and went over to the small table beside the chair where Abigail had been found. There wasn't much to see. Everything had been removed by the investigators, leaving only a dusting of fingerprint powder behind.

"Do you mind if I look around a bit?" she asked Philip.

Philip made a sweeping motion. "Please do."

Annie wandered into the kitchen, trying to get a feel for things. The kitchen was tidy. Better than it had been last time they were here. Had Philip been cleaning up? Or was Abigail feeling more up to doing it herself? She checked the door leading from the kitchen to the backyard. As well as the regular keyed lock, it had a sliding deadbolt on it, fastened securely from the inside.

She noticed a handbag on the end of the counter. Had the police missed that? She opened it up and dumped its contents on the kitchen table. A pair of sunglasses, a wallet, some lipstick and a small compact. Not much else. A cash register receipt. She looked at it. It was for a bottle of vodka, purchased that morning. The timestamp on the receipt said 10:23. She stuffed it between the pages of her notepad and continued looking.

There was a pot of brewed coffee in the coffeemaker. She examined it closely, frowning. There seemed to be two cups gone. She looked in the sink. No cups there.

She went back to the living room and stood in the doorway. "Philip, did Abigail drink coffee?"

"She would have the occasional cup. Maybe every couple of days or so."

"And you?"

"I would drink coffee here in the morning before work, but lately I have been stopping at a coffee shop on the way to work." He smiled. "I drink too much coffee."

Annie thought a moment and then said, "There's a pot of coffee in the kitchen. Did you make that?"

"No, I haven't had anything to eat or drink since I got home about an hour ago."

Annie nodded. "Is there anything else you can think of that may help us?"

"Actually, yes. Abby always puts the chain on the door when she's here alone. But today when I came home, it wasn't on. It was locked, but no chain."

Annie made a note in her pad. She twiddled the pen a moment and then asked, "Philip, what was your wife wearing when you came home?"

"She was wearing her housecoat."

Annie made another note and paced the living room floor, thinking. Finally she said, "That's all I can think of now." She looked at Jake.

Jake shrugged. "I can't think of anything else." He stood and followed Annie to the door.

Philip saw them out. "Please let me know if you find out anything."

"We will," Jake said.

CHAPTER 14

Thursday, August 18th, 9:00 a.m.

"CAN I SEE YOU a minute, Captain?"

"Sure. Come on in."

Detective Hank Corning stepped into the office, pulled back a chair, and dropped down. He glanced across the desk at Captain Alano Diego and waved some papers in the air.

"Captain, I just have a gut feeling there's something more going on here."

Diego dropped his pen and sat back. "Listen, Hank, I know what you're saying. You're the best detective I have and I respect your gut, but it's all there in black and white." He was a few pounds overweight, and his jowls quivered as he talked.

Hank frowned and pointed at the papers he was still holding. "But there's more to it than this. And they didn't do a full autopsy."

He waited as Diego reached to the side of his desk for a manila folder, dropped it in front of him, and flipped it open. "The coroner didn't think a full autopsy was necessary," he said.

"I believe there's more than just what's in the report," Hank said.

Diego shrugged his shoulders and brushed down his bristling mustache with his finger. "Maybe. Maybe not. But I can't justify keeping you on it." He looked down at the open folder. "The drug screen came back positive for Lorazepam. The coroner's report labeled the cause of death as suicide, and the investigators at the scene found no evidence to the contrary."

Hank stared at him.

Diego continued, "Add that to the fact Mrs. Macy was experiencing mental and emotional problems at the time. Her psychiatrist said she might have been suicidal." He paused and looked up. "There's just nothing to go on. Except your gut."

"My gut is telling me there's something here."

Diego continued, "Even the manner of death is consistent with suicide. I think the figure is something like, thirty-eight percent of women who attempt suicide do it with something toxic. Usually an overdose."

"If this was a homicide," Hank said, "the killer may have known that figure and knew an overdose was the best way to avoid suspicion."

Diego ignored the assumption. "Hank, we've known each other for a long time. I know you're a good cop." He leaned forward. "What you do on your own time is up to you, but officially, this file is closed."

"The Lincolns are looking into this. If they, or we, come up with something solid, can we take another look?"

"Not meaning to disrespect the Lincolns in any way, but they're looking into this because they're paid to look into it. Not because they necessarily think there's anything to go on." He paused. "However, if they come up with something solid. I mean solid. Real proof a crime has been committed here. Something that will stand up in court, then we'll take another look. But until then …" He closed the file folder in front of him with a swish, sat back, adjusted his navy-blue tie, and looked at Hank.

Hank studied Diego a moment and then finally stood. "All right. Thanks Captain," he said reluctantly as he turned and left the room.

Hank knew Diego had done the logical thing. As head of the Richmond Hill Police Department, Captain Diego had worked his way up through the ranks and was well respected by the men under him. That wasn't to say Diego was always right, of course, but he was the captain.

He sighed and stabbed speed dial on his cell phone.

"Jake here."

"Hey, Jake, the captain closed the file. Mrs. Macy's death has officially been labeled a suicide by the coroner."

"So the investigators found nothing either?" Jake asked.

"Nope. I have all the reports right here. If you guys are going to be home for a while, I'll drop them over."

"Sure," Jake said. "We're here now. Come on over."

"Be right there." Hank touched the cell phone and ended the call, shoving it into his pocket. He made photocopies of the papers, went to his desk, and slipped them into his briefcase.

Before leaving, he poked his head back into Diego's office. "Can we at least have an autopsy done?" he asked.

Diego sighed. "All right. I'll get the coroner to do a full autopsy. Then we'll close the case."

"Thanks, Captain," Hank said. He turned and left the precinct.

Thursday, August 18th, 9:22 a.m.

JAKE SWUNG the front door open when Hank knocked. "Come on in. Annie's in the kitchen. There's some fresh coffee on." He led the way and Hank followed.

Annie greeted Hank with a smile as he and Jake dropped into chairs at the kitchen table. Jake slouched back, using another chair to prop up his feet, while Annie poured three steaming mugs of coffee. She set them on the table with cream and sugar and sat at the end.

Hank opened his briefcase and removed the folder of reports. He dropped them on the table in front of Annie. "It's all here," he said. "Police report. Coroner's report. Doctor's report. Drug screen."

Annie flipped open the folder and browsed the papers while Hank and Jake prepared their coffee. Lots of sugar in Hank's. Not too much cream.

Jake looked at Annie. "Hank said the investigators found nothing suspicious."

Hank nodded. "That's what they say, but …"

Annie turned to Hank. "You don't think it's a suicide either, do you?"

Hank shook his head. "I'm not sure, but the captain closed the file. He said he had no choice as there's nothing there to indicate it was anything other than suicide." He shrugged and took a gulp of coffee. "But I was able to convince him to do a full autopsy first."

Jake sat up and picked up one of the reports. He browsed the pages, sipping thoughtfully at his coffee.

"Outside of these reports, there're a lot of little things that don't make sense," Annie said.

"Such as?" Hank asked.

"For starters, Philip Macy said his wife would always keep the front door chained when he's not home. But today, when he came home, the chain was off. The door was locked, but the chain was off."

"That's a little slim," Hank said.

"Not to me, it's not," Annie said. "We know how afraid she had been the last few days. She didn't even want to leave the house. The back door, leading from the kitchen to the backyard, had a manual lock on it, as well as the regular lock.

Both were secured. And yet, the front door was not so secure. That doesn't make sense to me, considering Mrs. Macy's state of mind and the fact she always kept that door chained."

"Okay, that's a good point," Hank said. "But she could have just forgotten to chain it."

Annie shook her head. "I don't think so."

Jake said, "I was wondering why she would sit in the chair. It just seems to me if she was going to kill herself, she would more than likely lie down on the couch." He shrugged. "It just makes sense to me."

Hank nodded dubiously. "Perhaps, but I don't know how much weight I would give to that assumption."

Annie looked at Hank. "From a woman's point of view," she said, "that makes a bit of sense. Woman commit suicide differently than men. They never shoot themselves and rarely hang themselves. They do things nice and neatly. Jake may have a point there. I think she would have taken the pills, and then lain down on the couch or perhaps in bed."

Hank squinted, looking thoughtful, and nodded slowly.

"And I have a problem with the coffee," Annie said.

Hank raised his cup. "Mine's okay," he said, taking another gulp.

Annie laughed. "Not that coffee."

Hank cocked his head.

Annie continued, "The coffee at Macy's. There was a pot of coffee in their kitchen, in the coffeemaker. It was turned off but it smelled fresh."

"So?"

"I looked at it carefully. There appeared to be two cups missing. Philip said his wife rarely drank coffee, and yet there were two cups gone."

"So you think the killer made some coffee and drank it?" Jake asked.

"No, but maybe Mrs. Macy made a cup of coffee for him or her."

Jake frowned. "So that means she knew who he was, let him in, they drank coffee together and then …"

"And then he killed her and left," Annie said.

Hank looked at her. "Makes sense," he said, "but don't forget the alcohol. The tox screen showed a high level of alcohol in her system. When and how did that get there?"

"Maybe before the killer came, or perhaps she was drinking while he was there," Annie replied.

Hank shrugged. "So, how did he get the pills into her system?"

"In the coffee," Jake suggested.

"Maybe."

"Granted," Annie said, "all of these things out of place don't mean a lot individually, but taken all together, it makes me suspect something happened we can't prove. At least, not yet."

"My big problem is with the note," Hank said, "or lack thereof." He guzzled the rest of his coffee and pushed the cup away.

"What about it?" Jake asked.

"Suicide victims almost always leave a note. Occasionally they don't, but with a suicide note, the person who's committing suicide has the last word, explaining why they felt they had to end their life, and to bring closure to others, especially their loved ones, so there's no guilt. And usually there's someone they want to forgive and someone or something they want to blame."

"Knowing what we do about Abigail Macy, I'm sure she wouldn't want her husband to feel at blame," said Jake. "I have to agree with you, Hank. It seems out of character for her."

"But again, it's nothing conclusive. Certainly not enough to reopen her file."

Annie said, "Maybe not, but it's enough for us."

"Annie and I are planning to see her psychiatrist this morning, Dr. Boris Hoffman," Jake said and shrugged. "Maybe he can tell us something we don't know."

"We talked to him before, regarding Mrs. Macy's report she had seen a murder," Hank said. "At that time, he stated she was showing tendencies to be delusional and paranoid. Another talk with him might be a good idea." He shrugged and added, "I guess it wouldn't hurt, anyway."

Annie was browsing the forensics report. She looked up. "We don't have much else at this point. We can talk to any friends or acquaintances she may have as well. If Mrs. Macy was murdered, as we suspect, then it was by someone she knew. I think she let him into the house."

"We need to get a list of everyone she knew," Jake said. "One of them is likely her killer."

"What's the motive?" Hank asked.

"She witnessed a murder," Annie said. "I believe he thinks she could identify him, and he had to eliminate her as a precaution."

"So find out who was murdered—if there was truly a murder—and then you have your suspect," Hank said.

"That's our best bet," Annie said.

"I have a problem with the pills," Jake said. "How did he, or she, get Abby to down all those pills?"

"Perhaps she was drunk, and then he forced them down her throat," Annie said.

"Or dissolved them in her drink," Jake said, and then looked at Hank. "Do any of those reports say whether or not there was anything in the glass? Any residue of Lorazepam?"

Hank shook his head. "There was no residue in the glass. She had to have taken them directly in pill form."

"Or in the coffee," Annie added.

Hank agreed. "Perhaps."

"Funny thing is, though," Annie said, "there were no dirty cups."

Jake shrugged. "She washed up."

Annie nodded slowly. "Maybe, but then why didn't she wash up the coffeepot? She would have dumped out the rest of the pot. She didn't drink much coffee and likely had no plans to have another cup." She paused and added, "And I believe the killer is a he, not a she. Remember, Abigail Macy said it was a man she saw killing a woman."

"Yeah, good point," Jake said.

Annie glanced at the clock on the kitchen wall. "We need to see Hoffman this morning. He said he could allow us a few minutes. And then, we need to find out who Mrs. Macy saw being killed."

"Good luck, guys. I gotta run," Hank said as he stood and picked up his briefcase. "You can keep those reports. They're just copies." He turned to leave.

"Oh, Hank," Annie stood and asked, "can you get me any reports of missing persons from Sunday night on?"

"Sure," Hank said. "I'll see what I can come up with." He waved over his shoulder as he left, and said, "Thanks for the coffee."

CHAPTER 15

Thursday, August 18th, 9:50 a.m.

THE SUN WAS blinking in and out from behind inky clouds. A few drops of rain were already splashing onto the windshield of the Ford Escort as Jake and Annie climbed inside. Thunder smacked a few miles away, rumbling through the air, promising to bring more rain. It boomed again, this time closer.

Annie tossed her handbag and umbrella into the backseat, fastened her seat belt, and turned the key. The engine spun and came alive.

She glared up at the sky and touched the wiper control, slipping it into intermittent. It squeaked across the glass and settled again into place.

Jake's machine was parked in the garage, safely out of the way of the rain that had been threatened that morning. It wasn't used to seeing rain. Annie's car was. Jake wanted to keep it that way.

Annie looked over. "Fasten your seat belt," she said.

Jake could never get used to wearing seat belts. They didn't seem safe to him. All tied in like that. Hard to control a vehicle when you couldn't move around. Nonetheless, he wasn't driving, so he snapped his belt on and powered down his window. Not enough rain yet to worry about a few drops. He stuck his elbow out and settled back.

Annie tugged on the shifter and touched the gas pedal. She drove carefully from the driveway, down the street, and took a left turn.

Traffic was thin. Usually was this time of day. Most people were either at work already or didn't work at all. There wasn't enough rain to slow things down yet, just a dampening of the streets making the tires squish as they turned onto Main Street.

Dr. Boris Hoffman's office was located on the second floor of Midtown Plaza above a pizza restaurant. Eat in, take out, and delivery, the sign promised. Jake had ordered pizza there once. It was as good as any.

The steps to the second floor were to the right of the restaurant. Annie slipped into a parking space directly in front of the doors leading up and they stepped from the vehicle.

Inside the lobby, a placard on the wall listed the establishments occupying the second floor.

Annie pointed. Dr. Boris Hoffman. Suite 204.

There was no elevator, just stairs, and they climbed them, entering through a door leading into a wide hallway extending for a distance in both directions. An arrow led them to the right. They passed a few suites and stopped in front of a door with a shiny faux gold banner, the doctor's name stenciled in plain black letters. A handwritten sign below said, "Ring Bell and Come In."

They did.

A pretty young receptionist looked up as they entered. She smiled. "Can I help you?"

"Jake and Annie Lincoln. We have an appointment to see Dr. Hoffman," Annie said.

The receptionist consulted a ledger. She frowned. "I don't see anything here."

"We're not patients," Annie said. "We called earlier and

were promised we could see him for a few minutes at ten o'clock."

The girl peeled off a sticky note stuck to the computer monitor. "Here it is," she said, looking up. "If you would like to take a seat, Dr. Hoffman will be right with you."

She picked up a phone and stabbed a button. She spoke into it as Jake and Annie took a seat along a wall of chairs, packed together in a row of four or five.

Jake browsed through a stack of magazines on a table in front of them. *Psychiatric Times. Journal of the American Psychiatric Association.* He looked for something worth reading and settled on a three-month-old copy of *Time.*

Annie was already browsing a magazine, flipping impatiently through the pages.

The receptionist looked up. "You may go in now," she said as she stood and went to a door to their left.

They dropped their magazines back onto the pile and stood, and the girl swung the door open, motioning inside as they approached it. They stepped inside the room, Annie leading, Jake behind her.

Dr. Boris Hoffman was seated behind a large, intricately carved walnut desk, containing only a delicately decorated lamp, a photo, and a pen resting on the blotter in front of him. Jake glanced at the photo. It was a woman, nice looking, sophisticated, probably his wife.

Hoffman was resting back, his elbows on the armrests, his hands in a praying position tucked under his neatly trimmed dark beard. He motioned toward a pair of guest chairs in front of the desk.

They sat.

Jake studied Hoffman. Maybe about forty years old, slightly thinning hair with no gray. Probably touched up. Looked like an expensive suit. Maybe Armani, or Gucci. Jake didn't know the brands too well. Nice tie, too.

He took a quick look around the spacious area. Dark paneling on the walls. Maybe walnut or mahogany. A bookcase filled with rows of matching books. A few paintings on the walls. Could be originals. Jake didn't know. There was a comfortable-looking couch to the right with a pair of matching armchairs. The whole room had a rich, elegant look.

Hoffman spoke. His voice was slightly deeper than most. "I promised you a few minutes. However, I don't know what I can tell you that might help." He sounded refined, well educated. Rich.

"Thank you for your time, Dr. Hoffman," Annie said. "We'll try not to take up too much of it."

Hoffman nodded slightly.

Annie continued, "As you're aware, a patient of yours, Abigail Macy, was found dead yesterday. An apparent suicide."

Hoffman nodded again. "I am aware," he said.

"We don't think it was suicide."

Hoffman's brows shot up.

"We believe she was murdered," Jake said.

Hoffman looked thoughtfully at Jake. "What brought you to that conclusion?"

"There's some evidence. A few things don't make sense."

"Such as?"

Jake ignored the question. They weren't here to answer questions. They were here to get answers to their own. "Dr. Hoffman, we had hoped to get some insight into Abigail Macy."

Hoffman frowned. "I can't tell you a whole lot," he said. "Patient confidentiality precludes me from discussing certain areas."

Annie spoke. "I understand Doctor, but Mrs. Macy is dead now. Confidentiality in many areas doesn't apply, such as—"

Hoffman interrupted, "I am well aware of the exclusions. I will conduct our conversation accordingly."

Jake thought the guy was a bit of a jerk, but didn't say anything.

Annie spoke, "Dr. Hoffman, Mrs. Macy had an appointment to see you yesterday morning. We're trying to piece together her day. Could you tell us, did she keep her appointment?"

Hoffman shook his head. "No, she never showed up."

"Was that unusual for her?"

Hoffman nodded. "I believe it was the only time."

"She had been seeing you quite often over the last month," Annie said. "Can you tell us a little bit about her state of mind?"

"I already spoke to the detectives regarding this." He frowned.

"Yes, I realize that, but we would like to hear it firsthand. And perhaps there may be something you can add."

Hoffman thought a moment. "As I stated, she had anxiety disorder brought on by the death of her child. This had been making her delusional and paranoid at times."

"Did she express any of her delusional thoughts to you?"

"Not explicitly, but her overall state of mind suggested it."

"Did she ever appear suicidal or have any thoughts of suicide?" Jake asked.

"Yes. She certainly did. She occasionally expressed her lack of the will to live. She was very depressed at times, and a deep depression can cause you to take actions you wouldn't normally consider."

Annie nodded. "Yes, I understand that. However, did she ever mention specifically any attempts she had made?"

"No, she never specified any attempt. I believe she had been considering it for some time, however, before finally acting on it."

"So it's your professional opinion, then, that she took her own life?"

"Yes. I believe she did. She felt she was to blame for the death of her child."

"And yet, she didn't leave a note. Isn't that unusual, Doctor?"

"I can't speak to that. I don't have any information on why suicide victims do or do not write notes. Frankly, in the years I have been involved in this field, I have only counseled one other person, many years ago, who eventually took his own life."

Annie hesitated. She looked at Jake for a moment before looking back at Hoffman. "Dr. Hoffman, Mrs. Macy had claimed to have witnessed a murder on Sunday evening. What's your opinion of that claim?"

"Again, I believe she was delusional. When the police interviewed me, they told me she had consumed a significant amount of alcohol. I believe the alcohol, coupled with the medications, had caused her delusion and paranoia."

Annie nodded. "Is there anything else you could tell us, Doctor?"

"I really can't think of anything else. Unfortunately, Abigail Macy was in an unwell state of mind. Her death is sad but not totally surprising."

Annie looked at Jake and then stood. She offered her hand to Hoffman and they shook. Jake stood and shook as well.

"Thank you, Doctor," Jake said as they turned and left. They smiled and thanked the receptionist as they left the office.

CHAPTER 16

Thursday, August 18th, 10:43 a.m.

ANNIE SLIPPED the paper from the fax machine and glanced at it. It was from Hank. It was a list of persons reported missing in the last month.

She sat at the desk, dropped the paper in front of her, and studied it.

There were five names on the list.

The first name she was able to eliminate immediately. It was a twelve-year-old boy who had been reported missing two weeks ago. She grabbed a red marker from the penholder and crossed it out. Immediately, she felt guilty about slashing his name out as if he didn't matter and felt sorry for the boy and his parents, hoping he would be found safe.

She paused a moment before continuing down the list.

The second name was Betty Barnoble. Thirty years old. A possibility. She ticked the name.

The third one. Nope. An eighty-four-year-old man had gone missing two weeks ago. A note beside his name said he had turned up two days later, wandering in the park.

She stroked that one out and was glad he was safe.

The fourth name looked possible. Thirty-eight-year-old Vera Blackley. She put a tick beside the name.

The last name was another man. Abigail Macy had said it was a woman she had seen murdered. She crossed out the name and sat back, twiddling the marker in her fingers.

She realized the victim could have been from anywhere—from another city or town—but she suspected they were local. That left two distinct possibilities: Vera Blackley and Betty Barnoble.

She leaned in and powered up her Mac. In a couple of minutes, a picture of Matty and Jake wrestling in the backyard appeared on her monitor. She smiled at the sight of her two boys. It always made her smile.

She booted up Safari and went to Google, performing a Boolean search. "'Vera Blackley" AND "Richmond Hill.'" Nothing. Another search. "'Betty Barnoble" AND "Richmond Hill.'" Nothing. It seemed missing persons were not big enough stories to rate mentioning, even in the local papers.

She picked up the desk phone and dialed Hank's cell.

He answered on the first ring. "Detective Hank Corning."

"Hi, Hank. It's Annie. I got the list of names you faxed me and I see a couple of possibilities. There're two local women on the list. Do you have the police reports on Betty Barnoble and Vera Blackley?"

"One second," Hank replied. She could hear the faint tapping of computer keys, then he said, "Betty Barnoble. Thirty years old. Reported missing by her husband on August ninth. Last Tuesday. According to the report by the attending officers, Mrs. Barnoble had gone shopping out of town the day before and never returned. Because there was no evidence of wrongdoing, only the basic investigations were done. She was unable to be reached via her cell phone, and after contacting her friends and family, there was still no trace of her."

Annie was furiously taking notes. "Is she still missing?" she asked.

"According to a follow-up by the investigating officer, she was still missing as of yesterday."

"And the other one?" Annie asked.

"What's the name again?"

"Vera Blackley."

A few more key taps could be heard, and then, "Vera Blackley. Thirty-eight years old. Reported missing this Monday, August fifteenth, by her husband. He was out of town for several days and came back on the fifteenth. He was unable to reach her by phone and he had tried calling her friends and family. No one had heard from her since Sunday, the fourteenth. Again, there was no evidence of foul play, so after the basic investigations, it was filed away. A follow-up yesterday showed she was still missing."

Annie scribbled a few notes on the paper beside Vera Blackley's name.

"There's a note here by the attending officer," Hank continued. "The officer was of the opinion the husband didn't seem concerned. The husband stated, and this is a quote, 'She probably just left me again.' Unquote."

Annie laughed and then said, "Okay, that's great, Hank. This gives me somewhere to start. Will you fax me over those two reports?"

"Sure. Right away."

"Oh, and Hank?"

"Yes?"

"That twelve-year-old boy on the list. Jerry Farnsworth. Did they ever find him?"

Hank tapped the keys and a moment later said, "Yup. He showed up three days later. According to the report, he had run away from home and found out life on the street wasn't all he had expected and returned on his own."

Annie smiled. "A happy ending."

Hank chuckled. "Yes. And a lesson learned."

Annie laughed and then said, "Thanks, Hank. Take care."

Annie studied the notes she had made. She realized if the

murdered woman had been killed by her husband, then she may not have been reported missing. But at least these two names were a place to begin. It was all she had.

The fax machine rang and then squealed. She would have to get a new machine one day. That one was pretty ancient. But it still worked. She stood and went to the fax and waited. She watched a paper come from the machine and slide into the tray. Then another one. She scooped them up and sat at the desk. Leaning back, she studied the reports.

She was looking for the addresses of the missing persons.

Betty Barnoble, 18 Maverly Court. She tapped a few keys on the keyboard. Google Maps showed Maverly Court to be on the other side of Main. She used the satellite view and studied the area, trying to get a feel for things.

Next, Vera Blackley, 90 Berrymore Street. Again, she did a search on Google Maps. Berrymore Street was just a few blocks away. She zoomed in closer and her mouth dropped open.

Berrymore Street ran parallel to Silverpine Street, where Kevin Rand lived. Where Abigail Macy had seen the murder take place.

More than just a coincidence? Annie thought so.

She slid open the side drawer of the desk and dug out a file folder, looking for the address of Kevin Rand's house. Number 76. She stabbed a few more keys and zoomed in on the map.

She sat back, a triumphant smile on her face.

The house where Vera Blackley lived on Berrymore, and Kevin Rand's house on Silverpine, touched each other back to back, and except for a few bushes, the two lots joined in seamlessly with each other.

CHAPTER 17

Five Days Ago

VERA BLACKLEY wasn't happy. She knew the man she was having an affair with was married. And of course, she was married as well.

But she wanted more.

Her marriage had long been on the rocks, and it meant nothing to her anymore. Anderson was her second husband. A loser, and a poor excuse for a man. He was just a mistake she had made, and she wanted out.

Her first marriage had lasted several years, but it had been a disaster, and she was surprised they had kept up appearances as long as they did. The best years of her life had been given to a man who gave nothing in return. She couldn't spare any more time when life was short and she wanted to get all she could from it. She wanted everything she deserved, and he just couldn't give it to her. So, when Anderson had come along with promises of eternal love, she'd been swept right up.

And so, she'd married Anderson three years ago. The honeymoon was good, and so were the first couple of months or so, but everything had slipped downhill since then. Now it was just a facade, just a brittle shell that protected their doomed marriage. Doomed from the start. Why she hadn't been able to see him for what he really was, she couldn't understand. She had been misled. He had treated her well when they were seeing each other, so she hadn't hesitated in divorcing her first husband and marrying Anderson. She'd thought he was the love of her life.

How wrong she was. What a fool she had been.

And now at thirty-eight years old, she wanted more. Was she always destined to meet failures? She knew she was still attractive. Her long, thick hair hung down below her shoulders. She had nice full lips. A perfect nose. The wrinkles around her eyes and on her forehead were barely noticeable. And she took good care of her body. Still a nice flat stomach, unspoiled all these years by being careful she didn't get pregnant. She shuddered at the thought.

She stood and let her housecoat slip to the floor, naked, inspecting herself in the full-length mirror on her bedroom wall. She still had a great figure. Long legs and well shaped. She suspected there wasn't a man alive who wouldn't turn and watch her as she walked by. She was pleased with what she saw.

She smiled as she thought of her new love. She had met him six months ago, and he was not a failure like the last two. He was successful, and she knew she loved him. And he loved her. He had told her so on many occasions.

She was thankful Anderson was often out of town, seemingly on business. She suspected he was seeing someone else as well. She didn't really care. She didn't love him anymore, and she knew he didn't bother himself in the least worrying about what she did.

But she wasn't happy.

She wanted her latest lover to marry her. She had told him on many occasions she would gladly divorce Anderson and marry him, but he had never expressed the same desire. At least not outright, just in a vague way now and then. But she couldn't wait forever. Why was he holding on to his marriage when he had no feelings for his wife?

She hated this running around, hiding, not being able to say anything. She had never been to his house even though his wife was away for extended periods of time. No, he always came here. It wasn't fair. She didn't feel as though he loved her as much as he said he did. She wasn't going to take it anymore.

Sure, she loved him and didn't want to lose him, but she could find another man any time. They were a dime a dozen, and of course, it wouldn't take much to make them want her. She had that way about her. Most men would do anything to get a chance with her. She spun around and admired herself from the back. It looked good. She still had it.

And now, she was fed up. She wanted a commitment. And tonight she was going to get it. She would lay it all out in front of him. It was now or never. She would give him an ultimatum.

But subtly, of course.

She looked at her watch. Still some time before he came.

She would have to seduce him using her many and ample charms, and show him what he would be missing if he chose to ignore their love.

Sure, he'd seen her body before, but tonight, she was going to keep it covered, showing just enough to make him hungry, and then deny him.

She laughed out loud. This was going to work. She'd had experience in the past with just this sort of thing. She knew how to get her way.

Humming to herself now, anticipating the evening, she went to her closet. She browsed through the long row of clothing. She knew what he liked. She chose a sleek red dress with a plunging neckline and a back that left her naked to the waist, tight enough to show her beautiful figure, and short enough to reveal the tops of her silk stockings. Perfect. She removed it from the hanger and dropped it on the bed.

She went to the vanity beside the door and slipped open the top drawer. Forget the pantyhose. She pulled out a pair of red stockings and a garter belt, the same color as the dress. She admired them and dropped them on the bed.

And of course, a pair of red panties. She laughed. He wouldn't see those tonight, and maybe never again if he didn't make the right decision.

And then to the closet again. A pair of red shoes with heels like towers. And a pair of nice earrings, black, to complement the color of her eyes, with a matching necklace.

She set them aside and went to the shower. She washed her long black hair and then toweled off and flicked on her hair dryer, drying her hair and curling it at the tips the way she knew he liked it.

She spent the next half hour getting dressed, adjusting everything perfectly, painting her lips bright red and spraying on a little Victoria's Secret body spray.

She stood back and admired herself, smiling grimly, determined to make her plan work.

Tonight's the night.

Do, or die.

CHAPTER 18

Thursday, August 18th, 11:05 a.m.

ANNIE TOOK a more thorough look at the police report filed by Anderson Blackley regarding his missing wife, Vera.

She was sure now there was a connection. She believed Vera Blackley might have been the woman Abigail Macy had seen murdered on her way home late Sunday evening. Actually, in the wee hours of Monday morning.

She didn't believe Dr. Hoffman had been correct when he'd said Mrs. Macy was delusional and paranoid. Maybe she was at times, but not concerning what she had claimed to have seen take place that night.

It was too much of a coincidence that the two houses were back to back and Vera Blackley was reported missing the day after.

The report listed her name and address, as well as vital statistics such as hair color, weight, age, etcetera.

Under the heading "Circumstances leading to disappearance," a statement had been filled out by Anderson Blackley.

> *I was out of town on business for several days and returned home on the morning of Monday, August 15th. At that time, my wife was not at home. I was not immediately concerned, but when she didn't return by late afternoon, I phoned around to her friends and family. No one had seen her since Sunday, so I called the police.*

Not much to go on there. It wasn't a crime to be missing. Anderson Blackley wasn't suspected of anything, and if there was no evidence harm had come to Vera Blackley, then the police would only do preliminary investigations.

She would have to arrange to interview Anderson Blackley directly.

The report said he was the National Sales Manager for a company called "Proper Shoes," and he was introducing a new line of footwear for the elderly. There was a contact phone number. She called it.

A receptionist answered. Blackley was there and Annie was put through to him immediately. She introduced herself and asked if she and Jake could arrange to see him later that day.

Blackley sounded confused. "Why're you involved in this?" he asked. "I didn't hire any private investigators."

"We were hired by your neighbor, Philip Macy, to look into the death of his wife. She had earlier reported seeing someone killed on the property behind your house, and we think there may be a connection to the disappearance of your wife."

"You don't think she's dead, do you?" He didn't seem to sound concerned.

"It's too soon to say anything, Mr. Blackley, but we would like to speak to you if possible."

"Hmm. Well, okay. I can see you at one o'clock today, if that's good for you."

"That would be perfect," Annie replied.

She hung up and sat back in the swivel chair, formulating a plan. First, she wanted to check something out. She had a couple of hours before their appointment with Blackley.

Jake was in the basement doing his daily workout routine. She went from the office and swung open the basement door leading off the kitchen. She could hear him grunting and straining. She stood and admired him for a minute, his muscles bulging under his shirt, soaked with sweat, before she headed down the stairs.

He looked up and grinned when he saw her, then dropped the barbell he was lifting. It thumped and settled into place. He grabbed a towel, wiped off his face, tossed it aside, and looked at her.

"What's up?" he asked.

Annie sat down on the bottom step. "We have an appointment with Anderson Blackley at one o'clock."

He cocked his head. "Who's Anderson Blackley?"

Annie filled him in on her conversation with Hank, the missing persons list, the police reports, and her suspicions regarding Vera Blackley's disappearance.

Jake whistled. "And she lives right behind Kevin Rand?"

"Yes. I thought I would drop over there first and take a look around the property again. I just want to get a better feel for the area."

He shrugged. "Sounds like a plan. Do you want me to come with you?"

Annie shook her head. "No, I won't be long. I just need to see for myself."

"Okay." He went back to his weights.

Annie stood and went upstairs to the kitchen. She grabbed her keys from the basket on the counter and her umbrella from the stand in the foyer, then slipped on an old pair of shoes—practically worn out, but they would be perfect for today. She made her way out the door and looked at the sky.

The rain had been falling intermittently all morning. Right now, the sun had forced itself out from behind the low-lying clouds, but all around was the evidence of earlier showers. She caught an unmistakable whiff of ozone in the air.

Annie climbed into her Ford Escort, fastened her seat belt,

and brought the engine to life, pulling away. In a few minutes, she came to a stop in front of the Blackley house on Berrymore Street. She stepped out and surveyed the house. Nothing remarkable about it. Just a normal middle-class house in a middle-class neighborhood—a garage in front, a nicely manicured lawn, and a small flowerbed under the front window.

She took the narrow pathway to the front steps, climbed up onto a small porch, and knocked on the door. She waited. There was no answer, just as she'd hoped. Anderson Blackley was at work, but she wanted to make sure no one else was here before she went snooping around.

Stepping off the porch, Annie moved along the front of the house and made her way up the side to the property at the back. There was a back door to the house, and she climbed the steps to the small deck and peeked in through the sliding double doors. She could see the kitchen and down a hallway beyond, probably to the living area.

She turned around, facing the back of the property. She could plainly see Kevin Rand's house behind. She crossed the wet lawn, her shoes now making a squishing sound as she walked. She heard thunder far off to the north. She went about fifty feet, and then onto the Rand property, walking along the side of the house, then crossed the front lawn and approached the street beyond.

A couple of young girls, chattering away, walked by on the other side of the street. They should be in school. An old woman hustled past holding an umbrella. She smiled a sweet hello to Annie and scurried away, probably hurrying to get home before it rained again.

Annie stood on the sidewalk and looked back. This was near where Abigail Macy would have been standing. This was where she'd seen the murder take place. She had seen the victim run from the side of the house to the front lawn of the

Macy house, where she was caught, strangled, and then dragged back.

Dragged back to the Blackley house.

She was sure of it now. The victim had been Vera Blackley.

But who was the killer? Anderson Blackley? Or somebody else? Was Blackley really out of town?

That was what she had to find out.

A few drops of rain slapped into her hair. She raised her head and looked for the sun, now behind a black cloud. The rain started more seriously. She had left her umbrella in the car.

She ran around the Rand house, crossed the backyard, and hurried through to the Blackley residence, up the side of the house, and back to her car. The rain was falling in earnest now, and she jumped into her car and started it up, turning the wipers on.

The tires hummed on the wet pavement as she touched the gas and splashed up the street toward home.

CHAPTER 19

Five Days Ago

SHE WAS READY for him. Her mind was made up. He couldn't play with her emotions anymore and expect her to keep following him around like a dim-witted floozy forever.

She looked at her watch and sat on the couch, pulling back the curtains. He should be here any minute. She watched and waited. Finally, she saw his car pull into the driveway.

She smiled grimly to herself as she stood and went to the front door.

She opened it and watched as he stepped from his vehicle. He looked around as if to be sure no one was watching, and then strode up the path.

Vera Blackley opened the door and greeted him with a smile before he had a chance to knock.

He stepped in, carrying a bottle of wine which he set on a stand by the door. He looked her over and whistled, his gaze moving down slowly, taking in the sight of the tempting woman in front of him.

She smiled again as his gaze stopped on her face. He moved in, holding her close, and they kissed passionately for a moment. His hands wandered and she pulled back. She left him staring as she wiggled into the living room.

He grabbed the wine from the table and followed, not moving his eyes from her, watching her walk.

She took a seat on the couch, crossed her legs, and looked at him seductively. She finally spoke. "It's good to see you again, darling."

He set the bottle on the coffee table and sat beside her, leaning in, his hands reaching to touch her all over, but she pushed him away again. He sat back. "What's wrong?" he asked, frowning slightly.

"Nothing," she said. "Why don't you open the wine and pour us a couple of glasses?"

He looked at her thoughtfully a moment and then answered with a shrug, "Okay." He stood, swept up the bottle and headed for the kitchen.

She went to the stereo and chose a CD. She slipped it in the player and a mix of some 80s music came quietly from the speakers. Some soft love ballads she liked.

She heard the cork pop in the kitchen. A cabinet door slammed. She took a seat on the couch again, crossed her legs, and waited until he returned.

She had a plan and she was going to stick to it. She must have an answer tonight. She didn't see any reason for prolonging it and was determined to know what their future was—that was, if they had any future together at all.

He came back in the room, set the glasses on the coffee table, and poured the wine. He handed her one glass and picked up the other, raising it as if to make a toast before taking a taste.

She sipped at her glass, watching him.

"My wife's out of town again," he said. "Gone to see her mother." He shrugged. "It's better that way. It makes it easier for us to get together."

She nodded and smiled.

Now's the time. "When are you going to divorce her?" she asked quietly, sweetly.

He studied her and then said, "Soon."

"You've been promising me that for a long time."

"Vera, darling, it's just not good timing right now."

"You've been saying that for a long time as well," she said, not so sweetly, and then asked in a demanding voice, "When will it be the right time?"

"I don't really know."

"And when will you know?" Her voice was sharper now. "You say you love me. You know I love you, so what's standing in the way?"

He groaned. "You know I love you, Vera. Do we have to have this conversation again?"

"Yes, we do. I need an answer."

He set his glass on the table and stood up. He began pacing slowly.

"I need an answer, now," she said.

He stopped and looked at her. He opened his mouth to speak, and then shut it again with a sigh.

She waited.

"Can we just go upstairs?" he asked. "Then I can think about it later."

She shook her head. "No."

He stared at her, pleading, "Come on, Vera, I missed you. Let's go." He sat beside her and reached out to hold her, but she held up her hands. He stopped abruptly and scowled, and then he sat back and glared at her.

She said, "I have promised you before, I will divorce Anderson as soon as I'm sure you will divorce your wife. He doesn't love me anyway, and I don't love him."

He sighed.

"Look," she said, "I'm not just someone you can come to any time you please and have sex with. I want more than that. You have to prove you love me." She raised her voice. "Divorce your wife."

He frowned. "Come on, Vera. I said I would. Don't you trust me?"

She looked at him doubtfully. "I'm not sure."

He stood and gave her an angry stare. "What do you mean, you're not sure?"

"I'm not sure if you love me," she said as she crossed her arms, glaring back at him.

"All right. Here's the truth," he said slowly, deliberately. "I can't divorce her right now. It would ruin me financially."

"And is money more important to you than I am?" she asked indignantly.

"No, of course not, but …"

"But? No but. Either you love me or you don't. Which is it? Either you divorce her now, or …"

He narrowed his eyes. "Or what?" he demanded.

"Or I will have to tell her … about us," she said flatly. She raised her nose and looked at him unemotionally.

He threw his hands in the air in exasperation and began pacing furiously back and forth again, turning to glare at her, and then pacing again. Finally, he stopped and turned to her, his arms folded tightly. "You wouldn't do that," he said.

"Oh, yes, I would."

"And then your husband would know about us."

"I don't care," she said calmly, and then screamed, "I don't care anymore."

"Well, I do," he shouted.

Vera glared at him, her lips thin, her nose in the air. Then in a menacing voice, low, threatening, and calm, she said, "I will tell her."

"You will do what?" he shouted.

"I will tell her about us."

He leaned in, pointing at her, anger in his eyes. "If you do that, then it's all over for us."

"It may be all over for us anyway."

"What do you mean by that?" he demanded.

"I mean," she said,"it looks like we're through."

He swore at her, savagely, angry, fuming. "You wouldn't do that."

"Yes, I would. And I will. That's a promise," she said smugly.

"But I love you," he said, begging, whining.

Vera stood and walked over to him, her hands on her hips, her eyes flaming. She leaned in and said coolly, "I'll give you two days to do something about us or I'll tell your wife."

He raised his hand as if to strike her. She stepped back, unruffled. "Don't you dare touch me." She turned and sat, her back straight, her head up, her eyes narrow, angry.

He strode from the room and, in a moment, a door slammed.

She had stuck to her plan. She had given him an ultimatum, and she was determined to see it through.

CHAPTER 20

Thursday, August 18th, 12:55 p.m.

THE RAIN SHOWERS that had earlier dampened the day had been chased away by the gentle breeze now sweeping down Richmond Valley. The sun was out in full, the pavement steaming as the wet city dried off.

Annie pulled the Escort into an industrial complex on Magnetic Drive. A towering sign at the street had a long list of businesses occupying the cookie-cutter units. She drove slowly down the long row, eyeing the small signs attached to the front of each unit. They found Proper Shoes down near the far end, at 22b. She slid into one of the slots in front, and they climbed from the vehicle and approached the unit.

Jake pulled on the front door and swung it open. Annie stepped in and Jake followed her into a small reception area. They approached a woman sitting behind a counter, guarding the entrance into the room beyond. Behind her, in a larger area, were half a dozen desks occupied by sales people, talking on phones, taking orders, the room humming with activity as business was done. The woman looked at them over the top of her tiny reading glasses. She frowned, as if they had interrupted her in the middle of an urgent matter.

"Yes?" she asked, sounding bored.

"Annie and Jake Lincoln to see Anderson Blackley. We have an appointment at one o'clock."

Without a word, the receptionist stabbed a button on the bank of phones beside her. "Your one o'clock is here."

"Send them in," came from the speaker.

The woman pointed to a door at the back of the room. "Straight through there," she said as she went back to the papers on her desk.

They stepped through a door-sized space at the end of the counter, and weaving around desks and workers, they approached Blackley's office. A gold sign on the door said "Anderson Blackley. National Sales Manager." The door swung open as they approached it.

Blackley waved them in.

The brightly lit room had three or four bulging filing cabinets that appeared to have served many years. There were shoeboxes stacked along one wall. Piles of stuff along another. The small desk had papers and folders piled high, a monitor at one end, and a phone at the other. There was a small window along the left wall, the blinds closed.

Annie looked at Blackley, sizing him up. He was in his late thirties, maybe early forties, and rather handsome. Dark hair, nice blue eyes, a good physique. He was dressed in a suit with no tie. His top button was undone, the jacket hanging loosely around his shoulders.

They sat in a pair of guest chairs on the near side of the desk. Blackley went behind his desk and sat in a stuffed leather chair. He leaned back, dropped his elbows on the armrests, and looked at them, waiting.

Annie smiled. "Thank you for seeing us, Mr. Blackley," she said.

Blackley gave a slight nod and said nothing.

"As I told you on the phone, we were hired by your neighbor, Philip Macy, to look into the death of his wife."

"Tragic," Blackley said, "but as I understand it, she committed suicide." His voice was full, mellow, and not unfriendly.

"We don't think so," Annie said. "We think perhaps she was murdered."

"And you think this somehow involves my wife?"

"We're not sure," Annie said, "but we're looking into the possibility. Mrs. Macy reported seeing a murder take place on the Rand property, behind your house. We checked for missing persons in the area, and your wife seems to have gone missing about the same time."

Blackley looked back and forth from Annie to Jake. "I have no idea when Vera went missing. I was away since last Thursday, and when I came home Monday, she was gone."

"Did you talk to her at all during that period?" Jake asked.

Blackley shook his head. "No, I didn't call her and she didn't call me."

"Is that unusual?"

"Not at all. We're not a happily married couple, Mr. Lincoln." He shrugged. "Haven't been for some time."

"So you think she may have just left you?"

"Maybe. I don't know for sure. That's what I thought at first." He sighed deeply. "It wouldn't be the first time."

"And you checked around with people she knows?" Annie asked.

Blackley nodded. "I called her family and some friends, but no one had heard from her for quite some time. Her car is still parked in the garage."

"What about extra clothes?"

Blackley shrugged. "I have no idea. She has so many clothes. I would have no way of knowing if she took anything or not."

"Jewelry? Suitcases?" Annie asked.

"Again, I don't know," Blackley said.

"What about money? Did she take any money? Did you check your personal bank accounts?"

Blackley looked at the ceiling a minute. "She has her credit cards but hasn't used them as far as I know. And she didn't touch the bank accounts."

"Doesn't that seem unusual?"

"Not really. The last time she left, she had met some rich guy. She just dropped everything and up and left. Gone for about three months. She didn't take anything with her that time either."

"So," Jake asked, "you assume she has done the same again?"

Blackley nodded.

"Do you know if she's currently having an affair?"

"I can't say for sure. Maybe."

Annie was confused. "So, Mr. Blackley, if she's having affairs, why are you still together?"

"I don't really know." He paused. "I'm busy a lot. We live separate lives. She does her thing and I do mine. I expect we'll get divorced eventually."

Annie studied him. She noticed he was still wearing a wedding ring. He seemed calm about his wife's disappearance. Could that be because he had accepted his wife was unfaithful and was resigned to it? Or had he killed his wife in cold blood and hidden her body somewhere? Maybe buried it, or dumped it in the lake? Was he the killer Mrs. Macy had seen?

Blackley leaned forward and dropped his arms on the desk. "So let me get this straight. You think the woman murdered may have been Vera?"

Annie nodded. "Perhaps."

"Then where is she? Where's her body?"

"We don't know. If her body had been found, then the police would be involved. As it is, she's just missing."

"Yeah, the police didn't do much," Blackley said, leaning back again.

"Mr. Blackley, can you tell us where you were Sunday evening?"

Blackley frowned. "You're asking me for an alibi?"

Annie nodded.

"I gave all of this to the police."

"Yes, I know, but we don't have that information." Annie slipped a notepad and pen from her handbag.

Blackley sighed. "I stayed at the Nights Inn at St. Catherines. I had a meeting with our regional manager on Friday, and I stayed for an extra day and then drove home on Monday morning."

She looked up at Blackley. "What time did you get home?"

"About two o'clock in the afternoon," he said, and then leaned forward. He looked Jake in the eye, and then turned to Annie. "Look, I didn't kill my wife. That is, if she has even been killed."

Annie wrote the date and time in her notepad.

"We're just trying to piece everything together," Jake said. "We don't necessarily suspect you had anything to do with it. And like you said, we don't even know if anything happened to your wife. Hopefully, she will return."

Blackley shrugged. "Yeah, maybe. I don't really care if she's run off again, but I do hope she's okay. I don't love the woman, but I don't wish her any harm."

"Mr. Blackley, would you have a picture of your wife we could borrow?" Annie asked.

Blackley shook his head. "No, not here. If you drop by the house I should have something there I can give you."

Annie nodded. "Okay. And Mr. Blackley, we would like to contact her friends and family. Could you give us a list of names?"

Blackley nodded and grabbed a pad and pen from the side of his desk. He wrote for a while and then said, "There're some people here I don't have any phone numbers for. You can probably look them up." He ripped the paper from the pad and handed it to Annie.

Annie took the list and glanced at it briefly before slipping it into her handbag. She found a business card and handed it to him. "If your wife returns, or if you think of anything else, please call us."

Blackley took the card and glanced at it briefly before tucking it under the edge of the phone. "Okay," he said.

They stood and shook hands.

"Thank you, Mr. Blackley," Annie said as they turned to leave.

The receptionist didn't look up as they slipped past her and made their way out the door to the car. They climbed in and fastened their seat belts. Annie pushed the key into the ignition and sat back, her hands on the steering wheel.

Jake looked at Annie. "Do you think he did it?"

Annie stared thoughtfully at the unit in front of them, and then at Jake. "I don't know," she said. "But did you notice he was still wearing his wedding ring?"

"Yeah, I saw that. Maybe he's wearing it to avoid suspicion."

Annie wrinkled her brow. "Maybe, but if he's trying so hard to avoid suspicion, then why would he freely admit he didn't love his wife and she was having affairs?"

"Because that information would come out anyway. Eventually. So, if he took his ring off, then that might make it look worse for him. Like everything was final."

"Maybe." Annie shrugged. "Or maybe it doesn't mean anything at all."

"And why hasn't he divorced her?" Jake asked.

"Could be it's just like he said. He doesn't really care."

"Doesn't make sense to me either way." Jake thought a moment before continuing, "The way I see it, we're going under a bunch of assumptions here."

Annie nodded. "I realize that."

Jake continued, "We're assuming Mrs. Macy saw someone

murdered. We're assuming Mrs. Macy was also murdered. And now, we're assuming Vera Blackley was the one murdered. And maybe it was Anderson Blackley who did it."

"Yes, and if any of our assumptions are incorrect, then our whole theory breaks down."

"Exactly," Jake said. "If Mrs. Macy didn't really see someone murdered, then it's likely she wasn't murdered either."

Annie finished Jake's thought. "And perhaps Vera Blackley is alive somewhere."

"Right. But assuming Mrs. Macy really did see someone murdered, then who was it, if not Vera Blackley?"

"She's the only one missing who seems like a possibility. And here, again, I'm assuming the victim was someone local."

Jake shrugged. "I dunno. We don't really have any firm proof of anything."

Annie smiled. "Don't forget about women's intuition. I just have a real feeling we're on the right track."

"Sure. I agree. I think you're right, but we need some proof."

"That's a problem," Annie said as she leaned forward and turned the key. "We need to find something."

CHAPTER 21

Four Days Ago

DR. BORIS HOFFMAN was angry. He knew once Vera had made up her mind there was no changing it. He knew she would tell his wife about their affair. He couldn't let that happen.

It would ruin him.

The big mansion he lived in. The fancy cars he drove. All of it belonged to his wife. She had inherited it from her father, and he would have no claim to it should she divorce him. Sure, his practice did okay, but it was struggling. He couldn't get enough clients to live the lifestyle he wanted.

And now, it was all in danger.

He had to do something.

He had come into the bathroom to get away from her and perhaps calm down a bit, to think clearly. He was tempted to just leave and go home, but that wouldn't solve his problem.

Could he convince her not to say anything? She could ruin his life.

He tried to calm down. He splashed water on his face and looked intently at himself in the mirror, not seeing his true reflection, just the image of a now desperate man.

He tried to shake it off and swore at himself for being so stupid. He should never have gotten involved with a patient.

He was caught up in her charms. She had seduced him and was now playing with him.

He wiped his face on a towel and strode back to the front room. Vera was watching him as he came in. He stopped short and glared at her as she sat on the couch.

"Have you changed your mind?" she asked calmly. She no longer looked attractive. She looked devious and ugly. He hated her now.

He stood still, scowling at her, his hands on his hips. "No, I haven't," he said firmly.

She stood suddenly and stepped toward him, unafraid, standing a few inches away, her eyes flaming. She pointed to the front door and demanded, "Then get out of my house."

He pushed her away viciously. She fell back, flailing wildly to catch herself. She hit the floor, landing on her back. She looked up at him, loathing in her eyes as he stood over her, an uncontrollable wrath sweeping over him, swallowing him whole, commanding him now.

Hate. Hate. Hate.

He dropped to his knees beside her. His hands reached. Reaching for her neck. Her throat. She struggled to her knees and rolled away as he dived for her. A crazed snarl erupted from deep inside as he lunged again, catching her by the leg as she fought to get away.

I've got you now.

Vera had the wine bottle in her hand, its contents splashing to the floor as she swung it high. It came down. He felt a jolt run through him and he fell back, dazed.

She twisted free, tearing her stocking, and stumbled to her feet.

He hated her. Wanted to kill her.

He shook his head, trying to clear his foggy mind. His head was sore where the bottle had landed. He paid no attention to the throbbing as he rose slowly.

Hate. Hate. Kill.

She stood a few feet away, the bottle still in her hand, high above her head, ready, waiting.

"Get back," she screamed. "I'll hit you again."

They stood, facing one other, studying each other, like opponents in a ring, looking for an opening, panting, waiting, calculating.

He lunged at her. She stepped aside, twisting, and swung the bottle. It missed and went whistling across the room, hitting the floor and rolling to a stop against the wall.

He lunged again. She moved and he caught her by the dress. She pulled away and left it dangling from his fist. In a rage, he threw it aside and chased her as she ran wildly from the room.

Kill. Kill. Kill.

Half-naked now, she stumbled down the hallway to the kitchen. He followed, cursing, desperate.

Vera scrambled for the knife holder on the counter, snatched up a large blade, and spun around as he reached her. She swung the weapon wildly. It grazed his head as he ducked, the momentum knocking her off balance. He swung around behind her, grabbing her around the shoulders.

She still had the knife, and she twisted her arm back over her shoulder, trying to stab him. "Let go of me," she shrieked. The knife barely missed his face as she thrust it at him, again and again.

He pushed her away and grabbed her arm. The knife hit the floor. She turned and hit him desperately across the face with her other fist, breaking free as he raised his arm to protect himself. She ran toward the back door.

Can't let her get outside. Have to stop her. Now.

He dove. Missed. She was out the door.

He chased after her in a frenzied attempt. He couldn't let her get away.

She ran across the back lawn as he pursued frantically.

She was on the next property behind now, heading up the side of the neighboring house.

He almost had her, his hand reaching for her, brushing against her back with his fingertips. As she rounded the front corner of the house, he made a desperate leap and caught her by the hair. She stopped short, stumbled, and was brought to the ground.

Kill. Kill. Kill.

She lay on her back and attempted to scream for help, struggling and clawing feebly at her attacker as he knelt beside her, his hands about her throat, gritting his teeth, growling like an animal, squeezing, squeezing.

Until her final scream was cut short and all was still and quiet.

He dropped her lifeless body, rose to his feet, and then leaned over and grabbed her hands. He dragged her across the grass, back toward the darkness at the edge of the home.

He had to get her body out of here. Get to safety before someone came and saw.

He heard branches rustling and snapping, coming from the hedge along the side of the property, near the sidewalk. He looked up from the shadows. Someone was watching. Someone he knew and someone who knew him.

It was Abigail Macy. One of his patients.

She stared open-mouthed as he looked into her frightened eyes.

She turned and ran.

He dropped the body and followed instinctively, like a rabid dog after its prey. He was behind her now and she glanced over her shoulder. He was close and getting closer with each step.

She stumbled the last few feet, crossed the lawn of her house, and then fell onto the brightly lit front steps of her home.

He stopped suddenly, ducking behind a tree as a car went by. He looked across the street. A light was coming from a house window. He could see someone moving about inside. He looked up at a bright streetlight directly overhead.

His anger had faded enough now for his head to clear. He had to think logically. He should have waited and planned this a little better. But he had been furious, and now he had to do something about Abigail Macy. He cursed at the way his luck had turned. His bad luck, getting worse.

He couldn't chance doing anything about her now. He had more urgent matters to attend to. But she may have recognized him, and he would have to deal with her later.

He moved carefully back down the street, keeping in the shadows as much as possible. He glanced over his shoulder and saw Abigail dig in her handbag for her key and then disappear inside the house.

He made it unseen back to the spot beside the house where Vera's body lay. He hoped the sounds of the struggle hadn't been heard. He listened for a while. All was quiet. There were no lights on in the house beside him. It was well after midnight and the city was asleep.

As quietly as possible, he hoisted the body over his shoulder, and then, stumbling under the weight, he carried it back to the Blackley house, up the steps, across the deck, and into the kitchen.

He carried it through the house and dropped it onto the floor by the front door. He looked around. The struggle had made a bit of a mess. He straightened things up, meticulously checking everything. Put the knife back in the kitchen. Adjusted the coffee table. He found a garbage bag in the kitchen. He wiped off the empty wine bottle and the glasses with a dry cloth, and then dumped them into the bag. He found the cork. That went into the bag as well.

The spilled wine had spread across the floor where the

bottle had landed and had splashed onto the hardwood floor in several areas as Vera had swung it about. He dug under the kitchen sink for something to clean it with. A cloth and some water. He spent some time, making sure he had cleaned it thoroughly. It appeared to be acceptable. It was a good thing it was white wine. He dumped the cloth into the garbage bag.

He took a last look around and then, carefully using the dry cloth, he wiped down any areas he may have touched. He didn't want to leave any fingerprints.

He stopped to think for a moment. One last thing to do.

There was a door to the garage off the kitchen. He went into the garage and looked around. He saw just what he needed and smiled grimly, chuckling to himself.

Using the same cloth, he reached to the wall and removed a hammer, careful not to touch the handle. He hurried back into the kitchen and found a small knife. He went to where the body lay.

He made a small cut on her wrist, just enough to make it bleed. The heart had stopped pumping, so the blood didn't flow. He squeezed her wrist and a few drops fell onto the head of the hammer. He smeared it around, and then pulling a hair from her head, he rubbed it into the blood. It stuck.

He went back to the garage and hung the hammer back up on the wall. Anderson Blackley's fingerprints would surely be on that hammer. He had covered his tracks.

Just in case.

He locked the back door, switched off the lights, and then, after first digging out his car keys, he hoisted the body over his shoulder. Checking to be sure no one was about, he carried it quickly to his car. He popped the trunk and dropped Vera's body inside, snapping it closed quietly.

Hurrying back to the house, he grabbed the garbage bag full of the items he had collected, locked the door from the inside, closed it, and tested it. It was locked securely. He hurried to his car, tossed the bag in the backseat, and backed out.

The street was bare. All was quiet. He drove away slowly, finally breathing freely once he had turned onto the next street.

Now, what to do with the body? Have to think.

A plan began to form.

He knew where Blackley worked.

Winding his way through the city, watching carefully in case any cops were about, he found Magnetic Drive. At the rear of the row of units was a service driveway, used for deliveries, garbage pickup, and employee parking. He saw the back door for Proper Shoes. Beside the door was a massive garbage bin. He looked around and saw no one.

He backed up to the bin, climbed out, and popped the trunk. Removing the cooling body of his former lover, he dumped it into the big green bin. The bag from the backseat was tossed inside as well.

The truck would pick that up. If the body wasn't seen, then it would be buried in a landfill somewhere. Forever.

But … if they found it, Blackley would look guilty.

He jumped in the car, well pleased with his plan as he drove away, heading for home.

He would sleep well tonight.

CHAPTER 22

Thursday, August 18th, 2:20 p.m.

ANNIE HAD SPENT the last hour on the phone contacting the names on the short list given to her by Anderson Blackley.

Vera Blackley's father, who lived locally, hadn't seen her for some time and was of no help. Her mother had disappeared out of her life many years ago and her father had no idea where she was now.

"We're not very close," he had said. "She has very little time for her family."

She had few friends. None of them had heard from her for several days, and they didn't know where she might be. Only one woman, Diane Henderson, had been any help at all. Annie had called her and spoken to her briefly.

Diane hadn't been aware that Vera Blackley was still missing. Anderson Blackley had called her on Monday, but he'd given no indication there was anything to be concerned about. Now, Diane sounded anxious. "I haven't seen her or heard from her since last week," she had said.

"Do you know where she may have gone? Did she know anyone out of town?" Annie asked.

"Not that I know of."

"Ms. Henderson, would you have any idea if Vera was having an affair?"

There was silence on the line for a moment, and then reluctantly, Diane answered, "I think so."

"Do you know who she was having an affair with?" Annie asked.

"No, she didn't say."

Annie hesitated. "Ms. Henderson, we have reason to believe some harm may have come to Vera."

Diane caught her breath.

Annie continued, "And so, it's important we find anyone who may have seen her or talked to her lately."

"Do … do you think she's been murdered?"

"I hope not," Annie replied, "but we're trying to find out." She hesitated. "What can you tell me about Anderson Blackley?"

"I have only met him a couple of times. I don't know much about him. Only what Vera mentioned."

"What did she say about him? Is he capable of hurting her? Did she seem afraid of anything or anyone?"

"No, she never expressed any concern about him. I know she didn't care about him, but she never said she felt threatened in any way," Diane said.

"Is there anything else you could tell me?" Annie asked.

"Mrs. Lincoln, Vera is a good friend and I've known her for a long time. I love her, but to be honest, she's rather impulsive. Especially when it comes to men. She can fall in and out of love without a moment's notice. And that's why I'm not positive whether she's having an affair or not."

"But you think it's possible?"

"Oh, yes, it's very possible. More like probable." She paused. "Oh, I do hope she's all right. Please let me know if you find her. I am very concerned."

"I certainly will. And please, Ms. Henderson, give me a call if there's anything else you can think of that might help locate her."

"Yes, yes, I will."

Annie gave her cell and office phone numbers to Diane and then hung up.

She sat back and glanced at the list again. She had contacted them all and had nothing new to go on. Only one thing was evident. No one knew where Vera Blackley was, and it seemed as if few people even cared.

Thursday, August 18th, 4:18 p.m.

SAMMY FISHER was homeless.

Not that it mattered to him. He found life on the streets was a lot better than working for a living. For the last ten of his forty-five years, he had been his own boss, and certainly not a demanding one.

He preferred life in the suburbs to the inner city. A lot less competition for his daily necessities, few though they were. He never had to scramble for a place in front of a heat register, or a sewer grate, in order to get warm on a cold night. And the food that could be found here was more to his liking and far surpassed the meager pickings that were to be found downtown.

He never had to push one of those grocery carts, slugging around his stuff with him wherever he went. He had his own little place under Richmond River overpass, way up high and tucked back behind the concrete pillars. He had found a little cave, his own nest, as it were, just room for himself and his possessions.

No one, other than himself, knew about the place, and so he never had to fend off any invaders, and except for a few insects and the occasional rat, he was left alone. The place was so well insulated by the earth around it, it could be heated by a candle on the coldest winter night. And it was cool in the summer. Once he got used to the musty smell, it was home, sweet home.

He liked it that way.

Sammy awoke and stretched, scratching himself in a few places before finally sitting up. That afternoon nap had done him good. He swept back the canvas and peered out.

Time to find supper.

He slapped on his baseball cap and crawled from his refuge. The concrete-colored canvas swung back into place, perfectly camouflaging the entrance. He scrambled down a few feet on all fours before having enough space to stand.

He brushed himself off and checked his back pocket. He always carried a couple of plastic grocery bags jammed in there, one for his supper, and an extra one just in case he stumbled across anything he couldn't live without. That was rare, but you never knew.

He kicked up dust with his tattered running shoes as he hobbled down the embankment to the river below. It flowed from north of the city and went a few miles south before finally slamming into the lake. But here, the water was fresh enough. It hadn't picked up a lot of pollution yet on this part of its journey south, and Sammy found it good enough to drink.

He slipped his cap off and took his daily bath, consisting of kneeling down and soaking his head. He felt refreshed. He cupped his hands and slurped up a few mouthfuls of water. It was cold and tasted good. He wiped his mouth on his sleeve, and then stood and shook his bushy head like a shaggy dog shaking off water.

It was time to go.

Sticking his hat back on the knotted mess, he climbed up the embankment and around the side of the overpass, and soon he was standing on the sidewalk of a busy city street.

People pointed and stared at his tattered clothes, his

laceless shoes, and his heavily bearded face as he ambled along. A few conspicuously looked the other way as they passed, avoiding his eyes and holding their breath in case the man carried something contagious.

He pretended not to see, and on occasion, he would get even by accidentally bumping into someone who was particularly offended by him. And then he would touch his cap, give a hearty apology, and chuckle to himself as he continued on his way.

He'd had a part-time job as a party clown many years ago and had loved it. There wasn't much call any more for his expertise, but he had learned long ago that little children never seemed to be offended by him. And now, on occasion, he would stop and do a happy dance, entertaining the kids, enjoying their giggles, until their mothers sternly steered them away, probably lecturing them about the eminent dangers of homeless strangers.

He wandered on.

At the next intersection, he turned down Magnetic Drive, an industrial area. There were a couple of diners here, catering to the local warehousing and shipping industries that littered the street. They depended solely on local customers and did a roaring business during office hours, but usually closed up by five o'clock or so. The area was deserted after that, and there was always an abundance of leftover good stuff to choose from in the bins behind the restaurants. Plenty to satisfy his taste buds and fill his slightly rounded tummy.

It was rumbling now.

Humming to himself, he slipped down an alleyway between two buildings and took a left. By now, he could already smell his supper waiting for him in the big green bin dead ahead.

A sign above the bin said, "Jackie's Diner, No Dumping."

He stepped onto a ledge at the end of the bin, about halfway up, then hoisted himself the rest of the way and peered in. He grinned.

"Supper is ready. Come and get it."

There were enough goodies here to open his own diner. There always were. Well, not always. Not on the weekends. The place was closed then, and Sammy was too particular to eat two-day-old food, especially after the rats and other rodents had browsed through it.

He was a frequent visitor to this establishment and knew how everything was packaged. The leftover meat was in small white bags, probably to keep the eventual smell down. Fries, bread rolls, and pastries were usually packed neatly in a cardboard box along with prepackaged sandwiches that hadn't been purchased. And then the whole lot of tidily packaged leftovers was tossed untidily into the waiting bin.

It didn't take him long to find what he needed. He dug a grocery bag from his back pocket. He would take what he wanted for supper and enough for breakfast and lunch tomorrow, and leave the rest to the rodents already skittering around inside the bin.

He packed his choices carefully inside the bag, tied the top, and dropped from the bin.

Life was good.

As usual, he would go down a couple of streets and enjoy his feast in the park. A lovely little place where he could watch the kids and appreciate the afternoon.

But first, he would see what was in the other bins along there. He hadn't checked them for a while.

The next unit did commercial printing. There was never anything in there he needed, but if he ever wanted some writing paper in the future, he knew where to get it. He passed the bin by.

Next was a computer parts supplier. Never anything there.

Next. "Proper Shoes."

I don't really need any shoes. And these ones are for old people anyway. Maybe I'll come back in forty years or so and see what they have for me.

Suddenly, an overpowering stench filled his nose. He held his breath and moved away, shaking his head in disgust. It smelled like a dead cat or something was inside.

Drawn by curiosity, he plugged his nose and climbed up the end of the bin. He heaved himself up carefully, closed one eye, and looked.

What he saw made him change his mind about eating his supper real soon. His stomach wasn't up to it now. He dropped to the ground, backed up several feet, and stopped, staring in disbelief and slowly shaking his head.

The police'll want to know about that.

CHAPTER 23

Thursday, August 18th, 5:02 p.m.

ANNIE HAD DROPPED over next door to chat with Chrissy for a while. Jake had just brewed a fresh pot of coffee, its pleasant aroma filling his nose as he poured himself a big mugful. He carried it out the back door to the deck, slouched down in a chair, dropped his feet onto another one, and sipped carefully at his steaming drink.

He watched as Matty and Kyle kicked around a soccer ball on the lawn. Matty was showing Kyle how to do a hip fake, a deft little move that always seemed to fool his opponent. They practiced until Kyle had it right.

Jake was proud of Matty. He was pretty adept at most sports, taking to it naturally, just like his father. Jake had been mainly into football, though. His size had made him a formidable opponent. He'd tried to pass his football skills on to Matty, but Matty had taken more to soccer and baseball, and he seemed to be a natural at both.

The boys were tiring out and needed a rest. Matty skillfully kicked the ball, spinning it through the air, up onto the deck. He followed behind it, trudging up the steps. Kyle trailed, and they flopped, panting, into a couple of lawn chairs beside Jake.

"Hey, Dad."

"Hi, Mr. Lincoln."

"Hi, guys," Jake said, and then turned to Kyle, "Your footwork is starting to look pretty good."

Kyle grinned. "Matty's a good teacher."

"Keep at it and you'll both be stars."

The boys laughed. Kyle gave Matty a shove and said, "Matty's already a star."

Matty tapped Kyle playfully on the head. "I'll make you a star too. We'll show everybody how it's done."

Jake grinned at them and then asked, "So, guys, how'd it go at school today? Did that Jordan kid give you any more headaches?"

Matty laughed. "I think he learned his lesson, Dad. He wouldn't come near us today. At lunch break, I saw him standing across the yard with a couple of other guys watching Kyle and I, but he stayed plenty far enough away."

"Kyle and me."

"What?"

"Kyle and me. You have to say, Kyle and me. Not Kyle and I."

Matty gave his father a funny look. "You're starting to sound like Mom."

Jake laughed. "Is that such a bad thing?"

Matty shrugged. "Guess not," he said, and then, "You know I had to slug Kevin, right, Dad?"

Jake thought a minute before speaking carefully. "Sometimes there are other ways."

"Not this time. We tried other ways. We tried to just talk to him, but sometimes talk isn't enough. You know what Grandpa says—actions speak louder than words."

"Yeah, a lot of people say that," Jake admitted. "And I guess it's true sometimes."

Jake knew it firsthand. In his preteen days, he had been fairly small. At times, he'd been picked on and forced to defend himself physically. He had endured a bit of torture from some of the bigger boys, but as he'd hit his teen years, he'd begun to sprout like a weed and they'd stopped bothering him. He didn't seek revenge on his tormentors and had actually become good friends with a couple of them eventually.

Jake added, "But just try to do whatever you can to avoid fighting in the future, okay, guys?"

"Sure, Dad. But what if he starts bugging Kyle again and I'm not there?" Matty asked.

Kyle looked at Matty. "Don't worry, Matt, I'll just warn him I'll tell you. He won't do anything." Kyle grinned. "He's scared of you now."

Matty looked at Kyle, nodded slowly, and said seriously, "Yeah, I guess you're right, but I don't want him to be afraid of me. Just respect us and leave us alone."

Jake listened to the wise words from his eight-year-old son and felt even prouder.

Annie had returned home from her visit with Chrissy. She stepped out onto the deck, sipping a coffee. "What are you guys talking about?" she asked.

Jake looked up. "Just asking them how their day was. Matty said the Jordan kid is staying away from them now."

Annie looked at the boys. "Just be careful in the future, okay?"

"Yes, Mom. Dad already lectured us," Matty said as he turned to Kyle and slugged him on the arm. "Come on, Kyle, let's go." He jumped up, retrieved the soccer ball, and hit the lawn with a leap. Kyle stopped long enough to mash a spider and then was right behind him.

Annie sat in a deck chair and watched the boys for a moment before turning to Jake. "I've been thinking about Philip Macy," she said. "He must be going through such a terrible time. First he loses a child, and now his wife." She sighed. "What's the poor man going to do?"

Jake thought of his own family. Of Matty, and Annie. He couldn't imagine what it would be like to lose them both, or even one of them. He shook his head slowly and looked at his wife. He could tell she knew his thoughts and was probably thinking the same as him. "Yeah," he said and sighed before adding, "It must be rough."

They were quiet for a moment, each with their own thoughts. Finally Annie spoke. "We have to find out what happened to Abigail Macy. Philip needs to know. If he's left hanging, it will drive him crazy for the rest of his life."

"Like they say, he needs closure." He shrugged. "I don't know what on earth closure is. Nothing's going to bring her back, but at least he needs to know why and how."

"And who," Annie added.

Jake looked at her and cocked his head.

"Who," she said. "He needs to know who killed her."

"Yeah. That's the big question."

Jake's iPhone buzzed. He kept it in a holder on his belt now. The new purchase made his phone a lot easier to get at. He slipped it from the holder.

"Jake here."

"Jake, it's Hank. I just got a call. It looks like they found Vera Blackley. She's dead. I'm on my way to the scene now. Apparently a homeless guy found her in a bin behind Proper Shoes."

Jake whistled and looked at Annie. "It's Hank. They found Vera Blackley." Then he whispered, "Dead."

Annie leaned forward as Jake put the phone on speaker.

Hank continued, "I haven't talked to the homeless guy yet. I thought you might want to be here when I take his statement. You know where Proper Shoes is, right?"

"Yup, we were just there a couple of hours ago."

"Go behind the building, to the service area."

Jake and Annie were standing now.

"We'll be right there," Jake said as he hung up and slipped the phone back in its holder.

Annie reached out. "I need your phone for a second."

Jake handed it to her. Annie dialed. One ring. Two.

"Hello?"

"Chrissy, it's Annie. Can you watch Matty for a while? Jake and I have a bit of an emergency."

"Sure. What kind of emergency?"

"Remember I told you about Vera Blackley? They just found her body."

"Ohhh. Sounds exciting."

Annie laughed and scolded her gently. "Chrissy, a woman is dead."

"Yeah, I know," Chrissy said meekly, and then, "Send the boys over."

Annie hung up the phone and handed it back. She looked toward the yard and called, "Matty, come here a minute, please."

Matty gave the ball a final kick across the yard and ran toward the deck. "What is it, Mom?"

"Your dad and I have to go out for a while. Can you guys run next door until we get back? Let Chrissy know you're there."

"Sure, Mom," Matty said. Then they sprinted across the lawn, squeezed through the hedge, and ran in through back entrance of the house next door.

Jake gulped the rest of his coffee and set the cup on the table. "Ready?" he asked.

"Ready."

CHAPTER 24

Thursday, August 18th, 5:15 p.m.

WHEN HANK pulled into the parking lot at the rear of the building that housed Proper Shoes, the first responders, as well as the crime scene investigators, had already arrived. He pulled up next to the forensic van and climbed out. Officers were stretching yellow tape around the area and investigators were busy.

A group of four or five bystanders were watching from a distance, undoubtedly curious.

Hank saw the lead crime scene investigator, Rod Jameson, standing back a distance from the big green bin that was the center of attention. He was busy giving orders, making sure the area was secure. Jameson looked at Hank as he approached and nodded. "Afternoon, Hank."

"Hey, Rod, what can you tell me about this one?" Hank asked.

"The body has been here a while," Jameson answered. He pointed over to the side, behind the tape, where a man was sitting on a crate watching proceedings. "That's Sammy Fisher. I asked him to stick around for a while. He's the one who discovered the body. You may want to talk to him."

Hank glanced over briefly and nodded, then asked, "How do you know it's Vera Blackley? Is there some ID on the body?"

"Nope. The place wasn't deserted yet. There were still a couple of people inside the building and I showed them a photo of her face I snapped on my cell. One of them recognized her as Vera Blackley, the wife of one of the people who works here." He consulted a clipboard. "Anderson Blackley, the husband."

Hank thanked him and moved in a little closer to the bin. An unpleasant odor hit him. A police photographer had climbed up onto the bin and was snapping pictures. Evidence markers had been placed in a few spots around the bin, marking items that might be of interest.

The medical examiner, Nancy Pietek, had just arrived. Hank watched as she approached the bin and talked to the photographer, who now seemed to have taken all the pictures he needed. He jumped down and helped her climb the bin, and she dropped carefully inside.

Hank turned as he heard the rumble of a familiar car approaching. It was Jake's Firebird. He grinned as he saw the car. He dipped under the yellow tape officers had finished putting in place and approached the vehicle. Jake and Annie climbed out and came toward him.

Jake slapped him on the back. "What's up, Hank?"

"Hey, Jake," Hank said, and then looked at Annie and smiled hello before pointing to the bin. "She's in there."

Jake followed his gaze and whistled. "Thrown away like trash."

The ME was being helped from the bin. Jake and Annie followed Hank as he walked back to the taped-off area and motioned her over.

Nancy Pietek gave a wave of recognition and came to where they were standing. She smiled grimly. "I didn't expect to see you again so soon, Hank."

"Hi, Nancy," he said. "It's always nice to see you."

She greeted Jake and Annie and turned back to Hank.

"Looks like she was strangled. The body is almost naked, so there may have been a rape or some other sexual abuse involved. I'll know more after I do a complete examination, but right now, I'd say the cause of death is definitely asphyxia caused by strangulation."

"How long has she been dead?" Hank asked.

Nancy thought a moment. "I'd say about four days at the most."

Hank did the math. "That would make it Sunday," he said and then asked, "Any defensive wounds?"

"Sure are. Not hard to see, considering the lack of clothing. It won't take me too long to do the report once they get her back to the lab. Things aren't so busy right now, fortunately."

Hank heard the crunching of tires on gravel. He turned and frowned, then shook his head in disgust as he saw the van for Channel 7 Action News pull up. The local newspapers and TV stations monitored the police bands and were always quick to respond to anything sensational that would boost their ratings. Channel 7 was the first to arrive.

The van screeched to a quick stop near where they were standing. The doors opened and the driver jumped out, slipping open the side door and reappearing in a moment with a camera. He slung it on his shoulder and chased after the passenger, a woman, who had already shot from the van and was heading toward Hank.

Hank knew exactly who she was. Lisa Krunk considered herself to be a world-class reporter, destined someday to be a newspaper journalist and win a Pulitzer. But Hank knew better. They had had some recent run-ins with her, and he knew her as someone who would do just about anything to get a story.

"Come on Don," Lisa said, beckoning impatiently at the cameraman.

Don hustled behind her, flicking his camera on. A red light glowed and the camera was aimed toward the action around the bin, panning, zooming, humming.

Hank chuckled as he saw Nancy catch sight of Lisa. The ME knew Lisa Krunk well, and she spun around and left in a hurry, back to the crime scene.

Lisa reached Hank and shoved a microphone at him. The camera swung his way. Lisa said, "Detective Corning, I understand the body of a woman was found here." Her extra wide mouth flapped as she continued, "What can you tell me about this situation?"

The city would see this, so Hank had to hold back his disdain for Lisa. "We don't know much at this point," he said politely and pointed toward the bin. "The body of a woman was reported to have been found in that bin. We don't know any more yet, as the investigators are still working the scene."

"Do you know who the woman is?"

"Not at this point." Hank wasn't about to release the name of the victim until they were certain who it was and her husband, Anderson Blackley, had been notified.

"Was it a murder?"

"We think so, but that hasn't been determined for certain yet."

"Can you tell the viewers anything else?"

"No. Nothing more at this point."

The microphone was withdrawn and poked at Annie. The camera followed. "Annie Lincoln," Lisa said. "We know you and your husband are private investigators. Can you tell us why you're here?"

Annie hesitated. "All I can say is this may be related to something we're currently involved in."

Lisa Krunk looked down her thin, sharp nose. "Did you know the victim?"

Annie shook her head. "The victim hasn't been identified yet."

The coroner's van was backed up close to the bin. The back doors were open and a gurney was being removed from the vehicle, ready to be put to use.

Lisa pulled the microphone back and pointed to the bin. Don swiveled and the camera zoomed to catch the action.

They watched as two officers climbed inside the bin and, with some difficulty, hoisted the body out. It was placed on the gurney, maneuvered into a body bag, and rolled to the waiting doors of the van. The gurney was slipped inside and the doors slammed.

Nancy Pietek climbed into the passenger side. The camera watched as the vehicle pulled away, out of sight.

"Come on, Don." Lisa hurried over to the group of people who were watching. Don clicked off the camera and chased behind.

Hank looked at Annie and shook his head. Annie rolled her eyes. "That woman is a pain," she said.

Hank laughed. "You got that right." He looked over to where Sammy Fisher was sitting, still watching. Better not to keep him waiting too long. Hopefully Lisa wouldn't get to him.

The bin was being emptied now. Everything was carefully bagged and loaded into the forensics van. It would all be taken back to the lab and gone over meticulously.

The items on the ground around the bin that were being guarded by the evidence markers were bagged and marked as well. Nothing was missed.

It was time to interview Sammy Fisher, but first, Hank had to make a phone call.

He hit speed dial one and waited.

"Hello?"

"Hi, Amelia."

The voice on the other end brightened. He could hear the smile as she said, "Hi, Hank. We're waiting for you here."

Hank hesitated. Amelia had been a victim in a recent case he had worked on with Jake and Annie. They had become much more than friends since then. She knew he was a cop, of course, and his work sometimes demanded odd hours and forced him to be on call any time night or day.

"I'm so sorry, darling," he said. "I may be a little late. I have a situation here."

"We'll wait for you. I'll keep dinner in the oven. Do you know how long you might be?"

Hank thought a moment. "A couple of hours at the most."

They said goodbye and Hank hung up.

"It's good to see you found someone who will put up with you," Jake said.

Hank laughed. "She's a keeper," he said as he turned and glanced at Sammy. He beckoned to Jake and Annie. "It's time to talk to Fisher."

Sammy stood as they approached. "Sammy Fisher?" Hank asked.

Sammy nodded. "Yup." He bowed slightly toward Annie and touched his cap. "Good day, ma'am."

Hank introduced them and offered his hand. Sammy shook it furiously. He had a good firm grip. Hank studied him a moment, his tattered clothes, worn-out cap, big bushy beard, but clear, almost beautiful blue eyes. He was a rough-looking character but immediately likeable.

"Sorry to keep you waiting," Hank said.

"That's okay." He beckoned toward the bin. "I know you're busy and I have nothing better to do anyway. And please call me Sammy." Hank noticed he was well spoken despite his rough exterior.

"Let's go around the corner here," Hank said. He wanted to be out of sight of Lisa Krunk. She would be sure to interfere if she saw them talking to Sammy.

They walked around the corner of the building and stopped.

Hank turned to Sammy. "I understand you're the one who found the body and called it in?"

"Yes, I did. I ran to a pay phone as soon as I saw it. It took half of my current life savings to make the call." He laughed. "But that's okay."

Hank smiled, then said, "Tell me how you came about discovering the body."

Sammy glanced briefly at the sky a moment before speaking. "I was just gathering up my daily necessities." He pointed down the row to the green bin by the restaurant. "Down there. And I checked a couple of the other bins. You never know what you might find. Anyway, when I got over to that one"—he nodded toward the taped-off area and wrinkled his nose—"well, I was going to pass it by until I caught a whiff. So I climbed up and looked inside, and voila."

"I assume you didn't go in the bin?"

Sammy frowned. "Not a chance."

"Or touch anything inside?"

"Nope."

"Did you see anyone around at the time?"

"No, I think everything was closed up by then and I didn't see anybody at all."

Hank reached into his pocket and pulled out a small roll of bills. He peeled off a twenty and handed it to Sammy. "Here's for your trouble," he said.

Sammy held up his hands in protest. "Uh uh. No, thanks. I don't need to get paid for doing the right thing."

"Take it anyway," Hank urged.

Sammy stuffed his hands in his pockets and shook his head.

Hank put the bill away and retrieved a business card and a single dollar. "All right, here's my card and enough money for a call if you think of anything else. You can take that much, right?"

"Yeah, I think that would be okay." Sammy stuffed the money in his pocket and glanced briefly at the card before tucking it in his shirt pocket.

"Is there any way I can get ahold of you if necessary?" Hank asked.

Sammy laughed. "Nope. I cut my phone service off ten years ago and the place where I'm staying has no address."

"Is there any place we can find you?" Jake asked.

Sammy though a moment. "I'd rather not say. It's kind of a secret place, and I wouldn't want the city to make me leave."

"Trust me, Sammy," Hank said. "No one else would know. I have no desire to cause you any trouble."

Annie added, "We're just glad you have a safe place." Hank could see she was drawn to this character as well. He had a certain good-natured charm about him that made him appealing.

Sammy squinted slightly and scrutinized them carefully. "All right," he said slowly. "But you gotta promise you won't say anything."

They promised.

Sammy paused, pushed his cap back, and scratched his head before saying, "If you go under the overpass, where Front Street crosses Richmond River, on the north side of the river, right up the slope until you hit your head on the bridge. You won't see it unless you're right up under there." He grinned. "That's my current residence. It's not much, but it's all mine."

Jake nodded. "I know the area," he said.

"Are you sure you don't want some money? Enough for supper?" Annie asked.

"Thank you, Detective Annie." He patted the bag over his

shoulder and smiled. “I have my supper right here. And enough for tomorrow.” His smile turned to a slight frown as he glanced at the bin and back. “Do you know who she was?”

“We’re pretty sure,” Hank said. “But we can’t say anything yet until we notify her husband.”

“Sure, I understand.” He looked at Jake. “If you need any help, Detective Jake, just drop by my mansion and I’ll check my calendar. I may be able to fit you in.”

Jake laughed. “I may just take you up on that.”

Hank said, “Sammy, you’ve been a big help and we appreciate it.”

“Any time.” He nodded at Jake and Annie. “Goodbye, Detective Jake, Detective Annie.” Then more seriously to Hank, he said, “I sure hope you find whoever did this.”

“We hope so, too.” Hank offered his hand. “Take care of yourself, Sammy.” They shook, and Sammy watched them as they walked away and then turned and ambled toward the street.

The forensics van was just leaving. Lisa Krunk and Don seemed to have vanished, the tape had been removed, and everything was back to normal.

Hank walked Jake and Annie to the Firebird. After the two had climbed inside, he leaned against Jake’s open window and said, “Now I have to tell Anderson Blackley about his wife.”

“That shouldn’t be as bad as it usually is,” Jake said as he brought the engine roaring to life. “He doesn’t seem to care much about her anyway.”

Hank nodded. “Yeah, but it’s still no fun,” he said, and then stepped back and watched the bright red Pontiac kick up a little gravel and roar from sight around the end of the row of units.

CHAPTER 25

Thursday, August 18th, 5:15 p.m.

SAMANTHA RIGGS had arrived at work that morning as usual. The only thing that wasn't usual was that Philip Macy wasn't there yet. He was always in before her.

And then he had called. He wouldn't be in today.

When Philip explained that his wife had committed suicide the day before, Samantha was distraught, almost hysterical, and was barely able to make it through the day. She couldn't keep her mind on her work.

It didn't seem like Abby to take an overdose and end her life. She knew Abby was depressed, but she had known her for a long time. It just didn't make sense. But, on the other hand, Philip had said the coroner ruled her death as suicide. Perhaps it was.

And now, as she shut down her computer, grabbed her purse from the bottom drawer of her desk, and flicked off the lights, she was feeling a little better. The blow that had overwhelmed her at first had now subsided to a numb sadness.

She felt sympathetic for Philip and had promised to take care of things at work for as long as he needed. She hoped it wouldn't be too long, though. It was a small firm, just the two of them now, and a receptionist. When Abby had stopped showing up a few weeks ago, it had put more pressure on the rest of them. And now, at least for a few days, Samantha would have to handle the client load by herself.

She locked the office suite behind her and waited for the elevator. She squeezed into the pack of departing workers. The elevator dropped two floors and the doors opened with a hiss. She stepped out, crossed the lobby, and followed the horde from the high-rise office building, through the spinning door to the street. She caught the first bus and crowded on, standing room only, holding on to an overhead bar as the bus jiggled her homeward.

Fifteen minutes later she stepped off, just a couple of minutes' walk from home. But first, she went to a nearby deli for a prepackaged sandwich and some soup in a cardboard container, and then made her way from the main thoroughfare and down a side street to her mundane apartment building, a big square block of bricks and mortar.

Inside the lobby, she checked her mailbox. A couple of bills, a lot of junk, and a hand-addressed envelope. No return address. She stuffed the stack under her arm and climbed one flight of stairs to her apartment.

She dropped everything on her tiny kitchen table, selected a can of Pepsi from the fridge and a glass from the cupboard, and sat down.

She went through the mail as she sipped her soup. The bills would go in a stack to be paid later. The rest was garbage. Except for the curious envelope.

She slit it open with her thumb and withdrew a single sheet of paper. She unfolded it and started to read, her mouth dropping open, her meal forgotten.

Dear Sam,

I am sending this letter to you because I know if nothing happens to me, if I am still okay when you receive this, then you will keep this note, just in case, and not show it to anyone.

However, I am afraid for my life. In the event something happens to me, then please take this letter to the police.

Sam, you're the only one I have told in detail about who I witnessed murdering a woman on Sunday evening. Philip, my dear Philip, believed I saw a murder, but the police did not. And so, I am hoping if this letter has to be revealed, then they will take it seriously now.

The man I saw was Dr. Boris Hoffman. I saw him strangle a woman on the lawn of a neighbor's house. The woman appeared to be half-naked, dressed only in a red bra and panties. I couldn't see her face and so couldn't tell who she was.

When he saw me watching him, he chased me, but left when I got to the front door of my home. I am afraid he will return. Since I am a patient of his, he knows me. He has already told the police I am delusional. Believe me, I'm not delusional. I know what I saw.

If I die, I know it will be by his hand. I have no proof. Only what I saw that night.

If I'm dead, they will have to believe me now.

The note was signed and dated.

Samantha sat still for a while, staring unseeing at the paper in her hand, and then folded it carefully, thoughtfully, and stuffed it back into the envelope.

Philip had told her Abby had committed suicide. Did he really believe that? Did the police believe that?

Samantha didn't believe it now.

She would have to call the police.

She stood and reached for the phone on the counter, picking up the receiver. She hesitated and then hung it up. She stood for a moment, the note in her hand, and then finally bent down and tucked it carefully into the bottom drawer of the cupboard, safely hidden underneath a stack of magazines.

Thursday, August 18th, 6:18 p.m.

DETECTIVE HANK CORNING drove down the tree-lined street and squeaked to a stop in front of 90 Berrymore. He had never been here before, but he knew the area well.

He squinted at the house. He wasn't sure if Anderson Blackley would be home, but when he saw the black Subaru parked in the driveway, he shut off his vehicle and stepped out.

He strode up the pathway, climbed the steps to the front door, and rang the bell.

Blackley came to the door dressed in a housecoat. His hair was damp and needed a comb. Probably just took a shower.

"Anderson Blackley?" Hank asked.

"Yes."

Hank showed his ID. "I'm Detective Hank Corning. May I come in for a minute?" he asked. "I need to speak to you."

Blackley stepped back and allowed Hank to enter, leading him into the front room. He motioned toward a chair by the large stone fireplace. Hank sat as Blackley tightened the belt of his housecoat snugly around him and dropped onto the couch. He looked at Hank and waited.

Hank cleared his throat. "Mr. Blackley," he said. "It's about your wife." He cleared his throat again and paused. "I'm sorry, but I have to inform you she has been found. She's dead."

Hank waited for Blackley's response.

Blackley just stared at Hank, unblinking. Finally, he glanced down for a moment, and then back up. "What happened to her?" he asked calmly.

"It appears she has been murdered."

"How?" Blackley's voice was low, unemotional.

"She appears to have been strangled."

Blackley crossed his legs and took a deep breath, letting it out slowly. He looked around the room, blinking furiously, as if holding back a tear.

Hank watched him, studying him.

Blackley took another deep breath and narrowed his eyes slightly. He looked directly at Hank. "Where did you find her?" he asked.

"She was left in a garbage bin. A homeless man found her there this afternoon and gave us a call."

Blackley's mouth dropped open and his eyes widened.

Hank continued, "She had been there for three or four days. I just came from there. She's been taken to the city morgue."

Blackley frowned and shook his head in disgust before saying, "I guess you know she and I were not on the best of terms. We pretty much lived separate lives." He shook his head slowly. "But I didn't expect this. I didn't want any harm to come to her. I certainly don't hate her."

Hank nodded. He understood how marriages could fall apart. His own marriage had not lasted long. Many years ago, after he and his wife had lost their own daughter, diagnosed with a brain tumor at six months old, they had drifted apart, never to get together again.

But he also knew, statistically speaking, most murders are for love or money, and in the death of a married woman, the husband is usually the first suspect. He watched Blackley carefully and said, "Mr. Blackley, the bin where she was found was behind Proper Shoes."

Blackley stared, his eyes popping. Then he frowned deeply, cocking his head. "You don't think … I had anything to do with this, do you?" he asked slowly.

"At this point we have no suspects," Hank said.

Anderson was quiet, unmoving.

Hank spoke again, "We'll need you to identify her body."

Anderson nodded. "Of course," he said.

Hank jotted the address down in his notepad and ripped out the page. He leaned forward and handed the paper to Blackley. "Please drop down there any time this evening if possible, or tomorrow morning. This evening would be preferable, before the autopsy is performed, if one is necessary."

Blackley took the paper and glanced at it briefly before setting it on a stand beside the couch. "I'll come down right away," he said.

CHAPTER 26

Thursday, August 18th, 6:22 p.m.

A BIG SIGN in front of the building said, "Office of the Chief Medical Examiner." Anderson Blackley pulled into the parking lot, slipped into a slot, and shut off his vehicle.

He sat there quietly, staring ahead.

What had Vera gotten herself into? He knew she was reckless at times, and her irresponsible nature had gotten her into difficult situations in the past, but he'd never suspected she would end up dead.

They'd had some good times in the past. When they had first met, he'd been sure she was the one. They'd seemed so much in love, he'd thought nothing could change that. But something had. It wasn't long after they were married before he'd suspected she was being unfaithful.

Little things. Like her not wanting to sleep with him as often. Or she was gone a lot with no explanation of where she had been. And when he was out of town on business, who knew what went on? The last two years had been especially bad, but he had closed his eyes and buried himself in his work.

He sighed and swung the car door open, climbing wearily from the vehicle. He walked slowly to the large front doors of the building and stepped inside.

"Can I help you?" a pretty young receptionist asked as he approached.

"I'm Anderson Blackley. I'm here to identify the body of my wife, Vera Blackley."

She smiled pleasantly at him. Not too much of a smile, but one probably aimed to put him at ease. She pointed to the side of the room. "If you would have a seat over there, Mr. Blackley, someone will be with you shortly."

He nodded his thanks and turned around. There was a row of comfortable seats against the wall. He chose one at the far end and sat down. Just like in a doctor's office, or maybe waiting to see the bank manager. Newspapers and magazines were stacked neatly on a small table in front of him. The smell of fresh flowers on an end table filled the air.

He glanced ahead to the doors leading into the bowels of the building. One would never know from appearances that the stench of death lurked just behind that polished stainless steel portal. Beautiful lives and happy families, suddenly replaced by despair and interrupted dreams.

Not that this would affect him so much in that way. Suddenly, a strange sense of joy at his newfound freedom washed over him. He immediately felt guilty, banishing the thought from his mind.

He grabbed a magazine and leafed through it absently. His thoughts were far away until he was startled back by a voice beside him. "Mr. Blackley?"

He looked up to see a young man wearing a long white lab coat, waiting for an answer.

Blackley nodded. "I'm Anderson Blackley," he said as he stood.

The young man smiled. "I'm Dr. Flanders. Please come with me."

Blackley followed Flanders across the waiting area, through a swinging door, and into a small room not much larger than his walk-in closet at home.

There was a window on the far wall, five feet ahead. The

doctor motioned him forward. As he approached the window, he could see into a large room, sparkling clean, all white and sterile, with gleaming stainless steel everywhere.

He dropped his eyes. A metal table had been pushed up to the window. A large white sheet revealed the distinct shape of a body beneath its snow-white covering. A woman stood behind the table, watching him, waiting until he was ready.

Dr. Flanders nodded. The sheet was lifted.

It was her.

There was no mistake. Even though it was white and lifeless, with pale, puckered lips, and shrunken features, he knew that face. The face that had beguiled him once, and had charmed and delighted so many others before him. The face that would attract men no more.

He felt a twinge of sadness. Not for himself, but for her. A small measure of pity for a life that was wasted and was now gone.

He didn't cry. He couldn't. She had drained all his tears long ago and there were none left. At least, not for her. The love he had once felt was now as cold and lifeless as the body in front of him.

He looked at the doctor and nodded. "It's her," he said.

Thursday, August 18th, 6:48 p.m.

LISA KRUNK was armed to the teeth. She had done her homework.

She hadn't gotten much from Detective Corning or the Lincolns, but after talking to the onlookers at the scene, she had gone around the building and banged relentlessly on the front door of Proper Shoes. An overtime office worker had finally succumbed and opened up. She'd barged in and, by asking the right questions, had managed to piece together what she needed.

She was pretty sure the body found was that of Vera Blackley.

Lisa supplied the name to her mole inside police headquarters, and a search through computer records had verified it. Vera Blackley, who had been missing since Monday, was now confirmed dead.

She had dropped off the Channel 7 van, and in order to gain the element of surprise, she and Don had used her personal vehicle, a nondescript gray Toyota that would be invisible as she waited at the curb for Anderson Blackley to return home.

It was a stakeout, and worth the wait if she was to be the first to get this story.

She tapped lightly at the steering wheel, her fingers drumming out the rhythm of the music softly pumping through the speakers. She glanced over at Don. He was dozing as usual, slumped over sideways against the door, snoring quietly, his hands resting on the camera in his lap.

Lisa sat up straight. A car had just pulled into the driveway. She slugged Don on the shoulder and he awoke with a start, shaking his head back to reality.

"He's here," Lisa said as she grabbed the microphone from the dashboard and shoved her door open. Don was right behind her as they dove out and hurried up the driveway to Blackley's car.

They approached their target just as he stepped from his vehicle and slammed the door behind him. "Anderson Blackley?" Lisa asked.

He spun around. "Yes?"

Lisa had the mike in the air. She pushed it at him. "Mr. Blackley, I'm Lisa Krunk from Channel 7 Action News. May I ask you a few questions?"

Don stood to one side, the camera was humming, red light glowing, waiting for something juicy.

Blackley frowned. "What's this about?" he asked.

"Mr. Blackley, the body of your wife was found today. What can you tell me about that?"

Blackley glanced back and forth from the red light to the mike and then at Lisa. "Yes," he said slowly. "Her body was found."

"Was she murdered, Mr. Blackley?"

Blackley hesitated. "Yes, she was," he said quietly.

"Can you tell us what happened?"

"She was … strangled," he said as he turned to leave.

Lisa persisted. "Mr. Blackley, do you have any idea who might have murdered her?"

He turned back. "No. How would I know?" He looked perplexed.

"Did you kill her?"

Blackley frowned. "Of course not."

"I understand you and your wife were estranged. Is that correct?"

"Look, my wife and I were fine. We were not estranged."

"You were out of town when the murder took place?"

"Yes, I was."

Lisa pressed on. "However, when her body was found, it was nearly naked. What can you say about that?"

"I don't know anything about that. The police are investigating and I'm sure they will be able to explain everything eventually."

"We have talked to witnesses who have stated she was having an affair, Mr. Blackley. Were you aware of that?" Lisa lied.

Blackley shouted, "No. She was not having an affair."

"They also said you may be having an affair?"

Blackley glared at her for a moment and then turned and strode up the walkway.

Don followed as Lisa ran after him. "Just one more question," she called.

Blackley stopped and turned around slowly. Lisa moved to the side as Don went between Blackley and the front steps, blocking his path to the house.

"Vera Blackley's body was found in a garbage bin behind the building where you work. Are you afraid you will be the number one suspect?"

"Why would I be? I told you, I was out of town on business at the time."

"The police may say you were somehow involved."

Blackley glared at her angrily. "This interview is over." He turned abruptly and bumped into Don, pushed him aside, and strode up the steps. The camera watched him as he struggled with the key and swung the door open, stepping inside and slamming the door.

Lisa stared after him. She didn't get as much as she had hoped, but it would have to do. She had the footage from the crime scene, and maybe a little clever editing would put a more interesting slant on the story.

"Come on, Don, let's go," she said, spinning around and striding down the driveway toward her car.

CHAPTER 27

Thursday, August 18th, 6:55 p.m.

HANK RANG THE doorbell of the Lincoln residence and waited.

The door swung open. "Hey, Uncle Hank. Catch any bad guys today?"

Hank looked down at the boy in front of him and laughed. "Not today, Matty. But I'm working on it."

Annie called from the living room. "We're in here, Hank."

Annie was curled up in a comfortable chair, a book in her lap. Jake was slouched on the couch, his feet on the coffee table, playing with his iPhone. They looked up as Hank entered the room and sat down on the other end of the couch, Matty popping in between them.

Hank slipped a folded paper from his pocket and held it up. "I have the autopsy report here on Abigail Macy."

Matty looked at Hank, and then at his mom. "I know, I have to leave now, right?"

Annie smiled at him. "Maybe you can go upstairs and do your homework."

Matty protested. "Mom, I think I'm old enough to hear about this stuff now. I know what you, and Dad, and Uncle Hank do. And I know people get killed sometimes."

Annie hesitated and looked at Jake. Jake just shrugged and looked back.

"I'm not a little kid anymore, Mom, and it won't give me nightmares if that's what you're afraid of."

Hank watched Matty's parents as they communicated silently with their eyes.

Matty continued, "I have to learn about this stuff some time, don't I? And I see worse stuff on TV."

Annie laughed and gave in. "All right. You can stay."

Matty grinned and sat back, a triumphant look on his face.

Hank unfolded the papers and glanced at them. "Unfortunately, there's nothing unusual in the autopsy report."

Matty looked at Hank. "What's an autopsy?"

"Um, that's when they check inside the person to see why they died."

Matty nodded his head as if he understood completely.

Hank continued, "As they initially found, the blood test showed a point zero eight five level of alcohol, so she was legally intoxicated. And that, coupled with a high level of Lorazepam, was a lethal combination. Everything else was normal."

"And the bottom line?" Jake asked.

"Other than that, the autopsy showed nothing unusual, and so the coroner concluded, again, the cause of death was suicide."

Matty's eyes were wide, glued on Hank, as he listened intently.

"It wasn't suicide," Annie said flatly.

Hank shrugged. "I think you're right, Annie, but there's nothing substantial to prove otherwise. Forensics came to the same conclusion."

"Vera Blackley's body is enough evidence for me," Annie said. "That proves Mrs. Macy saw what she said she saw."

"What did she see, Mom?" Matty asked.

Annie hesitated and looked at Jake.

"She saw a man, um …" He looked at Hank. "What did she see, Hank?"

Matty asked, "Did she see someone get killed?"

Hank laughed and looked at Matty. "I'm afraid that's exactly what she saw."

Matty's eyes were wide.

"That's enough of a lesson for tonight, Matty. Go upstairs and find something to do." Annie spoke gently, but her voice showed she meant business.

Matty tucked out his lower lip in a pretend pout and slipped from the couch. "See you later, Uncle Hank."

"See you, Matty." Hank watched him run from the room and listened as he tramped up the steps to his bedroom.

Hank chuckled. "That's a bright kid," he said. "He may make a good detective someday."

"Not too soon, I hope," Annie said.

"Now it seems we're right back where we started," Jake said, "Somebody killed Abigail Macy and Vera Blackley and we have no idea who."

"Maybe Anderson Blackley?" Annie asked.

"I don't think Blackley is stupid enough to dump the body in the bin where he works," Jake said.

Hank shrugged. "Dumber things than that have been done before. If he was in a rush to get rid of the body, that may have been the first place he thought of. Perhaps he assumed the bin would be dumped and her body gone forever."

"Yeah, but he was out of town."

"He could have driven home, killed her, and then driven back again," Annie said.

"Sure. He certainly could have," Hank agreed. "We don't know the exact time of death, and after four days, it's unlikely they will be able to narrow it down very close. It could have happened in the middle of the night." He paused. "That being said, I don't think Blackley did it."

"So what's the next step?" Jake asked.

"Hopefully forensics will come up with something from the crime scene," Hank said.

Thursday, August 18th, 7:15 p.m.

"CORNING," a voice called sharply.

Hank glanced toward the sound of the voice. Captain Diego was standing in the doorway of his office. He looked impatient.

As Hank stood and strode across the floor of the precinct, Diego disappeared into his office. When Hank went in, Diego was slouched in his high-back chair behind his desk, his elbows on the armrests, his fingertips tickling his mustache.

"Yes, Captain?"

Diego dropped his hands and frowned. "Corning, what're you waiting for? Get a warrant and search the Blackley house."

Hank took a seat and leaned forward. "I don't think he did it, Captain."

Diego sat forward, dropped his arms on the desk, and stared at Hank. "Maybe not, but I want his house searched." He spoke firmly. "Now."

Hank protested. "It just seems too pat to me," he said. "That wine bottle in the bag. And the glasses. And the body being found right behind Proper Shoes." He shook his head. "It wasn't him. Nobody is that stupid."

Diego had a file folder opened in front of him. The loose papers rustled as he slapped his hand on the desk. "Listen, Hank, this may be your case, but you still do as I say." He sounded irritated now.

Hank stared at Diego for a moment. "Are you really going to make me do this?"

The answer was firm. "Just get it done."

Hank sighed and stood. "Yes, Captain. I'll get a warrant right away."

"And get his car too," Diego added.

Hank nodded, left the office, and went back to his desk. He didn't like this approach, but he had no choice. Captain Diego wore the suit of authority, not him.

It wasn't hard to get the warrant. On the surface, there seemed to be enough evidence against Blackley, and the judge issued the order without hesitation.

He notified the forensics team to meet him there, and in a few minutes, Hank rang Blackley's doorbell.

"Good evening, Detective," Blackley said, and then frowned as he looked over Hank's shoulder. The forensics team was unloading equipment from their van and a couple of investigators were already coming up the sidewalk. "What's this?"

Hank held up the warrant. "Mr. Blackley, I have a warrant to search your house."

Blackley's frown deepened for a moment. Then he sighed and reluctantly stood back. "Do what you have to do."

Hank turned, gave a nod, and the search commenced. Police set up a cordon around the house. Two policewomen took boxes containing equipment and evidence bags into a tent erected in the front yard as the experts prepared to enter the house.

Blackley was escorted off the premises, and he paced back and forth outside the yellow barrier.

Soon, the investigators streamed into the house in their white coveralls. Nothing was left unscrutinized as the team made a rigorous examination. Items were packed and carried out. A thorough check for fingerprints was done. Luminol tests, swabs, and dyes were used. The main floor, upstairs, the basement, and the garage were probed, inspected, and studied.

A tow truck arrived and hooked up to Blackley's Subaru, carting it away. It would soon be in the pound and undergo a painstaking inspection.

Half an hour later, Hank stood in the makeshift lab, trying to stay out of the way of the technicians, when Rod Jameson approached him.

"Hank," Jameson said. "We're far from done here, but we have enough now for you to make an arrest."

"What do you have?"

"They found some wine glasses that look to be of the same style as the ones found in the bin. There were traces of dried drops of wine spattered in a few places throughout the living room. I think we'll find it to be consistent with the wine from the bottle we found in the bin." He grinned. "And here's the kicker."

Hank waited.

Jameson continued, "We found a hammer in the garage with blood on it."

Hank glanced through the opening of the tent. Blackley had stopped pacing and was now sitting on the grass, his head in his hands. Hank looked back at Jameson. "Any fingerprints?"

"Sure are. Blackley's fingerprints." He waved toward the technicians who were hunched over, busy with microscopes, chemicals, and lab tests. "They're still testing the blood residue on the hammer, but I think you'll find it belongs to Vera Blackley."

"So," Hank said slowly, "if that's the case, then the murder took place here."

"No doubt about it, in my mind."

"But still, nothing to show conclusively it was Blackley?"

Jameson shrugged. "What more do you want?"

Hank sighed. He knew that was enough. He would be lax if he didn't arrest Blackley under the weight of this evidence.

It was all circumstantial, sure, but it was enough. Besides, the captain would demand it. He had no choice.

"All right. Thanks, Rod," Hank said as he left the tent.

Blackley looked up as he approached, a worried look on his face. "Are you guys almost done here?"

Hank looked down at Blackley. He didn't want to do this. "Anderson Blackley," he said. "You are under arrest, charged with the murder of your wife, Vera Blackley."

Blackley's mouth dropped open in disbelief. "What?"

"Stand up, please," Hank said.

Blackley stood up slowly. "It wasn't me, Detective. I swear, you got the wrong guy."

"Put your hands behind your back."

Blackley obeyed quietly. The cuffs clicked and rattled as Hank secured them, then reluctantly read him his rights.

CHAPTER 28

Thursday, August 18th, 7:45 p.m.

SAMANTHA RIGGS had made up her mind what to do.

Her plan would ensure Dr. Boris Hoffman paid for his heinous crime, and at the same time, she could turn circumstances to her advantage. A financial advantage, that is.

She only had one unanswered question. How much should she ask? How much would he be willing to pay to be sure the note would never be found?

She didn't want to be greedy. A thousand dollars? Or ten thousand? Maybe more?

Or perhaps she *should* be greedy. He deserved it. Abigail Macy was dead now. Nothing would bring her back, so why not benefit from this? Make him pay and pay in full.

She pulled out the bottom drawer of the cupboard and, safely hidden underneath the stack of magazines, she found Abby's note where she had left it.

She sat at the table, opened the envelope, and laid the note out flat.

She read it once more, and then looked around her small kitchen. It could use a coat of paint. The cupboard doors were worn and faded. Her coffeemaker only worked half the time. She could use a new rug for her tiny living room. And, of course, some new clothes. The list never ended. She certainly could use the money.

She dug the rarely used phone book out of the cupboard and dropped it on the table. The chair leg scraped as she sat down and pulled it in closer. Hoffman. There were half a dozen of them listed. She thought he might have had an unlisted number, but there it was, Dr. Boris Hoffman's home number.

She sat back and stared at the book, and then at the phone on the wall, feeling uncertain about her plan. Should she really go ahead with it?

She jumped up, grabbed the phone receiver from its hook, and stretched it to the table. She sat and quickly dialed the number in the book before she could change her mind.

She held her breath.

One ring. Two. Three. Four. Maybe he wasn't home.

"Hello?"

Samantha caught her breath. She had made up her mind, thought she was ready, but …

"Hello?" The voice on the other end was more impatient now.

She exhaled quietly, then asked, "Is this Dr. Hoffman?"

"Yes."

"Dr. Boris Hoffman?"

"Yes. What is it?"

"I want to talk to you about Abigail Macy."

"Are you a reporter?"

"No … I am … was … a friend of hers."

The line hissed softly but was otherwise quiet.

Samantha closed her eyes and willed herself to continue. "Before she died, she left a note. In the note she explained she had seen a murder and was afraid for her life."

"I am aware of her death. It's sad, but how does that concern me?"

"In the note, she named you as the murderer, Dr. Hoffman."

"That's absurd," he said, but did she detect a hint of nervousness in his voice?

"I have the note," she said. "No one else has seen it."

He was quiet, then said, "And?"

"And." She paused. "No one else will ever see it, if …" She paused again. She could hear him breathing. She continued, "If you're willing to offer a suitable amount of money." There, she had said it. She waited.

"Who is this?" he asked.

Time to get serious. "I'm the one who's going to hand the note over to the police if we can't come to some arrangement."

"Hypothetically," she heard, "assuming you have such a note, what would be a suitable amount of money?" Yes, she was certain now she heard unease in his voice.

She blurted out, "Twenty-five thousand dollars." She held her breath. She hadn't planned on asking for so much, but there it was.

Silence again.

"How do I know there is such a note?" he asked, still in a worried tone, but apprehensive.

Samantha thought quickly and then asked, "Do you have a cell phone? I'll send a picture of it to your phone."

He paused and then gave her a number. He repeated it to be sure.

She knew she had him now. "Hold on," she said.

She jumped up and grabbed the cell phone from her handbag on the counter and, laying the note out flat, she snapped a picture, being careful to get the whole page. Then she hit the "Share" icon, and entered the number he had given her. She checked the number to make sure her shaking hands hadn't dialed wrong, and then touched "Send."

The photo went. She waited, breathing heavily. What had she gotten herself into?

"I have it," she finally heard from the phone.

"Did you read it?"

"Yes," he said quietly.

"Do you want the note?" she asked.

His voice was low and lifeless. "I will pay you."

Her heart thumped.

He continued, "If you come here, I can have the money ready this evening."

She thought a moment. "I will meet you somewhere else."

He sighed unevenly. "Where?"

"Richmond Valley Park. There's a bench at the south end, near the wading pool. I'll meet you there. Bring the cash."

"I can meet you at ten o'clock," he said. "With cash."

"I'll be there."

"How will I know you?"

She thought quickly. "I'll be wearing a red jacket and a red floppy hat. I'll be on the bench."

"Okay," he said. "I'll be there at ten. Bring the note."

"I will," she said and hung up. She was shaking all over now. She pushed a chair over to the fridge and climbed on. Opening the cupboard above, she pulled down a bottle of Irish whisky. That would help.

She jumped from the chair, her shaking hands finding a tumbler in the cupboard. She filled it half-full and took a long sip. It made her catch her breath, but it warmed her stomach and she immediately felt better.

She looked at the clock. A couple hours to get ready. She sat at the table and sipped at the drink, excited and nervous, planning ways to spend her future fortune.

CHAPTER 29

Thursday, August 18th, 8:36 p.m.

JAKE WAS SLOUCHED on the couch with Matty plunked beside him. They were watching television when his iPhone rang. He slipped it from its holder.

"Jake Lincoln."

"Mr. Lincoln, my name is Isaac Shorn. Anderson Blackley has retained me as legal counsel. He tells me you're fully aware of the circumstances surrounding his arrest, is that correct?"

Jake leaned forward and stood up. "Yes, we're well aware." Hank had called Jake and informed him immediately after the arrest.

"Mr. Blackley has asked me to contact you. He would like to avail himself of your services, if you're willing?"

"Certainly, Mr. Shorn. My wife and I are convinced Mr. Blackley had nothing to do with the death of his wife."

"Could you drop by the jail this evening? Immediately if possible. He's only allowed one visitor at a time, other than myself, and we would like to go over the case with either you or Mrs. Lincoln."

"Absolutely. One of us will be there within the half hour."

After he ended the call, Jake went to office where Annie was going over her notes. She looked up at him. "Who called?"

"Blackley's lawyer. He wants our help and would like one of us to talk to Blackley right away."

"Go ahead," Annie said. "I'll stay here with Matty."

Jake nodded. "Okay." He turned to leave.

"Don't forget your notepad," Annie called.

Jake glanced over his shoulder. "I keep my notes in my head."

In a few minutes, Jake was out the front door. The Firebird roared away and he made it to the precinct in record time.

He knew a lot of the cops in town and some of the officers on the evening shift were familiar faces. After a casual search, he was led through a secure door and downstairs to the holding cells.

There were six cells, three on each side of the passageway. Prisoners were held here awaiting arraignment or temporarily before transport to prison, and sometimes the cells were just used as an overnight "drunk tank."

He approached the central control room, staffed by deputies. A young cop looked up.

"I'm Jake Lincoln. I'm here to see Anderson Blackley. He's with his lawyer and has requested to see me."

The deputy consulted a sheet of paper. "No problem, come this way."

Jake followed him to a door guarded by an officer who swung it open, allowing him to enter.

The interview room was a small, soundproofed area, with one chair on the near side of a shiny metal table, and two on the other. The room was brightly lit, with barren, blank walls. Blackley was seated at the far side, his wrists cuffed to a ring on the table. The man sitting beside him stood and offered his hand. "I'm Isaac Shorn," he said.

Jake shook his hand. He had a firm grip, not unlike what one would expect from a good lawyer. The chains rattled as he shook Blackley's hand. He sat in an uncomfortable chair on the near side of the table and leaned forward, resting his arms on the cold metal.

Shorn was younger than Jake had expected. He looked like he was fresh out of law school. His dark-framed glasses sat neatly on his long straight nose. He was clean-shaven with a hundred-dollar haircut. His suit looked like money. He was either very good or came from a rich family. Jake decided he was the former. He just looked it.

"Thanks for coming so quickly," Shorn said.

Jake nodded.

"Mr. Lincoln, I am convinced of my client's innocence. My firm has done some work for Proper Shoes in the past, and we have had some dealings with Mr. Blackley as well."

"Then the three of us agree," Jake said. "Now all we have to do is convince the police."

"Mr. Blackley has been questioned briefly, under my supervision, and they have revealed the evidence against him. It's circumstantial, but it's enough for the DA. I expect he will be arraigned in the morning, and hopefully, bail will be set." He glanced at Blackley. "However, bail could very well be denied. Not unusual in the case of a charge of murder."

"And you need us to find the real guilty party ASAP."

"Correct."

"What do they have?" Jake asked.

Shorn consulted some notes. "For starters, they pulled a garbage bag from the bin where Mrs. Blackley's body was found. It contained an empty wine bottle, two wine glasses, and a cloth. The wine in the bottle was consistent with some droplets of wine found on the floor at Mr. Blackley's residence."

"Consistent?"

"The same alcohol content and other similar ingredients.

Not conclusive, but given the circumstances, it's clearly from the same bottle."

Jake nodded.

Shorn continued, "We're not disputing any of their evidence. The DA has to prove Mr. Blackley is guilty. The burden is on them. However, because of the weight of evidence, we need to prove, not that it wasn't him, but exactly who the guilty party is."

"We'll do our best, you can be sure of that. What else do they have?"

"They found a hammer in the garage with Mrs. Blackley's blood on the head, a strand of her hair, with Mr. Blackley's fingerprints on the handle."

Jake whistled and looked at Blackley.

"I have no idea how that got there," Blackley said. "It's my hammer, so certainly it could have my prints on it, but the blood …" He shrugged.

"Anything else?" Jake asked.

"His alibi is a problem. Since the time of death is unknown, Mr. Blackley could conceivably have driven home, killed his wife, and then driven back to his hotel."

"It's not looking too good," Jake said.

"It sure isn't, and unfortunately, the way I see it, none of this points to the real killer."

Jake looked at the ceiling a moment, and then said slowly, thinking out loud, "It points to the fact that Mr. Blackley was obviously framed. The question is, who framed him and why?"

Blackley spoke, "I think she was having an affair, it went bad, and he killed her. He framed me to cover his tracks."

"So," Jake said. "We need to find out who she was having an affair with, and then hopefully, we'll have our man."

"Exactly," Blackley said.

"Is that everything they have?" Jake asked.

"It appears so. They haven't done the autopsy on Mrs. Blackley yet, to the best of my knowledge. That may or may not help us."

"Then if there's nothing else you can tell me, let me get on this," Jake said. "I'll discuss it with my wife and we'll see where to go from here."

CHAPTER 30

Thursday, August 18th, 8:56 p.m.

THINGS WERE GETTING complicated. His burst of anger the other night was causing him all kinds of problems now.

He had been thinking about this since she had called him, and he could only see one way out of this messy situation.

The problem was, he was not totally convinced that he wasn't being set up.

Sure, she had the note. The picture she'd sent had left no doubt about that, but what if she was working with the police? Maybe they wanted to catch him in the act; cold proof the note was legit.

Twenty-five thousand dollars was ridiculous. There was no way he could lay his hands on that kind of money. He didn't intend to pay anyway. He had other plans.

He would cover his own butt and call Tommy. His nephew, Tommy Salamander, was a no-good, two-bit thug, but he would come in handy right now.

He hadn't seen or heard from Tommy in some time. He knew he was still in the city, hopefully not in jail, but didn't know exactly how to get ahold of him.

So, he called his sister. She was curious as to why he wanted to talk to Tommy. He rarely ever talked to her, his own sister. So, he told her a young cousin was in town and wanted to hire somebody who could show him around the city. Who better than Tommy?

His sister didn't think Tommy was the right guy for that, but she accepted his lame excuse and gave him Tommy's phone number.

He called it.

"Hello?" It was a woman.

"Is Tommy there?"

He heard her yell, "Tommy. Get the phone."

A pause.

"Yeah?"

"Tommy, it's your Uncle Boris."

"Uncle Boris. Hey, Uncle Boris, I hear you're a big-time doctor now. Some kind of psycho or something."

"A psychiatrist, Tommy. I'm a psychiatrist."

"Whatever. Now, why would you be calling me?" His voice was raspy like he had smoked too many cigarettes. Probably done too many drugs, too.

"I need you to do something for me."

"You need a favor? From me? Is this a paying gig?"

"It's worth a thousand dollars to me and it'll only take you an hour or so."

"A thousand bucks? What's the job?"

"I need you to pick something up for me."

"You're not into drugs, are you?" Tommy asked. "Cuz if you are, I can supply you any time. Good stuff. Good price."

Hoffman's voice was sharp and impatient. "No, I'm not into drugs, you idiot. It's just an envelope. A piece of paper. Can you do that?"

"I can do that."

Hoffman told Tommy who he should meet, how he would recognize her, and exactly where she would be waiting. "Make sure you're there by ten o'clock."

"No probs."

"Now, listen closely, Tommy. She's expecting you to bring her some cash. So, I want you to put together some kind of package that looks like it could contain a stack of cash and wrap it up. Make it look real. Got that so far?"

"Yeah, I got that."

"She will have a note on her. Maybe in an envelope. She's expecting the cash in exchange for the note. Now listen. I need you to make sure you get the note from her."

"Make sure I get the note. Okay, got that."

"And then scare her real good. Threaten her." Hoffman added sarcastically, "I'm sure you're good at that."

Tommy laughed. "I can do that. Should I hurt her?"

"If you have to, but just enough to scare her. Nothing serious. And then bring me the note right away. You know where I live?"

"Yup."

"Any questions?"

"What's her name?"

"I don't have her name. It doesn't matter anyway. Just look for the woman in the red floppy hat on the bench. She'll be expecting you. Tell her I sent you. Any more questions?"

"Not really. It sounds pretty straightforward." Tommy paused. "You'll pay me the thou as soon as I give you the note?"

"Yes, of course."

"Just wanted to be sure. You wouldn't consider making it two thou, would you?"

"I think a thousand dollars is pretty good for a couple hours of easy work."

"Yeah, okay."

"So, I should see you by eleven o'clock or so. Don't mess around. Come straight here."

"Yeah, yeah. Don't worry so much."

"Do you have transportation?"

"Sure. I got a bike. A sweet little Suzuki. Takes me anywhere."

Hoffman hesitated. He hoped he was doing the right thing. "Okay, Tommy. See you soon."

"So long, Unc."

What a mess. If this useless nephew of his screwed up, he could be in even worse trouble than he already was.

CHAPTER 31

Thursday, August 18th, 8:59 p.m.

WHEN ANNIE PUSHED the scaling wooden door open and stepped into Eddie's Bar, she was hit with the pungent odor of stale beer mingled with the smell of something like old eggs.

She squinted to see in the darkened, windowless room. A well-worn bar ran along one wall. A half dozen people sat on spindly towers, hunched over their beer, unmindful and uncaring of the presence of others. A jar or two of pickled eggs, plastic bowls of pretzels and peanuts, and a swiveling stand of dusty potato chips decorated the far edge of the bar. The smell of old grease and burnt french fries mingled in with the rest of the odors.

Rows of all kinds of favorite poisons lined a pair of shelves behind the bar, catching the flickering gleam of Schlitz, Bud, and Miller neon.

Stagnant cigarette smoke lingered below the ceiling, gently wafting around in places where the lazy overhead fan stirred the air.

Peanut shells and sawdust littered the floor, kicked around and never swept. The only place free of the cracking waste was the tiny dance floor that now entertained a couple of aged patrons. A quarter-a-play pool table sat forgotten a little further away.

Fake wood paneling could be seen on areas of the walls that were visible around dated posters and tacked up photographs, illuminated by the glow of more neon.

Eight or so precarious tables filled the center area, three now in use, patrons leaning forward, hands gripping tightly about their glasses, a look of yesterday's forgotten life in their unseeing eyes.

Quiet music filled the background, drowning out the silence. Hank Williams cried into his beer, moaning about a long-lost love.

Annie approached the bar, brushed a stool with her hand to avoid sitting on any lingering traces of its last occupant, and carefully climbed on. She looked at the bartender, now wandering her way.

She was a little past middle age, pleasantly overweight, with a friendly, but well-worn face. A warm spark in her eyes belied her obvious hopelessness of ever seeing better days, resigned to her mundane life, and eager to make the best of it.

She blew back a strand of her frizzy, wine-colored hair and asked, "What can I get you, honey?" Her voice contained a pleasant huskiness, like fine sandpaper.

Annie eyed the taps behind the counter. "Just a draft," she said.

The bartender selected a beer glass from the towering stack, gave it a final scrub with her apron, and filled it to the top. The head bubbled and flowed down the side, dripping onto the bar, as she carried it and set it on a Miller Lite coaster in front of Annie.

"How much?" Annie asked.

"Pay me when you leave. I don't expect you're gonna run out on me." She paused. "I'm Meg, by the way."

Annie smiled, "I'm Annie."

"You don't look like you belong here, honey. Is everything all right at home?"

"Oh yes. Actually, I was just looking for a little information."

"Well, sweetheart, if it happened here, you can bet I know about it." Meg grinned a friendly grin. With nice teeth, not expected.

Annie swung her handbag from her shoulder and snapped it open. She slid out a photograph. It was Abigail Macy. She flipped it around and held it up. "Do you remember this woman coming in here, Meg?"

Meg glanced at it briefly. "Sure, I know her. Name's Abby. She's been coming here a lot lately. Haven't seen her for a few days, though. She's like you. Doesn't look like she would frequent an establishment of this nature." She laughed. She had a pleasant, full laugh, probably often used.

A couple of pool balls cracked across the room, and then a curse. George Jones was crooning now. A man choked out a cough somewhere down the line, probably wasting the hours, waiting for his turn to die.

Meg's laugh faded as Annie said, "Unfortunately, she's dead now."

Meg touched Annie's hand and leaned in. "Ohhh. What happened, dear?"

A man barked across the room. Meg told him to shut up and wait, then poured another glass of the yellow liquid, delivering it to him. "You've just about had enough, Charlie," Annie heard her say.

Meg returned. "Sorry. Have to slop the hogs once in a while. Now, you were just about to tell me about Abby. Whatever happened to her?"

"She appeared to have committed suicide, but I know she didn't. I'm trying to find the truth."

"Sheesh. She seemed awful sad most of the time. Usually brightened up after a couple of drinks, though." She shook her head. "What a shame. She was such a nice gal. Real polite and all."

Annie nodded. “That’s what everyone said about her. She was well liked.”

A man tapped his glass on the bar. “Fill me up, Meg.”

Meg obeyed, took his money, dropped it in the register, and turned back to Annie.

“Did she always come here alone?” Annie asked.

“Yup. Always.”

“Did she ever meet anyone or talk to anyone?”

“She barely talked to any of the guys here.” She glanced around the bar. “Can’t say as I blame her. This pack of blokes ain’t worth a wooden nickel.”

“She just sat alone?”

“Well, Wilda comes in here a lot. Most every night.” She pointed across the room. “She usually sits right over there. She comes in about ten or so. Her and Abby would chat all the time. That’s about the only one she ever associated with.”

“Maybe I’ll come back a little later and see if Wilda comes in,” Annie said.

“Sure, honey. You’re welcome here any time. You kinda class up the joint a bit, if you know what I mean. Somebody intelligent to talk to. It gets awful lonely here sometimes, looking after these fools all the time.”

Annie smiled. “It’s been a pleasure to talk to you as well.” She pulled a ten-dollar bill from her handbag and dropped it on the bar. “I’ll see you later, Meg,” she said as she stood.

“Look forward to it, honey,” Meg replied.

CHAPTER 32

Thursday, August 18th, 9:45 p.m.

TOMMY SALAMANDER was nothing but a two-bit thug. And he looked the part.

His mother had had high hopes for him, but Tommy never wanted to conform to her plans. He didn't want to work for a living, and so, he never did.

This little task from Uncle Boris wasn't work. It was just what Tommy was good at. That and, of course, his little drug business. Oxy was big these days, but he could also supply coke, smack, and, for the more discriminating, some herbal refreshment.

He stood from the couch where he was slumped and glanced at his girlfriend, her eyes glued mindlessly to the television. "I have to go out," he said.

She didn't look at him, just shrugged one shoulder.

He threw on a worn leather jacket, slammed the door behind him, and tromped down the back steps, his jackboots thumping on the wooden stairs. Then around to an alley at the side of the shabby apartment building, where he unchained his bike, kicked it to life, and roared away, his stringy hair blowing back.

He knew where the wading pool was at Richmond Valley Park. He liked to hang around there sometimes and watch the young mothers with their kids. Not because he liked kids.

Not at all. Hated the little brats, in fact. He just liked to leer at the women. He had often sat on the very bench where he was heading; wasting away the afternoon, wishing his dim-witted girlfriend looked more like these women.

As he approached the park, but still some distance away, he could see the girl in a floppy red hat was already there waiting. Light from an overhead street lamp splashed onto the bench. He parked his bike about a hundred feet away, chained it to a tree, looked around, and strode over.

This should be easy. Just like a walk in the park. He grinned at his wit.

She was huddled at one end, clutching a handbag firmly on her lap. She watched as he approached and sat at the other end.

He glanced over at her. She was watching him carefully and looked a little frightened.

"Nice evening," he said.

"Yes … yes, it is." She looked away quickly.

"Did you bring the envelope?" he asked.

She stared at him, and frowned. "I … I was expecting someone else."

"Doesn't matter. He sent me. Give me the envelope and I'll give you the money."

"Did you bring it?" she asked timidly.

He pulled a grocery bag from his jacket pocket. He had stuffed in some paper and rolled it up to make it look pretty real. He showed her the packet briefly. "It's here." He shoved it back into his pocket.

"I need to see it," she said.

"I showed you."

"I mean, I need to see the money in … inside the package."

He frowned at her and spoke bluntly. "After I get the note."

She was quiet for a moment. He glared at her as she looked across the park, then at him, and finally down to her lap. Her hands trembled as she unsnapped the handbag and slowly withdrew an envelope.

She held it up. "Here it is," she said.

He reached for it but she pulled it back. "Give me the money first," she said.

Tommy looked around the park. Nobody seemed to be around at this time of the evening. He slid down the bench, squeezing her between himself and the armrest she huddled against. He put his arm around her shoulder and grinned at her. She was held fast, unable to move.

"Okay, now give me the envelope," he said.

She stared into his cruel face for a moment, and then handed it to him, an uneasy look in her eyes.

He snatched it from her and stuffed it in his pocket. "There, now, that didn't hurt, did it?" He laughed.

"The … money?"

He threw his head back, laughed again, and then leered at her. "What money?"

Her eyes narrowed. "The … the money … for the note."

He grinned and shook his head. "Sorry, I have no money for you. But I do have this." He reached under his jacket and slipped out a knife. It had a six-inch blade and had seen its share of action.

She began to tremble, her breath quick and short, as he tested the edge against his thumb, and then touched the tip to her throat.

He moved closer and gritted his teeth. "Who do you think you're playing with?"

She stared into his savage eyes, narrow now, his mouth sneering at her, and she trembled. The knife was hurting her. His arm still gripped her and she couldn't move.

Then he laughed and pulled the knife away. His hold

around her shoulder loosened a bit. Her left arm was free. She clutched her handbag tightly and swung it with all her force, catching him full in the face.

He was startled and reacted by pulling away, just enough for Samantha to slip out of his grip. She ran.

He had recovered and was right behind her, spitting out curses.

He was no fool. Sure, he had the note, and he hadn't had to give her any money, and she was scared, just like good old Uncle Boris wanted, but that fear would wear off and she could identify him. He had to catch her and finish the job.

He reached for her arm just as she spun around and swung her handbag again. He ducked, slipped on the grass, and rolled a couple of times. Cursing again, he stumbled to his feet and continued the chase.

She was moving toward the street. He couldn't let her get away. With one final burst of adrenaline, he shot forward and caught her by the arm that held her handbag. She stopped with a jerk and he spun her around. He moved the blade to her throat and dragged her behind a row of well-trimmed cedars, a more private place, to do what he had to do.

She struggled, but he held her firmly, his left arm around her back, his nose almost touching hers, his eyes on fire.

The body contains a remarkable amount of blood, and when a throat is slit, assuming the jugular veins and carotid artery are severed, blood will spray. If one stands too close, this spray can ruin a perfectly good set of clothes.

Tommy was well aware of that. He was no stranger to this type of thing. He was careful to stand back as soon as the razor-sharp blade had made its stroke.

Too bad. She was kinda cute.

He watched the process. She didn't die right away, of course. First, she tried to breathe. That didn't work. She was still on her feet, barely, now beginning to collapse. She might last a few more minutes. Eventually her brain would become completely deprived of oxygen, and if that didn't finish the job, then she would drown in her own blood.

Tommy didn't like to see that part, so he turned away, leaned down, wiped his blade on the grass, tucked it back into its sheath, and looked around.

All clear. Time to get paid.

In a final burst of inspiration, he turned around quickly, knelt down, freed the handbag from her dying hand, and stuffed it under his jacket. He sauntered toward his bike, humming to himself.

Tommy Salamander didn't see the bushes rustling just a few feet away. He didn't see the pair of bulging eyes that peered at the unbelievable scene, and he didn't see the eyes then disappear, or the dark figure that hustled across the park, into the darkness and out of sight.

He climbed on his bike, another job well done.

CHAPTER 33

Thursday, August 18th, 10:03 p.m.

ANNIE HAD SPENT the last half hour driving around town trying to make some sense of the case. She didn't know what she expected to get from Wilda, but she had nothing else to go on, and at least this was something.

She pulled her car into a slot directly in front of Eddie's, stepped out, and dug in her handbag for some coins, shoving them into the hungry meter.

She turned. A sign still beckoned patrons to come in, promising affordable beer and good times.

As Annie stepped back into the dinginess of Eddie's Bar, she was greeted by the familiar smells and sounds. The music still droned, the smoke still hung in the air, and the same patrons still hunched over.

Annie went to the counter where Meg was leaning on her elbows, chin in her hands, her fingers drumming on her cheek, keeping rhythm with the tune.

"Figured you'd show up again," Meg said with a wide smile. She stood and tucked her hands into her apron pockets.

"Couldn't stay away."

Meg pointed across the bar room floor to a small square

table near the wall. Annie saw a woman sitting alone, facing her way, sipping on a glass of beer. She appeared to be in her late sixties or so.

"That's Wilda," Meg said.

"Thanks. I'll go and talk to her for a while," Annie said.

Wilda set her glass down and watched Annie as she approached.

"Wilda?"

"That's what they call me." She had a cheerful face, and when she smiled, her bright red lipstick cut a wide slit across her slightly pudgy face.

"Can I talk to you a moment?" Annie asked.

Wilda waved to the chair opposite her. "You sure can, sweetie. Sit down."

Annie sat and pulled the chair in a little closer. Wilda looked at her, still smiling, and brushed back a strand of hair that had escaped from the graying, almost white bundle perched on the back of her head. "I'm Wilda," she said.

"My name's Annie." She offered her hand.

Wilda shook her hand. Annie noticed she had soft skin. Just like her grandmother.

"Meg told me you come in here a few times a week and you knew Abby Macy a little bit?" Annie asked.

Wilda sat back, adjusted her sweater at the shoulders, and crossed her legs. "Sure, sweetie, I know Abby," she said as she reached out, worked a cigarette out of the pack in front of her, and tucked it between her lips.

Annie didn't know exactly how to tell Wilda about the death of Abby. "Were you aware Abby is … dead?" she asked.

The cigarette hung, unlit, as Wilda's eyes popped. Finally, she removed the smoke. "What? Dead? How?"

"The police say she killed herself, but I am pretty convinced she was murdered."

"Murdered. My goodness, such a sweet girl. Who on earth would do a thing like that?"

"That's what I'm trying to find out. I was hoping you could help me."

"I don't know how I can help, but if I can, then I am certainly more than ready." She shook her head. "Gosh. This is so …" She searched for a word. "Unbelievable."

Annie nodded. "It sure is."

Wilda sat back and flicked her Zippo. A faint smell of lighter fluid hung in the air as the tobacco caught and glowed. She took a long drag and inhaled deeply. She puckered her lips and the smoke furled out and wafted up. "So how can I help, sweetie?"

Annie suppressed a cough. "Do you remember if you were here last Sunday evening?"

Wilda thought a moment, then replied, "Sure, I remember now. I was chatting with Abby. She was here when I came in. All dressed real fine. I was thinking she looked like one of those nice church ladies. Then I got to feeling guilty, cause here it is, Sunday again, and I should have went to church."

Annie smiled.

Wilda continued, "I ain't been to church since my Frankie passed. That's a good six years ago now, I guess. 'Stead, I just come here way too much." She paused. "Anyway, what were you askin' about, honey?"

"I just wondered if Abby was here on Sunday. You answered my question."

"Yeah, she was feelin' pretty down that night. Usually is, but gets better as the night goes on. But that night, she seemed worse than usual," Wilda said as she drained her glass. She set it down carefully and waved a hand toward Meg.

"Did she tell you why she was so down?"

"Oh, yes, sweetie, she told me all 'bout her son that

passed. It's a sad thing, that. Didn't have no kids myself, but I had a sister who died a long time ago. Just a young thing, she was. That's not a good feelin'."

Annie heard a snore. She turned and saw an old man, his head dropped on the table, one hand still wrapped around a glass, the other hanging by his side as if reaching for the floor.

Meg brought Wilda a fresh glass of beer and removed the empty one. "You two having a good chat?" she asked.

Wilda flashed her smile. "Sure are, Meg. Don't get to talk to anyone so decent too often."

A guy across the room was calling Meg. She nodded his way, shook the sleeper back to reality, and went back to the bar to pour another drink.

"Wilda, what did Abby drink when she was here?" Annie asked.

"Wine. Just wine."

"Did she ever drink vodka?"

"Oh, no. Always drank just the house wine. Sipped at it all night. Never touched any of the strong stuff." She chugged at her drink, took the last drag of her smoke, and tossed it in the ashtray. The smoke continued to curl up, slowly dying.

Annie listened to the six-foot-deep voice of Randy Travis for a moment. "Did she ever talk about Philip, her husband?"

"Oh, yes. She went on and on about that man. Never had a bad thing to say 'bout him. She always felt bad she was coming in here and leaving him alone. But still, she kept coming."

"Every night?"

"No, no. Just maybe two or three times a week. Can't be sure. I'm not here every night myself. Just when I get to feeling lonely." She looked around. "Not that this place gives me any company. But somehow, makes me feel better."

"Misery loves company," Annie quoted.

“Yeah, it does. Just seeing others worse than me makes me feel better.” She laughed, a little titter of a laugh, and asked, “So, were you a friend of Abby’s?”

“No, my husband and I are private investigators. Abby’s husband hired us to see what happened to her.”

“Ohhh. Private investigators, huh. Gee, is that as glamorous as on TV?”

Annie laughed. “Not quite. Mostly pretty dull stuff, but sometimes we get some excitement.”

“Well, I wish you all the luck in the world, sweetie. I sure hope you find out what happened to Abby. I’m gonna miss her, that’s for sure.”

“We’ll find out,” Annie said as she reached into her handbag and came up with a business card. She handed it to Wilda. “If you think of anything that might help, be sure to call me.”

“I sure will.”

Annie stood and offered her hand again. “Thanks very much, Wilda.”

“Come back any time.” Wilda shook her hand and flashed her smile.

Annie dropped a twenty on the table, waving thanks and goodbye to Meg on her way out.

CHAPTER 34

Thursday, August 18th, 10:53 p.m.

DR. BORIS HOFFMAN was pacing nervously in his favorite room of the mansion.

He looked at his watch. Not yet eleven. No need to worry yet, but that idiot had better not screw up.

He poured himself a double of scotch and fingered the glass, sipping slowly as he looked around the den. He admired the way the dark walnut floors offset the hue of the stone in the massive fireplace, the crimson curtains, made of the best fabric available, and the huge desk that dominated the center of the room.

It would be a shame to lose all of this.

He went to the window, pulled back the drapery and looked out. From here, he would be able to see anyone approaching up the long drive. No one was.

He dropped into the huge leather chair behind his desk and reached for the ornate cigar box, perched proudly on his desk. He flipped it open and slipped out a Cuban, holding it to his nose, breathing in the sweet, earthy smell. He clipped the end and, grabbing his gold lighter, lit the cigar and drew in a mouthful of expensive smoke. It relaxed him and he exhaled slowly. The smoke circled above his head, dancing in the light breeze wafting from the air conditioner before dissipating.

He was startled to his feet by a roar outside. Stepping to the window, he saw a motorcycle spinning up the long driveway. That must be Tommy. He hadn't seen Tommy for so long, he wasn't sure if he would recognize him, but of course, it was him.

Taking another quick breath of smoke from his cigar, he dropped it into the ashtray on his desk and strode from the room and into the foyer. He swung open one of the pair of huge solid oak doors and peered out.

Tommy had spun up onto the front lawn, damaging the well-manicured grass, and was now climbing off his bike. He turned around, shoved the key in his pocket, swaggered up the steps, and grinned. "Hi, Unc."

Hoffman frowned and beckoned him to come inside.

Tommy strutted in, looking around the foyer and then up at the ornamented ceiling. "Jeez, Unc. This is sure some fancy place you have here."

"Did you get the note?"

"Why are you in such a rush? Aren't you going to invite me in?" Tommy sauntered across the foyer, his head whipping back and forth as he took in the sights. He stepped into the den and whistled.

Hoffman followed him in and watched as Tommy strode across the room and slouched at the desk, dropping his feet onto the polished walnut top. The cigar still burned. Hoffman went over, picked it up, and butted it out.

"This your desk?" Tommy asked.

"Yes, yes. It's mine. Now where's the note?"

Tommy looked at his uncle. "I have it. Don't worry."

Hoffman reached out. "Give it to me."

"You're gonna pay me, right?"

Hoffman sighed, reached into an inner pocket of his smoking jacket, and pulled out a packet. He slapped it on the desk in front of Tommy. "Here's your money. Now give me the note."

"Relax, Unc," Tommy said as he picked up the packet of money and sniffed it. He grinned, reached into his pocket, and pulled out the envelope. He waved it in the air. "Here's your precious note."

Hoffman reached for it. Tommy pulled it back. "I think this information is worth a little more than a thou, don't you, Unc?"

"We agreed on a thousand dollars."

Tommy glared a minute, teasing him, before handing it to him with a laugh.

Hoffman snatched it from him and opened it, slipping out the paper. He studied it a moment, and then his face turned red and he shouted, "It's just a photocopy, you idiot."

Tommy shrugged. "That's what she gave me."

Hoffman paced frantically back and forth. Suddenly he stopped and spun around. "You have to get the original," he yelled.

"Maybe I can. That might cost a little more, though."

Hoffman glared. "I'll give you another thousand dollars."

"It's worth two. I have to find her now."

"Okay, idiot. Make it two. But get it done," he screamed.

"Calm down, Uncle. I'll get the note. Just relax."

Hoffman relaxed a bit. "How are you going to find her?"

Tommy laughed and pulled Samantha's handbag out from inside his jacket. "I'm betting her name is in here." He leaned forward and unclasped the handbag, dumping its contents onto the desk.

He sorted through the pile and found a small wallet. He grinned and flipped it open. He pulled out a driver's license and held it up triumphantly. "Ta dah," he sang out.

Hoffman scowled. "I hope she hasn't gone to the police already."

"Don't worry, Uncle."

"Did you scare her?"

"Yeah, I sure did. I don't think she'll be bothering you again." Tommy read from the license. "Samantha Riggs. That's her name. I'll find her apartment and get the note," he said as he slipped the license back into the wallet and dropped it into his pocket, along with a ring of keys that he pulled from the contents of the handbag.

"Make sure you do. And leave the rest of her stuff here. I'll get rid of it." He picked up her cell phone and tucked it into his breast pocket. "This has to be destroyed."

Tommy noticed the box of cigars. He smirked and flipped open the lid. "Oh boy," he said. He scooped up a couple and sat back. "You're in good hands," he said as he dropped his feet back on the desk and slipped the smokes into his top pocket.

Hoffman wrote his cell phone number on a piece of paper and handed it to Tommy. "Here's my cell. Call me as soon as you get the note. And make sure it's the real one this time."

Friday, August 19th, 8:25 a.m.

IT WAS A BRAND new day at the Lincolns'. Annie was cleaning up after breakfast and Jake was downstairs doing his workout.

Matty came charging into the kitchen. "Ready for school, Mom."

"Don't forget your lunch."

Matty grabbed his lunch, stuffed it into his backpack, and swung the pack into place. "Bye, Mom." He opened the door to the basement and yelled, "Bye, Dad," then slammed the door again.

Annie watched him go and heard the front door close behind him as he left. She finished cleaning up and went into the office, sat in the swivel chair, and leaned forward.

She had transcribed the notes from her notepad onto

several sheets of paper, laid out logically. She was trying to connect the dots, but there was little to go on, and she didn't know what her next move was.

She perused the paper, going over all of the details regarding the death of Abigail Macy and Vera Blackley.

The one little piece of information she had gotten the evening before from Wilda was that Mrs. Macy never drank vodka and never anything stronger than wine. And yet, when her blood had been examined, it had been shown that she had ingested a large amount of vodka. How had that gotten into her system?

She recalled Dr. Hoffman said Abby blamed herself for the death of their child. Therefore, she certainly would have left a note if it had been suicide. Yet there was no note.

Annie was now totally certain Abby had not killed herself. It just wasn't plausible, given the information in front of her. Abby had been killed to cover up what she saw.

If Blackley killed his wife, then how had he managed to kill Abby as well? No, Annie was not convinced Anderson Blackley was responsible for either death.

She looked up and leaned back as Jake came in. He plunked down into the guest chair. "Got anything there?" he asked.

Annie shook her head. "Still struggling to make some sense of this whole situation."

"It's not looking good for Blackley," Jake said. "I don't think he's responsible for any of this, but the evidence against him is pretty convincing."

"Too convincing," Annie said. "That's what you said last night and I think you're right. He was framed. He's not a stupid man, and not dumb enough to leave such obvious evidence lying around. That hammer they found in the garage with Vera's blood on it just seems too pat to me, and that's the piece of evidence that's the most convincing."

"The way I see it, whoever killed Vera knew her," Jake said. "It wasn't just a random killing, because he knew where Blackley worked, and exactly where to dump the body, and exactly how to make Blackley look guilty."

Annie nodded. "Vera Blackley must have had a lover. If we find out who that was, we've got our killer."

"So, how do we go about finding that out? We already talked to everyone who knew her."

Annie shrugged. "Everyone we know about. But if she had a lover, somebody, somewhere, must have seen them together."

"Stands to reason," Jake said. "But tracking him or her down is the problem right now. Where do we start?"

Annie sighed and looked back at her notes. "It's in here somewhere," she said.

CHAPTER 35

Friday, August 19th, 8:37 a.m.

TOMMY SALAMANDER drove slowly past the apartment building where Samantha Riggs used to live. He examined the building. It wasn't much better than the dive he had. Just a huge red eyesore, down a side street, somewhere in the middle of nowhere.

He coasted another half block, pulled his motorcycle to the curb, shut it down, and kicked the stand into place. He would leave his helmet on to cover his face. Just in case. One could never be too careful.

He pulled a pair of leather gloves from his jacket pocket and slipped them on, climbed from the bike, and strode back up the street toward his destination.

There were no security locks on the outer door, so Tommy turned the knob, pushed the door open, and slipped in. There was no elevator in the dump, but there was a set of stairs to his right. Apartment 202 would be up one flight. He took the steps two at a time, humming to himself, counting the money he would make.

He pushed open the upper stairwell door and peered in. The hallway was deserted, so he made his way down the dimly lit passageway and stood in front of 202. He dug inside his jacket pocket and found the ring of keys, took another glance around, and then tried the key that looked most likely to be the proper one. It was, and the door swung open. He stepped inside and closed the door quietly, locking it behind him.

He slipped his helmet off, set it on a table by the door, and fingered his hair back out of his eyes. He rubbed his hands together. Time to get to work.

It wasn't a large apartment: a front closet, a small living room, a bathroom, what looked like one bedroom, and a tiny kitchen. A thorough search shouldn't take long.

Start with the bathroom. All the obvious places. The medicine cabinet contained nothing of interest, just toothpaste, some Midol, Tylenol, and floss, but no note. He lifted the top off the toilet tank and peered inside. Nope. The cupboard under the sink was searched. Cleaning supplies and extra tissue. He felt around the edges, under the top, and moved things around. No note.

Next stop, the bedroom. The most obvious place was under the mattress. He flipped it up and peeked under. Then he went through her closet, moving things back and forth on the rod. He checked in the pockets of her dresses and sweaters. There were several pairs of shoes on the floor underneath, but he disregarded them and moved his eyes up. On the shelf above, he found a box holding some photos and a few envelopes. He opened the envelopes one at a time. Looked like a bunch of old love letters. The note he was looking for wasn't among them. He looked through the photos. Boring family stuff.

He slammed the closet door and turned around. The dresser, maybe.

He spent some time going through the drawers full of clothes. Her underwear drawer was especially interesting. He fantasized about her as he browsed her frilly things. He should have had a little fun with her before he killed her. That would have been a blast.

He slipped out all the drawers, checking in the cavity behind, and under the drawers to see if anything had been taped there. All he got was a sliver for his trouble, and he cursed as he kicked the drawer shut.

Nothing went untouched or unmoved as he searched the bedroom thoroughly. Behind pictures, under the alarm clock, under the bed, behind the faded curtains. No joy.

On a small nightstand by the bed he spied a little wooden box. He flipped it open. Just some junk jewelry and cheap earrings. Except for this. He picked up a necklace that looked like it could be gold. Might be worth a few bucks. He chuckled and slipped it into his pocket. Maybe he would give it to his girlfriend. Tell her he bought it especially for her. She was dumb enough to believe it.

Back to the note. He had to find it. He stood and looked around the bedroom, scratching his head. It must be in this apartment somewhere, maybe the kitchen. He would leave the living room for last. Nice TV, though. That would look good in his place, toss out the old piece of crap and drop this one in. Hmmm.

He strolled into the kitchen and went to the fridge. Not much food in there. Pepsi, water, some leftovers, a few veggies. He grabbed a carrot and munched on it as he slammed the door shut and opened the freezer. Sometimes people hid things in there. He rummaged around inside but came up empty.

Try the cupboards next. Start with the drawers, the most obvious place. One by one, he slipped them open and browsed through their contents. Finally, he was rewarded. In the bottom drawer of the cupboard, hidden underneath a stack of magazines, he found what he was looking for. He slipped the paper from the envelope and grinned.

That was it. That was the original.

He folded the paper again and dropped it back into the

envelope, then into his inner pocket. He laughed. Two thou, well earned.

He went to the front door, retrieved his helmet, fastened it on, and opened the apartment door carefully. Making sure no one was around, he left the apartment, locked the door behind him, and tromped down the steps to the front.

He made it down to the sidewalk unseen and hurried toward his bike, stopping long enough to turn his back, lean against a tree and wait until a tired young woman passed by, tugging two brats behind her. A ratty-looking dog followed them on a leash, yipping and barking. It stopped for a moment, sniffing at Tommy's heels, before being dragged along. They turned into an alley out of sight, and he walked briskly to his bike, otherwise unseen. He climbed on, kicked the motor to life, and rumbled away.

Finally making it home, he turned into the alley beside his building, parked his motorcycle in the usual spot, locked it up, went up to his crappy apartment and dropped on the couch. He pulled out his cell and the paper with his uncle's number. He dialed.

After the first ring he heard, "Dr. Hoffman."

"Hey, Unc."

"Did you get it?" Hoffman sounded anxious.

"Yup. I have it right here. Safe and sound."

"Are you sure it's the original?"

"I'm sure. It's in blue ink in a handwritten envelope. It's not a copy."

"Destroy it. Burn it."

"Okay. And what about my money?"

"Is money all you think about? Don't worry, you'll get your money." He paused, then added, "Come to the house this afternoon around four o'clock or so. I'll have it for you."

"Two thou, right, Unc?"

Hoffman sighed. "Yes, yes, two thousand dollars."

"Cash?"

"Of course, you idiot. Do you think I'd give you a check?"

Tommy laughed. "Just checking. Okay, see you then," he said and touched the "Hang Up" button.

He pulled the note from his inner pocket, withdrew it from the envelope, and unfolded it. He read through it again and grinned. "The way I see it, Dear Uncle has killed two women and he wants to give me two thou. That's only a thou per head. This information oughta be worth a lot more than two thousand dollars."

CHAPTER 36

Friday, August 19th, 9:10 a.m.

PHILIP MACY parked his car in the underground parking and took the stairs to the lobby of the office complex that housed Macy & Macy. He dodged people on phones, zombies with earbuds, everyone sipping coffee, rushing to work.

He took the crowded elevator to the second floor. The doors swished open and the silence of the quiet hallway calmed him. He didn't feel like being around a lot of people today. It just irritated him, watching their lives go on so peacefully when his had disintegrated into a million bits.

He went down the hallway, slipped the key into the lock of Macy & Macy, and opened the door. He was surprised the suite was still locked up. He had expected Samantha would be here by now. Especially when he had told her he might not be in for a few days.

He didn't feel much like working after Abby's death only two days ago, but his business was important to him, and he needed to take care of it, take care of clients. Abby certainly would have wanted it that way. She had put as much effort into building the firm as he had, and was proud of what they had accomplished together.

This was all he had left now.

He flicked on the lights, sighed deeply, and trudged

through the reception area to his office, slumping at his desk, leaning forward, his head in his hands.

After a while, he sat up and reached across his desk for a file he had been working on the last time he was here. He flipped it open, stared blindly at its contents, closed it again, and tossed it back on the small stack of waiting work.

He couldn't get his mind on business, now tossed between burying himself in his work, or just closing up and going home again. But that wouldn't help. He might as well be here as there. It wouldn't change how he felt.

He glanced at his watch, picked up the phone, and dialed Samantha's number. He let it ring a few times. There was no answer. She was probably on her way to work. He dropped the receiver in its cradle and sat back.

He stared at the wall, unseeing, recalling when he had met Abby. She had just graduated from the University of Toronto and he had been a first-year accountant in a growing firm. It had been love at first sight. He had never met anyone so beautiful and he'd considered himself lucky just to know her. Their future had looked wonderful, without a care in the world.

They had spent most of their free time together, and within six months of meeting, he had asked her to marry him. Of course, she'd said yes, and the happy event had taken place less than two months later. It wasn't a large wedding. Neither one of them cared about that; they just wanted to be together.

And then along came Timmy. Not exactly planned, but they were overjoyed when they found out Abby was pregnant. He went out of his way to spoil her, and together they spent months setting up the nursery, painting, decorating, shopping, laughing, and having a real adventure.

And when Timmy was born it was amazing. This little creature they had made. Life was even better. Timmy was just about the greatest little bundle he had ever seen and he loved helping Abby take care of him, feeding him, changing diapers, and tucking him in to sleep.

A few months later they opened their own accounting firm. Abby took to it naturally, and business, though slow at first, soon picked up and the future looked wide open.

Their business was growing, Timmy was growing, and their love was growing.

Then when tragedy struck just a few weeks ago and they lost little Timmy, they were devastated. Though Abby felt guilty, Philip never once blamed her. It was a tragic accident and no one was at fault.

And now, Abby was gone as well. The future looked dark, and without knowing what happened to her, it looked even darker.

His wife's body had been released and now he had funeral arrangements to take care of as well. He could use Samantha's help.

His eyes now glistening with moisture, he wiped them on his cuff and cleared his throat. Maybe he would call Detective Corning and see if there was any news. He was always supportive. He found his number, picked up the phone, and dialed.

"Detective Hank Corning."

"Detective Corning, it's Philip Macy. I … I was just wondering if anything had turned up."

Silence for a moment, then, "I'm sorry, Mr. Macy, but we have had no new evidence, and nothing that shows your wife's death was anything other than suicide."

Philip sighed. "I understand."

"But the Lincolns are still working on it," Hank said quickly. "If there's anything to be found, they'll find it."

"Thanks, Detective, I'll give them a call."

"Mr. Macy?"

"Yes?"

"I wish I could help you, but the coroner's report, and the forensic report … well, as you know, the captain has closed the file."

"Yes, I know you had already told me. However, I was just hoping …" Philip's voice trailed off. He couldn't give up hope. He had to know what had happened to his darling Abby.

Hank continued, "Officially, the case is closed, but personally, I believe there's more to this and I'm helping the Lincolns in every way I can. I want you to know I haven't given up on you."

"I appreciate that," Philip said and sighed.

"I'm truly sorry, Mr. Macy," Hank said. "But don't hesitate to call me any time."

They hung up and Philip sat back and closed his eyes, sitting quietly.

After a moment, he tried Samantha again. No answer. He looked at his watch and frowned. This wasn't like her at all. She was never late.

He dialed another number.

"Jake here."

"Jake, it's Philip Macy."

"Hello, Mr. Macy. How are you?" He sounded truly concerned.

"Not really so good. I just wanted to see if you had anything yet?"

Jake paused. "My wife and I had delayed calling you until we had something solid to go on. I don't know if you had heard about Vera Blackley. Her body was discovered yesterday afternoon." Jake told him the details.

Philip was stunned. He hadn't heard, had barely been mobile since Abby's death, and hadn't even switched on the television.

Jake continued, "We believe Mrs. Blackley is the woman your wife saw being murdered. They live on the property directly behind. We're sure if we find her killer then we'll know what happened to your wife. We believe it's the same man."

"So, then, you believe my wife was not delusional?"

"Absolutely."

"Do you have anything on Vera Blackley's murder yet?" he asked hopefully.

"I'm sorry, nothing concrete yet, but we're currently following up a few good leads, and we'll be sure to let you know what we find."

"Is there anything I can do to help?"

Silence, then, "Not really, but I'll certainly keep in touch, and if there's anything we need from you, I'll let you know," Jake said, adding firmly, "We're going to get to the bottom of this."

"Thanks, Jake," Philip said quietly.

They hung up. Philip was dejected and felt useless. He knew it had only been a couple of days, and these things take time, but he was anxious. He went to the outer office and started a pot of coffee. He had to get his mind off Abby.

CHAPTER 37

Friday, August 19th, 9:28 a.m.

DETECTIVE HANK CORNING had dropped by the precinct to pick up the reports on Vera Blackley. All around was the constant buzz of activity, rustling paper, phones buzzing, the prattle of chatter, and the tapping of duty boots on the time-honored hardwood floor. Officers scurried back and forth in their unceasing battle for law and order. A useless air conditioner droned behind him, kicking out a stingy amount of air, barely cooling the stifling atmosphere.

He slouched at his ancient desk and leafed through the paperwork. He wanted to have another go at Captain Diego. He saw a definite connection between the murder of Vera Blackley and the death of Abigail Macy.

But he knew any attempt to get Diego to rethink this thing would be fruitless. Abigail had committed suicide, and Anderson Blackley was in jail, charged with murdering his wife. Two separate and unrelated cases. At least, that's the way the captain saw it. It was nice and neat.

Too neat.

The autopsy of Vera Blackley had been finished and forensics had gone over everything from the crime scene and Blackley's house. The complete lab reports were in. It was all right there, sitting in front of him on his desk. All wrapped up.

After his talk with Philip, Hank had been concerned. Philip seemed to be so despondent. Who could blame him, really?

He closed the folder and dropped it into his briefcase. He had some other business to attend to. He was still working on the series of break-ins that had been taking place in the south end of the city. He would drop these reports to the Lincolns on his way there. He gave Jake a call to be sure he was at home. He was.

Grabbing his briefcase, he strode across the precinct floor and out the front door. His Chevy was parked behind the building where it always was, and he climbed in. The engine knocked a couple of times when he turned the key and then awoke.

In a few minutes, he slipped into the driveway behind Annie's Escort and shut down the motor. It crackled and popped as he stepped out and climbed the steps to the front door.

Annie answered his ring and invited him in. "We're just in the office," she said. "Going over our notes and trying to figure out our next move."

Hank followed Annie to the office and Jake grabbed a fold-up chair, flipped it open, and dropped it in front of him. "Have a seat," he said. "I'd take that one, but I'm afraid I might break it."

Annie parked behind the desk as Jake sat in the guest chair. Hank dropped into the fold-up, pulled out the reports, and set his briefcase on the floor beside him. He plopped the folder on the desk. "All of the reports on Vera Blackley are there," he said.

Jake grabbed the folder and pulled out the autopsy report, tossing the rest back on the desk. He leafed through the pages, making the occasional sound of interest as something caught his attention.

Annie flipped open the folder and studied the forensics report.

"One interesting thing there," Hank said, pointing to the paper Annie was reviewing. "Blackley's car came up clean. They also checked Vera Blackley's car. It was in the garage and it came up clean as well. There's no evidence either car was used to transport the body to the bin, or anywhere else for that matter."

Jake looked up. "If Blackley was the killer, then how did he get her body out of there?"

"Good question," Annie said. "And it bolsters my theory. I still think Blackley is innocent."

"And looky here," Jake said as he stabbed at the autopsy report with his finger. "The coroner reports no signs of sexual abuse or intercourse."

Annie looked at Jake with interest. "I think that tells us a lot."

"It sure does, cuz here's the question. If Blackley came home and killed his wife, then why was she half-naked? If she was dressed that way because some other guy was there, and Blackley killed her, then where's the other guy?"

Hank cut in. "And if she wasn't having an affair, then why was she half-naked?"

Annie added. "And why no signs of sexual intercourse?"

"On the other hand," Hank said, "if she wasn't having an affair, then was it an attempted rape gone wrong?"

"It doesn't seem like a rape to me," Annie said. "Because of the wine. A rapist doesn't usually bring wine with him. There were two glasses, remember?"

Hank nodded and said, "Going back to the way she was dressed, or rather not dressed, it seems obvious, given the Blackleys' failing marriage, she had not dressed that way for her husband. Therefore, I think we can conclude she was having an affair of some kind."

Jake added, "I think the wine stains found on the floor of Blackley's home show that as well. There was definitely some wine tasting going on that day."

"I talked to some of the neighbors as well," Hank said. "And the woman across the street remembers seeing a red Mercedes convertible parked in the Blackley driveway on occasion. She remembered it so well because she had often wanted one herself, but could never afford it."

"That's interesting," Jake said, "There's gotta be a lot of those cars around, but it does tell us she had a visitor. Somebody with some money." He paused. "He may be the other man."

"So," Annie added, "we're back where we started. Who's the other man and why did he kill her?"

"Here's the most interesting thing," Hank said as he glanced at Jake. "It's in the autopsy report you're holding, Jake. Remember the hammer?"

Jake nodded. Annie frowned and said, "Yes."

Hank continued, "There was blood on it, along with Blackley's fingerprints and a strand of hair from Mrs. Blackley. However, the coroner report states there was no blunt force trauma to her head or anywhere else on her body. There seems to be no way she had been hit with that hammer."

"And yet," Jake said, "her blood was on it."

"I had a problem with that hammer right from the start," Annie said. "Now I think it's part of the frame-up."

"You might be right, Annie," Hank said. "There was a small cut on her wrist. The only place blood was drawn."

"And that's where the blood came from," Annie concluded.

Hank shrugged. "Could be."

"Were there any defensive wounds on her body?" Annie asked.

Jake answered, "There seems to be a whole lot of them." He waved the report. "According to this."

"I'm not sure what that tells us," Annie said. "Except she tried to fight off her attacker."

Hank added, "There was nothing under her fingernails to show she scratched him or anything else on the body that would show exactly who he was."

"What about the stuff that was in the garbage bag in the bin?"

Hank said, "The wine glasses, the bottle, the cork, and the cloth, along with the wine stains on Blackley's floor, all came from the same source. And there were no prints on any of them."

"So they were wiped clean," Annie said.

"Almost," Hank said. "There were small traces of lipstick on one of them, consistent with the lipstick Vera Blackley had on."

"So one of the glasses was hers," Jake said. "No surprise there."

"True," said Annie. "But it does tell us they drank some of the wine. There had obviously been some conversation going on prior to the murder."

Jake interrupted. "And that proves to me she knew her killer."

"That rules out attempted rape," Hank added.

Annie laughed. "So we're back to our original theory. I think we'd better stick to that."

Jake and Hank agreed.

CHAPTER 38

Friday, August 19th, 9:32 a.m.

PIERRE BOUTIN was a perpetual tourist.

His grandfather had made an uncountable amount of money on a goldmine in northern Quebec and Pierre had never known what work was all about. He spent most of his days wandering around from city to city, country to country, enjoying the sights, sounds, and smells of the world. He used to call Montreal his home, but it had been so long since he had been there, he'd almost forgotten his old hometown.

This morning he was running a little late. He had partied too long last night and slept in. It wouldn't do to miss his morning run, so he donned the jogging bottoms he had picked up in Paris, along with a Nike sweatshirt, and running shoes that bore an American label.

He popped a couple of Tylenol and downed a bottle of water, grabbing one more for the road, and fast-walked from his hotel room. He took the stairs down five flights to the lobby. He drew stares from the front desk as he jogged across the Italian marble and out the door, giving a merci beaucoup to the doorman on the way through.

Without pausing, he took a deep breath of the city air, better than most, worse than some. He pounded up the sidewalk, twisted and weaved around the bustling pedestrians, heading for a place where he could go all out. He loved to run, and his destination was the park he had enjoyed the last few days, just a couple of blocks from the hotel.

He spun around a curve in the sidewalk and took a quick left onto a wide path leading into Richmond Valley Park. He sang lustily as he jogged, his clear voice catching the ear of a few curious people who were strolling about.

As he blurred past a row of cedars, something red caught his eye. It looked like somebody was sleeping back there. He continued on.

The pathway that wound through the trees, past benches and picnic tables, snaked in and around for almost a mile. He would take the route twice, and then head back to the hotel for a much-needed shower and an adult beverage. Or two.

As he passed the wading pool, near the park entrance, he paused and knelt down, cupped his hands, pouring some of the cool liquid over his head. It drenched his short hair, ran down his face, his neck and back, and refreshed him. Ready for another lap.

He rose to his feet, and as he began to pick up speed, he glanced again toward the sleeping guy behind the bush. Except, when he curiously pulled the bushes aside, it wasn't a guy, and she wasn't sleeping.

He stepped around the evergreens for a better view.

"*Sacré bleu*," he shouted. "*Qu'est-ce que c'est?*"

He stepped back onto the path and hurried past the wading pool and onto the sidewalk. A woman lugging two bags of groceries was hustling by, muttering to herself.

He stopped her. "Telephone, please."

She frowned at him, looked the other way, and hustled faster.

Along came a boy on a skateboard, leaning over, burning up the sidewalk. Pierre stepped in front of him, flagging him down. The boy spun to the side, almost wiping out in the grass. He looked angrily at Pierre and swore.

"*Bonjour*. Telephone, please?" Pierre asked.

The skateboarder cursed again. "I don't have a phone. Get out of my way, you idiot." He dropped back onto his board and rolled away.

Pierre sighed. Nobody wanted to help. He spun around, stepping through a row of parked cars and into the street. A taxi cruised up, looking for a fare. It squeaked to a stop as Pierre took another step forward and raised his arm.

He swung the front door of the cab open. "Police. Telephone, please. Need police."

The cabbie cocked his head and ogled him for a moment.

Pierre pointed toward the park. "Body. She dead."

The driver grunted, threw the car in park, and climbed from the cab. "Show me," he said.

Pierre rushed away, turning often to beckon the lumbering man to hurry.

The cabbie followed Pierre, jiggling and puffing, to the row of evergreens, and then behind. He stopped short when he saw where Pierre was pointing. He cursed and turned his head from the sight of a woman, rotting in the heat, covered with flies. The flow of blood from her almost severed head had spread out, dried, and been devoured by the rich soil beneath her lifeless body.

He called 9-1-1.

CHAPTER 39

Friday, August 19th, 10:05 a.m.

JAKE HAD BEEN discussing their plans for the day with Annie when his iPhone buzzed. It was Hank.

"There's been another murder," Hank said. "I thought you might want to come down here. It's a friend of Abigail Macy."

Jake's eyes popped. He leaned forward and looked at Annie. "Another murder," he whispered as he put the phone on speaker and set it on the desk. Annie leaned in.

"It's at Richmond Valley Park. I'm there now," Hank continued. "Near the wading pool."

"We'll be right there," Jake said, hanging up the phone and tucking it away.

Annie looked at Jake and raised a brow.

"A friend of Abigail Macy," he said. "Let's go."

Annie grabbed her handbag from the kitchen and followed Jake out the front door to the Firebird. They jumped in and the engine thundered, the tires squealed, and trees blurred by as they sped up the street.

The park was near the downtown core but traffic was light this time of day. In a few minutes, they saw flashing red and blue ahead of them. A dozen police cars were pulled over, one or two halfway on the sidewalk. A cop was directing traffic, the flow bogging down as drivers slowed and twisted their necks in the direction of the commotion.

Jake pulled up behind the line of cruisers and shut down the engine. They stepped from the vehicle and hurried into the park, past the wading pool.

An area to the left had been cordoned off with familiar yellow tape. Investigators were busy placing evidence cones as cameras clicked, evaluating and collecting physical specimens, studying and consulting with each other. Two or three officers guarded the area, making sure the gathering group of onlookers stayed well back.

Jake pointed. "There's Hank," he said.

Hank was just outside the yellow barrier talking to Rod Jameson, the lead investigator. He nodded a hello as they approached and pointed to a short row of evergreens. "She's right back there," he said. "You can circle around and take a look if you want, but I wouldn't suggest it. It's a pretty gruesome sight."

"What happened?" Annie asked.

"Her throat was slit. Her head is nearly half off. Pretty messy."

Annie wrinkled her nose and looked at Jake. "I guess we won't bother," she said.

Jake shook his head vigorously. He didn't want to see either.

Hank pointed to a man just inside the tape. He was sitting forward in a fold-up chair, his head in his hands. "That's Pierre Boutin," he said. "He discovered the body."

Annie looked over. Boutin sat up and rubbed his face, looked around, and dropped his head again. Annie looked at Hank. "Did she have ID on her?"

Hank shook his head. "No, she had no identification. Nothing at all, but I recognized her right away. Her name is

Samantha Riggs and she worked for Philip Macy. I talked to her briefly when I interviewed Macy a few days ago."

Jake whistled. "She knew who killed Mrs. Macy. That's why she's dead."

"I think you're right," Hank said. "Or perhaps she knew who killed Vera Blackley."

"Or both," Annie said.

Jake turned and scowled as he heard a familiar screech. It was the voice of Lisa Krunk. She was rushing toward them, microphone pushed ahead of her, Don bustling along behind.

The red light glowed. Lisa looked down her thin nose and spoke, "Detective Corning, can you tell me a little bit about what's happening here?"

Hank looked at the microphone three inches from his nose and then at Lisa. "A body of a woman was discovered here. We don't know much else at this point. The investigators have just arrived."

"Who was she, Detective?"

Hank frowned. "She had no identification with her," he said.

Lisa turned to Jake. The camera followed. "Mr. Lincoln, you and your wife are private investigators. Do you have an interest in this latest murder?"

Jake thought a moment before saying, "It's too early to tell. There may or may not be any relation to something we're working on now."

"Are you saying this may be related to the murder of Vera Blackley?"

Jake frowned. "No, I'm not saying that at all."

Hank spoke up. "I'll make a comment when we know more, but right now, excuse us please." He motioned toward Jake and Annie to follow him as he lifted the tape and stepped inside. They were right behind.

Lisa Krunk tried to pursue, but a uniform stepped up, cautioning her back.

"Detective Corning," she called. "Can you tell me who discovered the body?"

Hank disregarded Lisa and went over to Pierre, touching him on the shoulder. Pierre looked up. "Could you come with me?" Hank asked.

Pierre stood and followed.

Hank looked back at Lisa, and then led them to a spot where she couldn't overhear, out of the way of the investigators. He turned to Pierre.

"I'm Detective Hank Corning. I understand you found the body and reported it?"

"Oui. Oui."

Hank frowned. "Do you speak English?"

"*Oui*. Little bit. Yes."

"Your name is Pierre Boutin?"

"Yes."

"Can you tell me how you happened across the body?"

"How I find?"

"Yes."

"I run in park. Saw *le rouge*, red in bush. I move bush and find woman."

Hank studied Pierre for a moment, and asked, "Are you a tourist? Visitor?"

"*Oui*. Visitor. Nice city." He frowned and glanced toward the evergreens. "Not nice that."

Hank nodded. "It sure isn't. Pierre, where are you staying?"

Pierre pointed toward the street. "Hotel."

"The Hilton?"

"*Oui*. Hilton."

"Are you staying there for a few days?"

"Yes. One week."

Jake smiled. He knew Hank would need to get an interpreter to finish this.

"Someone will come to see you later. They will speak *en français*, okay?"

Pierre nodded his head vigorously. "Yes. I wait."

Hank walked him to the tape, lifted it, and Pierre jogged away.

Jake watched as Lisa Krunk ran up to him, cutting him off. She shoved the mike at him, asked him a question, and frowned at his reply. Pierre shrugged and Lisa watched him jog away again.

Hank laughed. "Lisa won't get much out of him."

Jake watched Lisa circle around, Don following, trying to get a better camera view of the victim. Trying to find another juicy tidbit.

They turned as the medical examiner, Nancy Pietek, approached. She greeted them and turned to Hank. "Looks pretty straightforward. I can't tell for sure yet, but it appears the cause of death is exsanguination. Basically, she bled to death."

"Any sexual abuse? Rape?" Hank asked.

Nancy shook her head. "I haven't checked her thoroughly, of course. I'll know when I get the body back to the morgue, but her clothes were intact. A few defensive wounds are visible, but otherwise it seems to be just as it appears."

"And the time of death?"

"Last evening. Looks like it happened somewhere between eight and eleven p.m."

Hank nodded. "Thanks, Nancy," he said as she turned and headed toward Jameson.

Hank sighed, letting the air out slowly. "I'll have to talk to Philip Macy as well," he said, thinking out loud. "Let him know about Samantha Riggs. Maybe find out a little bit more about her. Her family, etcetera. I need to see how Philip is doing, anyway." He shook his head. "It's been tough on him."

"And now he's lost his only employee," Annie added and sighed. "What more can happen to this poor man?"

CHAPTER 40

Friday, August 19th, 10:59 a.m.

DR. BORIS HOFFMAN showed the weird little man out of his office and shut the door. He had seen some strange patients, but this guy had fidgeted and squirmed for the last half hour and was really starting to get on his nerves.

He wondered why he had ever gotten into this business. He knew he wasn't a very good psychiatrist. He just pretended to listen to the lunatics as they ranted, then offered some useless advice and prescribed some medicine. And for that he got paid.

The thought was rather funny, but he didn't feel much like laughing right now. He had other things to think about. More important than the retards he had to see every day.

That nut-job was his last patient for the morning, so he dropped on the couch and flicked on the small overhead television.

Channel 7 Action News was just coming on.

The Barbie doll news anchor said, "The body of a woman was discovered this morning in Richmond Valley Park. Here's Lisa Krunk with the story."

Hoffman's attention was caught.

The view switched to a close-up of Lisa Krunk.

"I'm standing here in Richmond Valley Park where a woman was found murdered, her throat slit."

The camera panned across the park and zoomed into an area near the wading pool. Lisa continued talking. "Police have cordoned off the crime scene and are currently investigating."

Hoffman sat forward, intensely interested now.

Lisa continued, "I talked to Detective Corning, who said police had little information at this point and the victim has yet to be identified."

The camera view now showed a different angle. The body could be seen from a distance of about twenty feet. Hoffman could see a red floppy hat on the ground near the victim. She was also wearing a red jacket.

Hoffman swore and cursed Tommy Salamander.

The camera back on Lisa, she said, "Sources have indicated to me there may be a connection to the murder of Vera Blackley, the woman whose body was discovered in a dumpster yesterday afternoon."

Hoffman recognized Jake Lincoln when the camera showed his face. Jake said, "It's too early to tell. There may, or may not, be any relation to something we're working on now."

The camera view switched and Lisa's wide mouth flapped again. "The body was discovered by a French tourist, apparently staying in the city for a few days."

A view of a man in a jogging outfit. "Sir, I understand you found the body?"

The man shook his head. "No English," he said as he turned and jogged away.

Hoffman was on his feet now, angry.

Lisa Krunk said, "We will bring you breaking news as it happens. In an exclusive report, I'm Lisa Krunk for Channel 7 Action News."

Hoffman switched off the TV and paced the floor, back and forth, cursing and thinking. What had that idiot done? Things were bad enough now and this would only make things hotter.

He went behind his desk and swept up the telephone. He dialed, it rang, and in a moment, he heard, "Yeah?"

"Tommy, what did you do, you idiot?"

"Hey, Unc. What's up?"

Hoffman raised his voice. "You fool. Why did you kill her?"

"Relax, Uncle. They'll never figure out who did it. Besides, I was just protecting you. She was a threat to both of us." Tommy laughed. "And now she's not."

Hoffman lowered his voice. His secretary was in the outer office. It wouldn't do to have her hear. "I told you to just get the note and then scare her."

"Oh, sure, Unc. And then she would have gone straight to the police. With the letter. She was a little smarter than she seemed. That's why she just brought a photocopy. She was up to something."

Hoffman hesitated. Tommy might be right. At least Tommy was the one who had killed her. If investigators were able to find any evidence, then Tommy was the one it would lead to, not him.

Hopefully, he would be in the clear. And with the real note destroyed there was nothing to link him to any of this.

"Tommy?"

"Yeah?"

"Keep your mouth shut about this."

"No probs."

"I mean it. Don't tell a soul."

"Of course not. Why would I?"

"Because you're an idiot."

Tommy was quiet for a moment. The line hissed and then

he said, "I'll see you this afternoon for my payment."

Hoffman sighed. "All right." He slammed the phone down and cursed again.

Friday, August 19th, 11:03 a.m.

HANK STEPPED from the crowded lobby into the elevator and pressed the button for the second floor. The door hissed, and his stomach jumped; another hiss, and the elevator dropped him into a quiet hallway.

He moved down the passageway and stopped in front of a door. A sign said, "Ring and Come In," so he depressed the buzzer and opened the door.

Philip Macy stepped out of an office behind the reception area and came toward him. He looked haggard, his face showing the strain of the last few days.

And now, he would hear more bad news.

"Good morning, Detective," Philip said in a lifeless tone.

They shook hands and Hank asked, "Can we sit and talk a moment?"

Philip turned, beckoning Hank to follow, and they went into Philip's office. Philip dropped into his chair behind the desk as Hank sat in the guest chair, leaning forward, his arms resting on the desk.

The room wasn't exactly a mess, but things seemed to be uneasily disorganized. Work piling up and abandoned, bits of dust beginning to gather, with a stale smell of not enough fresh air.

Hank looked carefully at Philip. His arms were resting on the armrests of his chair, his hands clasped together, fidgeting restlessly with his fingers. He looked tired and needed a shave.

"I'm afraid I have some more bad news," Hank said.

Philip's expression didn't change as he waited for Hank to continue.

"It's about Samantha," Hank said. "I'm afraid she has been found … dead."

Hank studied Philip Macy. Philip stared back as if he'd forgotten Hank was there, and then dropped his head, his breath shooting out. He fell forward onto the desk, his head in his hands.

"I'm very sorry," Hank said.

Philip didn't move. The sound of his rapid breathing was all that could be heard. Finally, he lifted his head and looked blankly at Hank. "What happened?"

"She was murdered."

"Murdered?" Philip groaned. "Murdered?" The color drained from his face.

Hank nodded.

"Do you know who did it?" Philip asked as he sat up. His hands were shaking.

Hank shook his head. "Not yet." Hank always hated this part. Hated having to be the bearer of bad news. Samantha Riggs and Philip Macy weren't related, but she had worked for him for some time. "Do you know if she had any family?" he asked.

"I don't believe there's anyone locally. She has a mother she had mentioned from time to time. I believe she's out west, but that's all I know."

"Would you know how I could contact her?"

Philip shook his head. "I don't have any information on her."

"It's all right," Hank said. "I can find it."

Philip Macy spoke, his eyes on the ceiling. "She and Abby … were very close." When he looked back down at Hank, a tear or two escaped. He wiped them away and cleared his throat.

"Mr. Macy, do you have Samantha's address?"

Philip turned toward his monitor and his shaking fingers

tapped a few keys on the keyboard. "It's 33 Albert Street, apartment 202."

Hank found his notepad and pen in an inner pocket and jotted the information down. "I'll need to check her place, just in case."

Philip nodded.

"Is there anything I can do for you?" Hank asked, concern in his voice.

"Just find out who did this," Philip said. His voice was weak. He appeared about to collapse as he swung around and slid open a door in the wall unit behind him. He removed a bottle of scotch whisky and a glass, turned back, and set them on the desk. He smiled weakly. "I keep this for clients, but …" He poured a double and gulped it, catching his breath. He poured another and sat back, closing his eyes.

Hank didn't want to leave him alone. Philip was in bad condition, and Hank feared what might happen, or what he might do. "Do you want to come with me to Miss Riggs's apartment?" he asked.

Philip thought a moment before lowering his head and nodding. "Yes. I'm sure I won't be of much help to you, but I really need to get out of here now." He downed the rest of his scotch and set the glass down quietly. "Yes," he repeated. "I think that's a good idea."

Hank stood and waited, watching Philip as he spun around, put the alcohol and glass back into the unit, and rose to his feet.

Philip took a deep breath. "Let's go," he said.

CHAPTER 41

Friday, August 19th, 11:45 a.m.

ANDERSON BLACKLEY sat quietly in the holding cell beneath the Richmond Hill police precinct. The smell of fear, despair, and stale human sweat surrounded him. He was tired and he needed sleep. The iron bench in his small cage was cold, and the occasional curse, or insane yells from adjoining cells, hadn't allowed any rest.

He was scheduled to be arraigned this morning. His lawyer had been to see him and had no good news. The crown attorney was going ahead with the arraignment as planned, and Shorn had told him not to expect the judge to allow bail.

He'd had a lot of time to think. About Vera, his so-called marriage, and the events that had led to his incarceration. He had been set up pretty good. Whoever had killed Vera and framed him was out there somewhere and his only hope now was the Lincolns.

He looked up as he heard footsteps approaching his cage. It was Shorn, accompanied by a deputy. They were taking him to see the judge now. He stood slowly to his feet, fearful and uneasy about his future.

The door buzzed and the deputy squeaked it open.

Shorn was smiling faintly as he stepped in. "You're free," he said.

Blackley raised his brows. All he said was, "Free?"

Shorn nodded. "The crown attorney has withdrawn the charges. You're free to go."

Blackley's mouth fell open. He stared in unbelief, and then a wide grin split his face. He threw his arms around Shorn, and then stepped back and pumped his hand.

"You have a few papers to sign first," Shorn said, "and then we can leave."

Blackley stepped from the cell and followed Shorn and the deputy to the central control room outside of the holding area.

"Sign here and here," a deputy said, pointing to a pair of *x*'s on the bottom of two sheets of paper. Blackley signed and the deputy dumped out a bag in front of him. It contained his wallet, belt, cell phone, watch, and a few coins.

He slipped his belt and watch on, stuffed the rest in his pocket, and turned to Shorn. "Let's get out of here."

"You'll need this too," the deputy said, handing him a piece of paper. Blackley glanced at it. It was a release form for his vehicle, allowing him to pick it up at the pound. He took the paper, folded it, and tucked it in his breast pocket.

Suddenly moving from despair and uncertainty to freedom filled him with a strange elation. Like he had a whole new life. He took a deep breath of the warm fresh air as they stepped outside the front doors of the building. He turned to Shorn. "So fill me in. What's going on?" he asked.

Shorn looked at him with a smile. "The thing that was going to condemn you is the thing that set you free."

"Oh?"

"The hammer. The most damning piece of evidence suddenly became irrelevant. Since there was no evidence it had been used on Vera, there was zero proof it was even involved. The rest was circumstantial, and the crown attorney determined it was not enough to prove guilt."

"The wine splatters in the house?"

Shorn shrugged. "They could have been there for a while. They would have a hard time proving they weren't. And even if they could, it wouldn't indicate you were involved."

"So what's our next step?" Blackley asked.

"We get your car and you go home. Or back to work, or wherever you want." Shorn smiled. "You're a free man now."

"But I still want to find out who killed Vera."

"That's up to the police now."

"Or the Lincolns."

Shorn nodded. "You better let them know you're out."

Blackley found his cell and dialed. Annie answered.

"Annie, it's Anderson Blackley. They let me out." He couldn't hold back the overwhelming elation in his voice as he filled her in on the events and explained why they had released him.

"That's great news," Annie said. "I'd like to come and see you. What time will you be home?"

Blackley looked at his watch. "I just have to pick up my car. I should be home by one or shortly after."

"See you then," Annie said.

He stuffed the phone back in his pocket and turned to Shorn. "Let's get out of here," he said.

Friday, August 19th, 12:03 p.m.

HANK CRUISED slowly down Albert Street. Philip Macy sat in the passenger seat, eyeing the building numbers.

"There it is," Philip said as he pointed to an ugly brick-and-concrete apartment building.

Hank found a parking spot across the street from number 33. He shut down the engine, checked his service weapon, and slipped the keys from the ignition. "Let's go, Mr. Macy," he said, pushing his door open.

Philip turned to him. "Please, call me Philip."

Hank grinned. "Okay, and you can call me Hank," he said as he stepped from the vehicle. Philip climbed out and they crossed the street to the building.

Hank stepped up to the front door and held it open for an elderly woman coming out, struggling to open it. She mumbled thanks and worked her cane, puffing as she labored down the path to the sidewalk.

They stepped inside and looked at a handwritten sign on the wall: "J. Busby, Superintendent, Apt.101." They went down a short hallway, stopped in front of the first door, and rang the bell.

The door popped open a few inches, clunking when it reached the length of the security chain. A thin man peeked through the crack. He was probably midsixties, with a gray mustache and a few days of stubble on his gaunt face.

Hank showed his badge. "Mr. Busby?"

"Yup."

"Can I speak to you a moment?"

"What's this about?"

Hank frowned. "Will you open the door?"

The man sighed, the door slammed, the chain rattled, and the door swung open again.

Hank tucked his badge away and said, "I'm Detective Hank Corning. I need to speak to you about Samantha Riggs."

The man stared and then looked inquisitively at Philip. "Who's this?"

"This is my … associate, Philip Macy."

The guy looked them over carefully and finally asked, "What can I do for you?"

Hank said, "Unfortunately, Miss Riggs's body was found this morning. She had been murdered and we would like to see her apartment. Could you open it up for us, please?"

"Samantha? Dead?"

Hank nodded.

Busby shook his head slowly and said, "She was always a good tenant. Paid on time. Never caused no problems." He paused, then added, "That's a real shame."

Hank thought he didn't appear to be all that upset and was probably worried more about finding a new tenant.

"Just a minute," Busby said as he turned and went into another room. He appeared a moment later with a set of keys jingling and dangling from his hand. He put on a pair of slippers and stepped through the doorway, closing the door behind him. He selected a key from his ring and locked it, tested the lock, and said, "This way." He ambled down the hallway to a set of stairs and pointed. "Number 202. Up there."

Busby moved slowly, one step at a time, holding tightly to the railing. They followed him to the second floor and through another door into a hallway. Number 202 was the second apartment down and Busby fiddled with the keys, found one he liked, and unlocked the door. "Just lock up when you leave," he said as he toddled away.

It was obvious as soon as Hank stepped into the apartment, though it wasn't in total disarray, that someone other than Miss Riggs had recently been here. And it appeared they had been searching for something.

Philip followed Hank into the kitchen. A couple of drawers were hanging open and their contents rearranged. Hank browsed through them as Philip leaned against the wall watching.

He inspected the rest of the cupboards and drawers, peeked in the fridge, and rummaged through a basket of odds and ends on the countertop. There were a couple of unwashed dishes in the sink. Everything was otherwise normal.

The living room looked untouched. A TV sat in one

corner, propped up on a wooden box. An air conditioner was tucked into a window, humming and kicking out cool air. Hank shut it off. A vase of faded flowers sat on a coffee table, the water sucked up and dried away.

A cabinet had a couple of small drawers containing a few photos and other keepsakes. He inspected them and found nothing out of the ordinary. He tucked a clear photo of Samantha in his breast pocket.

He lifted the cushions on the couch, browsed through the CDs, and flipped through a bridal magazine on a small table beside the lazy chair.

Hank glanced at Philip. "Was Samantha getting married?"

Philip shook his head. "No. She didn't even have a boyfriend, as far as I know."

Philip picked up a framed photo from the coffee table. Hank took a peek at it. It was a photo of Samantha and Abby smiling at the camera. It appeared to have been taken in the office. Philip sighed softly and set it back on the stand.

"Why don't you keep that?" Hank suggested.

"Are you sure it's all right?"

Hank shrugged. "I won't tell anyone."

Philip looked at the photo again. "Okay," he said as he picked it up again.

Hank took a last look around and then went into the bathroom off the kitchen. He knelt down under the sink and opened the cupboard doors, then stood, flipped open the medicine cabinet, and studied the contents. Nothing was out of place.

He noticed the lid for the toilet tank was slightly awry. He lifted it, looked inside, and set the lid back.

Beside the bathroom, Hank saw what was obviously Samantha's bedroom. As he stepped inside and looked around, the bed immediately caught his eye. The comforter that was falling down so neatly all around had been caught, in one spot, between the mattress and the box spring. It appeared the mattress may have been lifted and dropped carelessly back into place. He knelt down and raised the mattress, peeking under. There was nothing of interest there.

The drawers of the nightstand were partially open. Hank peered inside and rummaged around, finding nothing unusual. The clock on top of the stand cast a faint red glow. A small lamp sat further back, a John Grisham novel beside it, a bookmark pushed in halfway. There was a little wooden box on the stand as well. Hank picked it up, opened it, and saw a few pair of earrings and some other costume jewelry. He snapped it shut and set it back.

The closet door was open. He explored the clothes on the rack. Sweaters, dresses, skirts, a gown or two. There was a row of shoes on the floor. Dress shoes, running shoes, high heels, and low heels. Looking up, he saw a shoebox on the top shelf. He retrieved it and popped it open. Photos, a bundle of letters, a few foreign coins. He browsed the letters briefly and flipped through the photos. Among them, there were a couple more of Abby and another one of Abby and Samantha. He slipped them from the pack and handed them to Philip.

There was a small dresser containing three drawers. Hank opened each drawer and went through its contents. Mostly underwear, socks, t-shirts. Nothing of interest.

He took a final glance around and turned to Philip. "There doesn't seem to be anything unusual here. Someone has searched this place, though. I wonder what they were looking for. Any ideas?"

"Not a clue," Philip said.

"It may be nothing, but we're assuming whoever killed Samantha knew who had … knew about what happened to Abby, and that's why she was targeted too."

"Abby may have told her something?"

"Perhaps." Hank frowned. "But we may never know if she did or not."

Philip dabbed at his eyes with the back of his hand and sighed deeply.

"Let's go," Hank said. "I want to drop by the Lincolns', and then I'll take you back to work."

CHAPTER 42

Friday, August 19th, 12:15 p.m.

ANNIE SET A TRAY with four glasses and a cold pitcher of fresh lemonade, dripping with moisture, on the deck table. The mound of ice crackled and popped as it met the early afternoon heat. The sun was scorching, but the back of the house cast a shade over the deck. She snuggled into one of the chairs and sat back.

Hank had called to say he was dropping by for a few minutes and bringing Philip Macy with him. She had told him to come around the side of the house. They would be on the back deck.

She looked over at Jake. He was scratching his head and frowning at some of Annie's notes.

"See anything interesting there?" she asked.

He looked up. "Not really, but I've been thinking, and it seems to me, since Samantha's murder was in such a public place, there might have been somebody around who saw a woman in a red hat and red jacket."

"You may be right," Annie said. "But how are you going to find them?"

"I thought I might hit the streets. Ask around the park. Who knows what might turn up?"

"It's a big park, and a lot of people go through that place every day. That could be a big job."

Jake shrugged. "Maybe. Either way, it won't hurt. I can't think of anything else right now." He paused. "Somebody had to have seen her at one point or another, but finding that someone may be the impossible task."

"But if you do find someone, that doesn't mean they saw the murderer," Annie told him.

"Yeah, I know," Jake said. "But I gotta try."

Annie looked vacantly across the backyard and nodded. She hoped something would break soon before anyone else got hurt, or worse … murdered.

She heard a shout. "Hello." Hank was coming across the back of the house. Philip Macy was with him, looking tired and glum.

"Sit down. Have a glass of lemonade," Annie said as Hank and Philip climbed the stairs to the deck. They took a seat as she filled four glasses and handed them around.

"Ah, that's good," Hank said as he took a gulp.

Annie sat and propped her arms on the rests, holding her drink with both hands. She looked at Philip, sitting forward, quietly sipping his refreshment. "What brings you here, Philip?"

He gave a faint smile. "I just couldn't stay in the office any more. I couldn't keep my mind on my work, and then when Hank came and told me about Samantha …" He paused and sighed. "It was pretty rough, and he asked if I wanted to go with him to her apartment." He shrugged. "And here I am."

"We just came from there," Hank said, taking another sip.

"Find anything?" Jake asked. He was cooling his forehead with the side of the frosty glass.

"I can't say I did. Her apartment had been searched before we got there. That much was obvious." He looked at Philip. "But we didn't find anything out of place. I don't know what I was looking for, but whatever it was, I didn't find it." He slipped the photo of Samantha from his pocket and handed it to Jake. "I brought this for you, anyway."

Jake took the photo, glanced at it, and stuffed it into his pocket.

"Did you hear about Blackley?" Annie asked Hank.

Hank looked at her, a question on his face.

"They let him go."

Hank frowned. "What? I mean, that's good news, but why am I the last to know?"

"It just happened. He called me. Apparently, the crown attorney withdrew the charges for lack of evidence. I'm sure they'll let you know soon."

"Diego won't like that," Hank said. "He had everything wrapped up nice and neatly."

"So what does this all mean?" Philip asked. "Is this going to help find Abby's killer?"

"Well," Hank said, "it means whoever killed Vera Blackley is still out there, and I think if we find him then we'll have Samantha's killer, the same person who killed your wife." He paused. "At least, that's our theory. And it's the only one that makes sense."

"I know it's the right theory," Jake put in.

Annie looked at her watch. "I'm dropping over to see Mr. Blackley in a few minutes. He should be home after one o'clock."

"And I'm going to the park," Jake said. "See if I can find anybody who saw something."

Hank grinned. "And I'm going to drop Philip home, and then I'll be out of touch for the rest of the day. We're trying to set up a sting downtown. See if we can catch the guys doing all the robberies." His grin faded and he glanced at Philip. "Sorry I can't do anything else on this right now Philip, but until the captain reopens this case …"

"I understand," Philip said.

Hank continued, "But the good news is, when he reopens

Vera's case, then that's as good as if he reopens your wife's case, because we're looking for the same guy."

Philip nodded.

"Right now, there are a couple of other detectives looking into the murder of Samantha, and I'll be on it hot and heavy first thing tomorrow," Hank said. "It's just that I have this thing right now that's been planned for a while." He slugged back the rest of his drink and set the glass on the table.

"What happened with Pierre Boutin?" Annie asked Hank, and then glanced at Philip and explained, "Boutin is the one who discovered Samantha's body." She smiled. "He didn't speak much English."

Hank laughed. "Somebody dropped by the hotel and took his statement. Somebody who speaks French, that is." He shrugged. "He didn't really have anything to add. He found the body, hailed a cab, and the cabbie called it in. End of story."

Jake gulped the rest of his lemonade, then stood and poured another one. He offered the pitcher around, but the others declined. He set it back down and took a long swig before asking, "Philip, what're your plans for the near future?"

Philip sighed and sat back. "I thought I might just close up the office for a few days and stay at home. There's no use being at work right now."

"You're welcome here any time," Annie said. "Please, don't feel like you're imposing."

"That's very kind." Philip smiled weakly.

Hank stood. "I had better get going. Are you ready, Philip?"

"I can drop Philip home," Jake said. "I'm going that way."

"You're sure?"

"Absolutely."

"I'll talk to you tomorrow, then." Hank gave a little wave,

stepped off the deck, and crossed the back of the house and out of sight.

"I have to go too," Annie said as she stood. "We'll keep in touch, Philip, and don't forget my offer." She slid open the back door of the house and went into the kitchen. She knew Jake would be leaving soon as well.

She wasn't satisfied with how slowly things were moving. She knew it had only been a couple of days but hoped they could get on the right track soon.

She picked her cell phone and car keys out of the wicker basket on the end of the counter, grabbed her handbag, and headed for the front door.

CHAPTER 43

Friday, August 19th, 1:00 p.m.

JAKE DROVE DOWN the boulevard bordering Richmond Valley Park and pulled into a spot across the street in front of a dry cleaner. He didn't really have a plan, just see who's around, show them Samantha's picture, and find out if anyone had seen her. He stepped out and crossed to the other side, approaching the park near the wading pool. The pool was busy. Mostly mothers with toddlers, splashing, laughing, and giggling.

Since the medical examiner had said the time of Samantha Riggs's death had been between eight p.m. and midnight, that would limit the number of people who may have been in the area at the time. By eight p.m. it would have been starting to get dark, and by midnight, it would have been pitch black except for the occasional streetlight. The question is, who would have been around at that time of the evening?

He ruled out picnickers, families, and splashing toddlers. Maybe joggers, dog walkers, a few teenagers, or those out for a late-night walk. Perhaps even Sammy Fisher, the homeless man who had found Vera Blackley's body. Or maybe some other street person.

He crossed the lawn and walked behind the hedge to

where Samantha Riggs had been found, looking around the area. Everything had been cleaned up, the tape was long gone, and the spot was deserted.

He glanced around the park. There was a mobile hotdog peddler down a little further. Jake approached the vendor, a dumpy man who looked like he had consumed too much of his own product.

"Were you set up here last night? In the evening?" Jake asked him.

Grease sizzled and spit as the vendor flipped some dogs on the grill. He spoke without looking up. "Sure was. I'm always here until it gets dark. Then I pack up for the night."

Jake pulled the photo from his pocket. "Did you happen to see this girl? She was wearing a red hat and jacket."

The vendor dropped the tongs, wiped his hands on his apron, and took the picture. He looked at it a moment, cocked his head in thought, and handed it back, shaking his head. "Nope, not that I can recall, and I know she never bought anything from me. I wouldn't forget a pretty face like that."

"Thanks, anyway." Jake took back the picture, wiped off a greasy fingerprint, and tucked it back into his pocket.

He wandered across the manicured lawn to an old man on a bench, sitting up straight as a stick, one hand resting on his lap, the other gripping a cane. The elderly man stopped whistling as Jake approached and sat beside him.

"Good afternoon, young fella," the old man said.

Jake smiled and nodded. "Did you happen to be in the park last night after eight?" he asked.

"Sheesh, no. That's way past my bedtime."

Jake thanked him and moved on. He approached a pair of joggers, a mother with a stroller carrying a whining baby, and several others who were wandering about alone, in pairs, or in groups of three or four. No one had seen a girl last night wearing a red hat and jacket.

He walked back to the wading pool and looked around. A homeless man was sitting cross-legged, leaning against a lamppost. He clutched a tattered cap, waiting for spare change.

Jake approached him. He was unkempt and his skin looked like horsehide from years of too much sun. Thin gray hair dripped down the side of his head, exaggerating his hairless and hardened crown. He stared blankly ahead, unmoving and unmindful of Jake's presence.

Jake dug in his pocket, came up with a handful of coins, and dropped them in the cap. He crouched down and held up the photo.

"Sir, did you happen to see this woman last night?"

Horsehide shrugged, looked away, and stared blankly across the park.

"She would have been wearing a red cap and jacket."

He stared at Jake for a moment. Something glinted in his eyes and then he looked away again.

Jake had seen the spark. "It's very important," he said. "This woman was murdered and I need to find out who killed her."

The wrinkled man paid no attention.

Jake pulled out his wallet and found a five-dollar bill. He snapped it between his fingers to draw attention. The weathered eyes turned back and ogled the bill. Jake folded it and dropped it into the cap.

"No cops." The man's voice was as rough as his skin.

"I'm not a cop. I'm a private investigator."

"No cops," he repeated and looked away.

Jake sensed the man knew something. He tried again, this time with a twenty-dollar bill. A hand shot up and snatched the bill, and Rawhide rolled to his feet, limping away, his hat still in his hand.

Jake watched him go and shook his head. He needed a new plan of attack. He sat on the bench by the wading pool and thought for a while.

"That's it." He snapped his fingers and jumped from the bench, striding across the park to the street. He crossed and climbed into the Pontiac, peeling away.

In five minutes or so, he turned onto Front Street, crossed an overpass, and pulled to the side. Jumping out, he walked back thirty feet and approached an embankment. He could see Richmond River below, flowing smoothly past on its way to lower ground. He was on the north side of the river. He climbed down a few feet, ducked under the overpass, and looked around.

Jake grinned. Sure enough, there was Sammy's castle. Barely noticeable, but he could see a concrete-colored canvas hanging loosely, the top wedged in under the overpass and held firmly.

He pulled the covering aside and laughed at what he saw.

The hole in front of him was about ten by ten and maybe four feet high. It appeared to have been burrowed into the side of the embankment like a cave. The floor had been covered with strips of wood, neatly laid side by side, making a solid base. Against one wall, a thick blanket and a tattered pillow served as a bed. The back wall was also shored up with wooden posts and covered with a piece of drywall. There was a small shelf unit containing several drawers, and a pot or two hung from the ceiling.

Sammy wasn't there.

Jake dropped the flap, made sure it fell properly in place, and climbed down the steep bank to the river.

"Detective Jake," a voice called.

Jake spun around. Sammy had just stepped from the overpass and was coming down the bank toward him. He carried a grocery bag over his shoulder. It jumped and rustled as he climbed. A grin split his face. "Did you ring my doorbell?"

Jake stepped forward to greet him. "Sammy. Good to see you again."

"It's good to see you too, Detective Jake. How's Detective Annie?"

Jake laughed. "She's doing great."

Sammy slipped his hat off, fanned his face with it, and wiped his brow before dropping the cap back in place. "Did you come to apply for an apartment?"

Jake grinned. "Not today, but I could use your help."

Sammy sat on a rock by the lip of the river and faced Jake. Jake crouched on the grass beside him.

"What can I do for you?" Sammy asked.

Jake tugged the photo of Samantha from his pocket and flipped it around. "This girl was murdered yesterday. We think it's related to the murder of that woman you found in the bin."

Sammy looked at the picture. "Oh, that's sad. Pretty girl, too." He squinted at Jake. "So how can I help?"

"The murder took place in Richmond Valley Park. I was in the park asking folks about it and I talked to a homeless guy. I think he saw something, but he won't talk to me."

"And you think he'll talk to me?"

Jake shrugged. "Maybe."

"I can give it a shot. Tell me about the guy."

"He had long thin hair. Bald. He was begging, with his cap."

Sammy wrinkled his brow. "That describes a lot of folks."

"He had a limp."

Sammy grinned. "Was he a little slow up here?" he asked, touching his temple with his forefinger.

"Yeah, I think so."

Sammy nodded his head slowly. "That's Lenny. Lenny Romeo. Not too bright, but he wouldn't hurt a flea. He lives in the park and keeps his stuff hidden in a group of thick bushes where he sleeps."

"So, do you think he'll talk to you?" Jake asked.

"I think so. I've known Lenny for a long time. Everybody knows him. He's been on the street longer than anyone can remember." Sammy stood. "You wanna go right now?"

Jake nodded. "If it's convenient."

"Just let me put my purchases in my pantry and I'll be right there," Sammy said as he hiked back up the mountain.

Jake followed him and waited on the street above until Sammy joined him. "Nice wheels," Sammy said as they climbed in the Firebird. He spun down the side window and stuck his arm out.

The tires protested a bit as they pulled a U-turn and peeled away. A few minutes later, as they drove up by the park, Jake could see Lenny Romeo had returned to his spot by the lamppost. They jumped from the Pontiac and dodged traffic, hurrying across the street.

As they approached Lenny, he looked up and dropped his hat into his lap. A hint of a smile touched his lips when he saw Sammy.

Sammy crouched down. "Hi, Lenny," he said gently.

Lenny didn't move or speak for a moment. Finally, he nodded his head slightly.

Sammy pointed at Jake. "This is Jake. He wants to talk to you."

"No cops." Lenny looked away.

"He's not a cop."

"Looks like cop."

Sammy sighed and stood up. "Why don't you sit over there for a minute, Detective Jake?" he said, pointing to the bench by the wading pool. "I'll see what I can get out of him."

Jake turned and went to the bench. He sat and watched Sammy as he knelt down beside Lenny, talking to him. Lenny didn't seem to want to speak. Finally, he opened his mouth and mumbled something.

Sammy stood and looked at Jake, then ambled over and said, "He wants twenty bucks and then he'll tell you what he saw."

"I already gave him twenty-five."

Sammy shrugged. "That's the best I can do."

Jake nodded. "All right." He slipped his wallet out, dug out a twenty, and followed Sammy back to the beggar.

They squatted beside him and Jake handed over the bill. Lenny took it, held it up to the sun, and then crumpled it and stuffed it in his pocket. He looked cautiously at Jake. "Salamander," he said quietly.

Jake looked at him, puzzled. "Pardon?"

"Salamander," Lenny repeated a little louder.

"Lenny," Sammy said. "You saw Tommy Salamander?"

Lenny nodded vigorously.

"What did you see him do?" Sammy asked.

Lenny looked around nervously and then at Jake. "Not cop?"

"I'm not a cop."

"Salamander kill girl."

Jake's mouth dropped open for a moment. He held up the photo so Lenny could see. "Is this the girl?"

Lenny nodded.

"Did you see what she was wearing?"

"Red. Wearing red."

"That's her," Jake said as he turned to Sammy. "Who is this Salamander character?"

Sammy looked at Lenny. "Thanks, Lenny." He straightened up and glanced around. Jake stood and waited. Sammy frowned and shook his head slowly. "He's bad news. A thug. He sells drugs, he's a petty thief, and if he killed Samantha, then I don't think she's his first victim."

Jake was elated. This's the break he was waiting for. "Where can I find him?" he asked.

"Can't say for sure. He could be anywhere right now. But I know where he lives. Well, not exactly, but I know the area he lives in."

"And?"

Sammy pointed toward the street. "Down here about four blocks, you'll see a street that has three or four old apartment buildings. Just small buildings and not very attractive. He lives in one of those." He shook his head and said slowly, "Not sure which one."

"I can find it," Jake said.

Sammy grinned. "Oh, I'm sure you can, Detective Jake."

"And how will I know him? What's he look like?"

"You can't miss him. He's got a tattoo of a cobra running down his arm." He stretched out his arm and demonstrated. "It runs from his shoulder and right down. The back of his fist represents the cobra's head." He twiddled his two forefingers. "And see these fingers here? That's the cobra's tongue. His nails are sharpened to a point, and his fingers are blood red." He paused. "It's actually quite impressive and realistic." He laughed. "Like I said, you can't miss him."

Jake chuckled, and then said, "Sammy, you've been a great help. I really appreciate this. Can I pay you for your time?"

"Not a penny," Sammy said. "But if you can get

Salamander off the street, then that's payment enough. He's bad for the whole neighborhood."

Jake slapped Sammy on the back and shook his hand. "I need to get going now. Do you want a lift home?"

"Nope, I'm fine. I'll just hang around here awhile."

"Remember, call me if you ever want anything."

"I will," Sammy said as he winked and walked away.

Jake watched him go for a moment. Sammy was a peculiar character, but in a good way. And a better man than many he had met.

CHAPTER 44

Friday, August 19th, 1:20 p.m.

ANDERSON BLACKLEY had arrived home. Annie saw his black Subaru in the driveway as she approached the house. She pulled in behind it, shut down the engine, and stepped out.

The grass needed to be cut and the flowerbed could use a little water. Understandable, considering Blackley's recent circumstances.

She took the short pathway to the front steps, climbed onto the small porch, and knocked. She assumed Blackley had been watching for her, as the door opened immediately.

She could see deepening lines on his face and dark shadows around his eyes. He looked tired and probably hadn't slept much in the last couple of days.

He motioned for her to come in as he stepped back, allowing her to move into the foyer.

She took a quick glance around. She remembered snooping outside the house yesterday, peeking in the windows and checking out the backyard, but she had never been inside before. She studied the living room as she followed Blackley in. It was a typical room, a little neater than she had expected, and any trace of the presence of the investigators the day before had been cleaned up.

Blackley motioned toward the couch. Annie took a seat while he sat in a straight-backed chair.

"Thanks for coming," he said.

Annie smiled. "It's good to see you've been released. I'm sure it's been a rather uncomfortable couple of days."

Blackley nodded. "Yes, it sure has been. And I hope you can help get rid of this black cloud hanging over my head." He shuddered. "I wouldn't want to spend another night in that place, never mind a few years." He cushioned his thoughts with an uneasy laugh. "And those orange jumpsuits are not to my liking either."

Annie chuckled before turning the conversation to more serious matters. He had not heard about Samantha Riggs, so she filled him in.

He was shocked and speechless for a moment. Finally, he asked, "Do you think her murder is related to Vera's?"

"I'm sure of it," Annie replied. "We're almost certain whoever killed your wife also killed Mrs. Macy. Miss Riggs was a friend and coworker of Mrs. Macy. I don't think there's any coincidence."

Blackley nodded. "I do believe you're right. Now, how are we going to find out who it was?"

"For starters, I'd like to know a little bit more about your wife. You told us before, you and Vera weren't close anymore, but do you know what she did in her spare time?"

Blackley laughed. "Her spare time. That's all she had." He thought a moment. "I don't really know. She got her hair done a lot, and she was always out shopping for new clothes. For some reason she bought a lot of fancy undergarments, but I never saw them on her." He chuckled. "I think that was reserved for somebody else."

Annie forced a smile before continuing. "Did she ever go to bars, or drink?"

"No, I don't believe so. She never was much of a drinker."

"Can you think of anyone she may have confided in? Any friends or relatives you may have forgotten to list before?"

Blackley shook his head. "I don't believe so, but then again, I don't really know for sure." He paused. "She was seeing a psychiatrist some time ago, but only for a few sessions."

Annie raised a brow. "A psychiatrist? Do you have his name?"

"Just a minute." He stood and walked into a small office off the living room. Annie could hear drawers opening and closing and the sounds of him rummaging around. In a few minutes, he returned with an invoice in his hand.

"His name is Dr. Hoffman," he said, reading from the paper as he took a seat.

Annie's jaw dropped. "Dr. Boris Hoffman?"

"Yup."

"Mrs. Macy was also seeing Dr. Hoffman," she said thoughtfully.

Blackley frowned deeply. "Do you think there's any connection?"

Annie scratched her head, thinking. "I don't know," she said slowly. "Maybe."

Blackley consulted the invoice again. "The last time she saw him was three months ago," he said.

Annie nodded and looked at her watch. "If there's nothing else you can tell me about your wife, Mr. Blackley, I'd like to cut this interview short. I have a few urgent matters I need to look into right away."

"That's all I can think of right now. If there's anything else, I'll call you."

He let her out the front door and she made her way to the Escort, climbed in, and fired up the engine. She sat for a few minutes, trying to wrap her brain around this new piece of information. Possibly a very big piece of information.

It was too early to say anything to Blackley, or to form any firm conclusions, but she had a nagging feeling Hoffman was deeply involved somehow.

She had to find out if he owned a red Mercedes convertible.

CHAPTER 45

Friday, August 19th, 1:28 p.m.

JAKE LEFT HIS car across the road from the park and strode the four blocks to the street where Sammy had directed him.

It was a nasty neighborhood, with lots of government-subsidized housing and a few crumbling two-floor apartment buildings.

A neglected old woman sat in a rocker on the front stoop of a squalid house, the roof dipping slightly in the middle as if ready to tumble at any moment. Her rocker squeaked in a rhythmic tone as she sat idling her time away. Across the street, a shabby house had a weed garden in front with a rusting car jacked up on cement blocks. The smell of something rotting was in the air. Jake put it down to the smoldering pile of garbage beside the tired house.

A few pedestrians ambled down the sidewalks, apparently going nowhere. The sound of a motorcycle almost deafened him as it flew by and spun around the corner. Groups of two or three were gathered on steps and makeshift benches or standing in driveways and doorways.

Four hoodlums in leather were carousing in front of a dilapidated garage. They quietened and stared curiously as Jake approached them.

"I'm looking for Tommy Salamander," Jake said.

An ugly one said, "Who's asking?"

Jake moved in a little closer to Ugly. "I am."

Ugly glanced at his companions, laughed, and then looked back at Jake. "And who are you?"

Jake moved in another step. He was just a few inches away, towering over him by a foot. "Never mind who I am. I want Tommy."

The guy dropped his head back and looked up at Jake but remained silent. The other three hoodlums had taken a step back and seemed on the verge of running away.

Jake put a massive hand on the guy's chest and propelled him backwards, slamming him against the garage door, pinned firmly. The tin door snapped and buckled. Ugly struggled vigorously, like a rabbit in a trap, but was held solid.

"Where is he?" Jake asked calmly.

Ugly stopped squirming, squinted at Jake, and then finally nodded toward an apartment building across the street. "He lives there." Jake detected a wobble of fear in his voice.

"Which apartment?"

"Second floor." He hesitated. "He's in 201, but don't tell him I sent you."

"Why, are you a friend of his?"

"Sure, we're friends. I've known him all my life, but he'll still kick my butt if he knows I talked to you."

Jake moved his hand and Ugly quickly slithered away, the others following him. Jake smiled grimly as he watched them tear around the side of the garage.

He turned and strode across the street, crossed the postage stamp lawn, and pushed the door of the building open. As he stepped in, his nostrils were assaulted with a strong odor of wet dog, mingled with stale cigarette smoke and moldy carpet.

The steps threatened to break through as he took them

two at a time to the second floor. He knocked on the door of 201.

"Who's there?" It sounded like a woman's voice.

He spoke gruffly, trying to imitate the lowlife across the street. "A friend of Tommy's."

"Come in," she said.

Jake turned the knob and pushed the door. It wedged at the top. He pushed a little harder and it sprang open, swung around, and thunked against the wall.

A girl slouched on the couch. She was probably early twenties, but looked as worn out, and burned out, as the guys outside. She didn't look at him, her eyes fastened to the soap on TV. She tilted her head, motioning down the hall. "He's in the can."

Jake stood and waited.

"Oh, Jessica, I have always loved you," the TV said.

"And I have always loved you too," the TV replied.

Jake slapped the television off and stepped back again, eyeing the girl. She looked to be entirely out of touch and unaware of him. She appeared not to notice the TV was no longer talking at her.

The toilet flushed, the bathroom door swung open, and Jake saw him. He looked as mean as Sammy had described. He was wearing a muscle shirt, and the tattoo was fully visible.

Tommy frowned when he saw Jake. His frown deepened as he moved closer. He stopped and spoke as if irritated. "What do you want, man?"

Jake was a daunting sight as he crossed his arms and glared at Tommy. "Why did you kill Samantha Riggs?" he asked flatly.

Tommy scowled. "What are you talking about?"

"I know it was you," Jake said. "We have an eyewitness."

Tommy hesitated. "If you're here to arrest me, then where's your gun?"

Jake pounded his right fist into his left palm a couple of times. "I don't need a gun."

Tommy wiped his hair back out of his wide eyes as he stared at the colossal pair of fists. He opened his mouth to say something and then closed it again.

Before Jake could react, Tommy spun around and dashed back down the hall, disappearing through a doorway. Jake sprinted forward and followed. It was a bedroom, messy, dirty, smelling like old laundry. An outside window was open and Tommy was climbing out.

Jake dashed to the window, but his prey was now on the fire escape, clattering down the metal steps. Jake squeezed his bulk out the window and hit the landing outside just as Tommy dropped to the ground, staggered, and fell to one knee. He recovered quickly and bolted down the alley, out of sight around the corner.

Jake thumped down the steps, hit the ground, and followed, but Tommy was gone.

He ran in the direction the killer had taken. He checked down a nearby alley, rounded the building, and continued on. A motorcycle roared nearby, and Jake turned in time to see it spinning out of the alley beside Tommy's apartment building. He ran to the street as it sped by and stood shaking his head as he watched him go. It appeared Tommy had circled back and grabbed his bike, and he was gone.

He'd had him in his hands, and he'd let him get away.

He followed on foot for a couple of blocks, running down the sidewalk, but gave up after a few minutes. He would never catch him this way. He would have to wait until Tommy came back home.

CHAPTER 46

Friday, August 19th, 1:41 p.m.

ANNIE PULLED into Midtown Plaza and drove around behind the complex. Employees and shopkeepers always parked around the back, leaving spots in front for customers. She drove slowly past the rear entrances of the tenants looking for Dr. Hoffman's reserved spot.

She touched the brakes and squinted at a sign posted on the brick wall beside a metal door. An arrow pointed downwards to the two slots below the notice. It said, "Reserved for Dr. Hoffman's Office."

One was filled by a ten-year-old Honda. That wouldn't be Hoffman's. It probably belonged to his receptionist. Not only was there no red Mercedes convertible in sight, but the other parking spot was empty.

It looked like Hoffman was not in.

She dug her cell phone from her handbag, turned on "Hide Caller ID," and dialed his office number.

"Dr. Hoffman's office. How may I help you?" asked a pleasant voice.

"Good afternoon. This is Annie Washington from Richmond Financial. I need to speak to Dr. Hoffman urgently regarding some papers he neglected to return."

"I'm sorry, but Dr. Hoffman is not in today."

"It's rather urgent," Annie said. "I need to see him today."

"I can have him get back to you when he calls in for messages," the girl offered.

Annie thought quickly. "I'm afraid that won't do. He has had an offer on his house, and it will fall through if I can't see him today."

"Oh, I didn't realize he was selling his home."

"Yes, he is. And this could be a real problem for him if we can't get this sorted out immediately. I would like to drop by his house. However, I don't have his home address." Annie made a face. That was dumb. What kind of bank wouldn't have the home address of its client?

She breathed a silent sigh of relief when she heard, "Just a moment. I'll get it for you."

Annie heard some paper rustling over the quiet hiss of the line. A moment later, the girl was back. "He lives at 133 Rambling Road. Do you need his home phone number?"

"Yes, please." Annie hurriedly dug the notepad from her handbag and wrote down the number. "Thank you. You've been very helpful."

She hit the "Hang Up" icon and shook her head. She hadn't thought that through well enough before she called. She laughed as she pictured the receptionist sitting at her desk, staring at the phone, suddenly realizing something was wrong.

She booted up the Google Maps app on her cell and punched in the address. The helpful map showed Hoffman's house was just on the outskirts of Richmond Hill, toward the north. She was familiar with the area and the variety of large homes on large lots along that road.

At least now she knew where Hoffman lived, and she had his phone number if necessary. Now it was time to put the next step of her plan into place.

Friday, August 19th, 1:45 p.m.

DR. BORIS HOFFMAN had been worried all day. He'd had a bit too much scotch whisky and was sipping a cup of steaming coffee, trying to clear his tangled brain.

He had canceled his appointments for the day. There were only two clients anyway, so he'd decided to stay home and relax. He didn't feel much like listening to wackos today; he had too much on his mind.

He was concerned the girl his idiot nephew had killed would come back from the grave and haunt him by means of another copy of the note. He was somewhat consoled by the knowledge that if there had, indeed, been another copy in her possession, the police would have found it and knocked his door down by now.

That at least, was somewhat of a relief, but he also knew the cops were pretty thorough, and there might be something else to connect Samantha Riggs back to him. That idiot, Tommy, had made a mess, and he didn't know if there was anything he could do to clean it up.

His thoughts disintegrated as he heard his cell phone buzz. He picked it up. It was the idiot himself. What could he want this time?

"What is it?" he said into the phone.

"We may have trouble."

Hoffman cursed. "What kind of trouble?"

"Some guy is snooping around my place."

"And?" Hoffman asked impatiently.

"He told me they have a witness who saw me kill the girl."

Hoffman clenched his teeth and cursed again. He wanted to strangle Tommy. He paced a moment, trying to think. Finally, he said, "Listen, idiot, if the cops had a witness, they would have been there by now."

"Maybe they're waiting."

"Waiting for what?"

"I don't know. Just waiting."

"Tommy, you're more of an idiot than I thought. Cops don't wait around. They'd be on you like a dog in heat."

"I don't know, but this is getting a bit hairy."

"Calm down," Hoffman said. "You're worrying about nothing."

"Uncle?"

Hoffman sighed. "What is it?"

"I think you could give me a bit more money. Two thou ain't enough, and I may have to get out of town."

"Running away is not going to help. That's only going to make you look guilty. And they would still track you down."

"Well, I need more money, anyway."

"No more money."

The line was quiet. Finally, Tommy said quietly, "I still have the note."

"I told you to destroy it," Hoffman yelled.

"Yeah, I know, but I read it, and it seems like it's worth more money."

Hoffman raised his voice even higher. "No more money. Just bring me the note."

"Listen, dear Uncle Boris, if I go down for this, then you go down too." He paused. "Unless I get more money."

Hoffman sighed. "How much more?"

"I want five grand. That's all."

"Oh, that's all, is it?"

"It's worth it."

"All right. Bring it over here and you'll get your money."

Hoffman felt like a fool for trusting that idiot. Now he was being blackmailed with a letter that was supposed to have been destroyed.

"I'll be there this afternoon," Tommy said. "Just like we planned."

Hoffman clicked off his phone, dropped it onto his desk, and slumped into his chair, shaking his head.

He cursed a moment and then leaned down and opened the bottom drawer of the desk, dug around at the back, and removed something wrapped in a soft linen napkin. He set it carefully on his desk, unfurled the cloth, and stared at his Glock pistol.

He might have to use this. If Tommy didn't give him the note this time, he would threaten him with it, or worse. Blow his brains out. The idiot deserved it.

He picked up the gun and slipped the ten-round magazine from the well. It was full. He rammed the magazine back in and snapped the MIC holster from the gun, setting the pistol back on the desk. He stood and fastened the cord of the holster to his belt, snapped the gun in, and slipped it behind the buckle, securely in place against his skin. He dropped his shirt over the weapon and sat down. It felt comfortable, and made him feel safe.

He flipped open the cigar box and selected a Cuban, clipped the end, and lit it. The warm smoke relaxed him, calmed him down. He laid his head back and closed his eyes, tasting the sweet earthiness in his mouth.

CHAPTER 47

Friday, August 19th, 1:54 p.m.

JAKE WALKED the four blocks back to the street where Salamander's apartment was located, slipping down the narrow driveway beside the building and around behind.

It led into a parking area where three or four cars were jammed into the narrow spaces. Tommy had sped away from here, so his bike must have been parked back here somewhere and he had retrieved it before taking off.

He knew in this kind of neighborhood, Tommy would chain his bike up securely. Jake looked around for a likely spot. The back door of the building had a small platform with a solid iron railing on one side. He leaned down and examined the railing. Otherwise covered with rust, there were some scratches where a chain had dug into the metal.

He stood and stepped onto the platform. The back door was unlocked, and it squealed as it scraped against the frame and swung open. He took the back stairs to the second floor and moved down the hallway toward the front of the building. He stopped in front of 201 and twisted the knob, and the door sprang open.

The smell of a freshly smoked cigarette hung in the air. The television was back on, and the girl appeared not to have moved. He shut the door quietly, crossed the room, and flicked off the TV. He turned and looked at her as she stared forward silently.

He kicked a small footstool over in front of her and sat down, leaning forward, facing her. She sat quietly, her hands in her lap, only her eyes moving briefly as they followed him.

"What's your name?" he asked.

She blinked. "Rachel," she answered in a husky voice, almost a whisper.

"I'm Jake," he said as he studied her. She had been quite attractive at one time. Maybe could be again, but not until she wanted to get out of this life and make something of herself.

"Do you know where Tommy would have gone to?"

As she shook her head, a long lock of blond hair fell forward and covered one eye. She reached up unconsciously and brushed it back into the tangled muddle on top of her head. She needed a hairbrush.

"Was he home yesterday evening?"

Instead of answering, she reached for a pack of cigarettes on a stand beside her and dumped one out, placing it between her lips. She fiddled with the lighter for a moment and couldn't get it to work. Jake took it gently from her, flicked it, and held it to the smoke. She puffed, inhaled deeply, and blew the smoke out the side of her mouth.

"Thanks," she said.

Jake dropped the lighter back on the stand and repeated. "Was Tommy home yesterday evening?"

She took another puff, blowing the smoke at him. "He went out."

"Do you know where he went?"

She shrugged. "He doesn't tell me. He just goes."

"What time did he leave?"

Her eyes moved up for a moment and then back at Jake. "Maybe eight or nine."

"Do you know what time he got home?"

"Late."

"How late?"

She shrugged again. "I was sleeping," she said and took another puff.

Jake sat back and studied her. Her eyes followed him, unafraid.

"Rachel, do you know if Tommy has ever hurt anyone?"

"Maybe."

"Does he ever hurt you?"

She looked away. "Sometimes. Not much."

He leaned forward and touched her cheek gently, moving her face back toward him. She didn't pull away or flinch at his touch.

"Why do you stay with him?" he asked.

Her eyes seemed to grow sad. "Nowhere else to go." She turned her head briefly and dropped her cigarette in the ashtray. The smoke curled up and was caught in the slight breeze from the open window.

He reached out and took her hand. She didn't protest. "Rachel, you could leave if you wanted to. Are you and Tommy married?"

She shook her head. "No, we're not married. Never."

"Do you love him?"

She frowned slightly. "Not really."

"If Tommy never comes home again, what will you do?"

She shrugged one shoulder. "Dunno."

"Tommy's a bad man," Jake said, observing her.

She nodded slowly. "I know," she said sadly.

"He kills people."

"Maybe. I don't know."

"Believe me, he does." Jake dropped her hand back in her lap and sat back. She seemed calm and relaxed. "Rachel, do you trust me?" he asked.

As she nodded, Jake thought he saw a slight smile touch her lips, making her look a little more attractive. He wasn't sure why she would trust him. He was just a guy who'd come into her home uninvited and started asking her a bunch of questions. Perhaps he looked trustworthy. He didn't know.

"Do you mind if I wait here until Tommy gets back?"

"I don't care."

"Do you mind if I look around the apartment?"

"Okay."

Jake patted her leg. "Thanks." He stood, turned around, and flicked the television back on, turning the volume down slightly.

He wasn't looking for anything in particular, just maybe snoop around a bit, get a feel for what Tommy was all about, and wait until he returned.

He went down the hall to the bedroom. The window leading to the fire escape was still open, but the air smelled stale and unclean.

He poked his head out the window and took a deep breath. He swung around as he heard a noise behind him. Rachel was in the doorway, leaning against the frame, watching him.

"Where's Tommy's stuff?" he asked.

She pointed to a rickety dresser by the unmade bed.

"Do you mind if I take a look?"

"I don't mind."

Jake went to the dresser and pulled the top handle. Wood squeaked against wood as he slid the drawer open and peered inside. He moved around some socks and felt something hard. He pulled it forward. It was a long knife tucked inside a sheath. He slipped it out and tested the edge against his thumb. Razor sharp. He put it back in its case and replaced it in the drawer.

He found a plastic box of Remington pistol and revolver cartridges. He turned to Rachel and held them up. "Does he have a gun?"

She nodded. "Yes."

"Do you know where he keeps it?"

She shook her head. "Sometimes he carries it, but not always. Sorry, I don't know where it is."

Jake smiled. "That's okay." He dumped the ammunition back into the drawer and squeaked it shut.

She stepped back into the hallway as he left the bedroom and went to the kitchen. The room was relatively clean. Jake assumed this was Rachel's territory.

She was behind him. "Are you hungry, Jake?"

He hesitated. He was always hungry, but he wasn't sure what to say.

"I can make you some eggs or something," she said. "Maybe a sandwich."

Jake smiled. "That's okay. But I would like a cup of coffee if you have some?"

She found a kettle beside the fridge, filled it, plugged it in, and waited for the water to boil. It was instant coffee, but it tasted fine.

He sat at the table and sipped it, hoping Tommy would return.

CHAPTER 48

Friday, August 19th, 2:00 p.m.

CAPTAIN ALANO DIEGO had been under pressure from the hungry media, starving for information. The two murders that had recently taken place were making headlines and many were demanding a resolution.

He had decided to hold a news conference. He preferred it when Hank stepped up and handled the press, but he was on another case right now and wasn't available.

He pushed the papers on his desk aside, stood, and went to the small mirror by the doorway of his office. He brushed his hand through his hair, flattened his mustache, and straightened his tie, adjusting the gold clip that pinned it to his shirt.

The crown attorney and the chief of police were waiting for him in the outer office. They stood and joined Diego, walked to the exit door, and stepped out into the warm air.

Out on the street, a cop directed traffic, the road now being reduced to one lane as cars and news vans lined both sides. Drivers slowed and rubbernecked until the officer impatiently blew his whistle, and they sped up again.

A small podium had been set up at the bottom of the precinct steps leading to a courtyard between the steps and the sidewalk. Reporters were bustling about. Cameras were ready to snap pictures, make video, and capture the occasion.

Notepads were poised, recorders were set, and the bank of microphones fastened to the podium was waiting, tuned, and tested.

Lisa Krunk was front and center, her sidekick close by. The camera was propped on his shoulder, loaded and ready to shoot the action, his finger on the trigger.

Four uniforms made a stern line in front of the stage, keeping the reporters from crowding in too close. Two more stood back further as if acting as bodyguards for the captain and his entourage.

As the chief, Diego, and the crown attorney came down the steps, the crowd hushed. As Diego stepped to the microphones, all eyes were on him.

He cleared his throat. "Ladies and gentlemen, thank you all for coming. I will make a brief statement and then accept your questions."

Recorders hummed, cameras clicked, red lights glowed, white lights flashed, and pencils worked.

"As you're aware, there have been two shocking murders in recent days. Yesterday, the body of Vera Blackley was found. She had been strangled and left in a dumpster for three to four days before finally being discovered." He paused. "This morning, the body of a female was found in Richmond Valley Park. Her throat had been slit, and apparently the murder had taken place last night."

Someone shouted, "Are the two murders related?"

Diego frowned. "I will take questions later." He looked over the eager crowd before continuing. "The city can rest assured we are doing everything to bring the killer, or killers, to justice. It's too early to know if the same perpetrator killed both victims or not. We are assuming there are two murderers out there, as the manner of death and other circumstances are completely different." He paused. "I will take your questions now."

Hands shot up and mouths spit questions. Diego pointed to a reporter near the back.

"Sir, do you have the name of the second victim?"

"All I can tell you is, it was a woman. Her name won't be released to the public until her next of kin can be notified." He pointed at another raised hand.

"Do you have any suspects?"

"Not at this point, but we have several persons of interest. We are expecting an arrest at any time, and this killer, or killers, will be caught and face the full extent of our judicial system."

"What about Blackley?"

Diego looked at the crown attorney before stepping to the mike. "Charges against Mr. Blackley have been withdrawn. There's no evidence he was involved in the death of his wife."

Diego pointed to Lisa Krunk.

Lisa said, "Captain Diego, informed sources have assured me the death of Abigail Macy is directly related to these two new murders. What do you have to say about that?"

Diego frowned. "Abigail Macy's death was ruled as suicide by the medical examiner. Her case is closed and there's no relation to the others."

Lisa was ready with a second question. "What are you doing to ensure the citizens of this city are safe?"

"We have no reason to believe the people are in any danger, but for any who are worried, I have this advice. Use your normal common sense. If you need to be outside after dark, make sure you're not alone, and stay away from unlit areas. Keep your doors locked, both at home and when in your vehicles."

Someone shouted, "Did the second victim know Vera Blackley?"

"I have already stated we don't think the murders are

related, and to the best of my knowledge, the victims did not know each other." Diego pointed to the reporter beside Lisa.

"Captain, have you been able to ascertain a motive in either murder?"

Diego thought a moment. "In the case of Vera Blackley, as she was strangled, it appears to be a crime of passion. In the case of … the second victim, it appears to have been a mugging gone wrong. The female victim had no handbag or identification with her, which is unusual, and at this point we are assuming she was robbed."

"So, you're looking for a male in both cases?"

"The manner of death in both cases is consistent with a male perpetrator, yes." He leaned into the mike. "We have no more information at this point, and there will be no more questions. Again, thank you all for coming," he said as he turned away.

He nodded to the crown attorney and the chief and they went back up the steps, ignoring the jumble of questions from the reporters below. As they stepped into the precinct, the shouts died out and all that could be heard was Diego's uneasy sigh.

CHAPTER 49

Friday, August 19th, 2:14 p.m.

TOMMY SALAMANDER idled his motorcycle into an alleyway two buildings away from his own. He dropped the kickstand and swung from the bike.

He was a little worried about that big guy who had come into his apartment and accused him of killing the girl. How did he find out? Tommy sure didn't want to see that clown again, and hoped he was gone, but he had to get into his apartment and get that note. It was worth five grand to him. He chuckled. Maybe more.

He hoped good old Uncle Boris was right, and if the cops knew something, they would have been here already. Well, they weren't, but the big guy was. So, what did he want?

He crept carefully back up the alley to the sidewalk, keeping a close watch in every direction as he made his way slowly to his building. He pushed the front door open and peeked inside. No one was around. He went in and took the steps as quietly as possible to the second floor. The floorboards squeaked a couple of times as he edged down the hall. He hesitated when he reached the door of 201, and then gradually turned the knob and eased the door open a few inches.

He peered inside. Rachel was sitting on the couch

watching TV like always. The door squeaked faintly as he pushed it further. She looked up.

"Is he gone?" he whispered.

She nodded and turned back to the TV.

He pushed the knob, opening the door enough to squeeze through. The knob was suddenly ripped from his hand as the door slammed behind him. He spun around.

The big guy was there. The clown had been waiting behind the door and his ugly girlfriend had betrayed him.

The mountain of a man looked at him and smiled. "Hi, I'm Jake," he said. "And I would like to talk to you."

Tommy tried to run but was caught by the shoulder.

"Sorry. Not this time," Jake said as he yanked on his arm and spun him back around.

Tommy tried to shake free but the grip was too tight. He swung his other hand but it was soon pinned as well. He stood still and stared up at the face of the guy who looked like he could tear him into strips.

He was spun around again, his arm wrenched behind his back. It felt like a bone might snap as he was propelled forward. Rachel rolled out of the way as he was swung around and thrust backward onto the couch.

He didn't move. He watched as Jake shut the television off, pushed the footstool over, and sat down facing him. Rachel went to the front door and sat in a straight-backed chair against the wall.

Tommy frowned at Jake. "What do you want?" he asked, fear beginning to control his voice.

"You killed Samantha Riggs."

"You're crazy."

"We have a witness who saw you and I just want to know why."

"I didn't kill anyone."

Jake sighed. "You're going to make this difficult for me.

See, Tommy, here's my problem. I'm a nice guy and I don't like to hurt people. I prefer not to make an exception in your case, but what can I do?" He shrugged.

Tommy glared and said nothing.

"I want you to know I'm not happy about doing this," Jake said as his hand shot forward and cuffed Tommy on the side of the head. It was only a slap, but he was knocked sideways, landing on his side against the couch.

Tommy rolled forward, stumbling to his feet in an attempt to get away, but was sent spinning, and fell back down with a whoosh of the cushion.

"Why did you kill her?" Jake asked.

"I didn't."

"Who hired you?"

"Nobody."

Whack. Tommy's head shot back. He brought his hand to his nose. It felt like it was broken. There was a warm trickle, tasting like blood, on his lip. He struggled to stand but was held firmly by a big hand on his chest.

"Sorry," Jake said. "Sometimes I just can't help myself. I hope that didn't hurt too much." He removed his hand, slipped a tissue from a box on the stand beside the couch, and handed it to Tommy. "Here, clean yourself up."

Tommy took the tissue and dabbed at his nose, keeping his eyes on his attacker.

"Is that better?" Jake asked. "Are we friends now?"

"We'll never be friends." His voice sounded nasal, the blood gathering in his nose.

Jake sighed. "Yeah, you're probably right."

Wham.

The blow caught Tommy on the other side of the head. He fell sideways but was quickly yanked to a sitting position by a pair of muscular hands.

"Who hired you to kill the girl?"

"Nobody." His voice trembled.

"You killed her, didn't you?"

Tommy was afraid now. He'd had enough. He needed to think of some way out of this. "Are you a cop?" he asked.

Jake shook his head. "No, I'm not a cop. Now, did you kill her?"

Tommy nodded slightly. "Maybe."

"Who hired you?"

Tommy shrugged. "Just some guy."

"Who was it?" Jake asked. "I don't care about you. I just want to know who hired you." He grabbed Tommy by the hands and bent them backward at the wrists.

Tommy howled in pain and tried to break out of Jake's hold. "I don't know. I don't know."

Jake relaxed his grip. "What do you mean, you don't know?"

"It was just some guy."

"What guy? Tell me who it was or I'll break both of your wrists."

The big guy looked like he meant what he said and Tommy had a feeling it would be rather easy to snap his wrists. The guy didn't look so mean, but the strength in his arms was impressive. "I don't know who it was. Honest." He shook his head and tried to make it look like he was telling the truth. "I don't know who it was. He paid me a hundred bucks. That's all I know."

Jake dropped Tommy's hands and sat back. "A hundred dollars. That's all her life was worth? A hundred dollars?"

Tommy tucked his hands under his armpits as if to protect them from further pain. He glowered at Jake, shaking furiously in fear, but determined not to say who had hired him.

Jake drew back his fist. "What did this guy look like?"

Tommy stared at the massive fist and his voice quivered.

"I don't know. I never saw him. He just called me, and we made a deal, and he dropped the money in my mailbox. That's all. I swear."

The big guy looked like he didn't believe him. He couldn't say who had hired him or he wouldn't get his five grand. He had to hold out no matter what.

Jake unfurled his fist and reached for his iPhone. "Smile for the camera," he said as he held it up.

Tommy looked sullen as the camera clicked.

Jake stood suddenly, knocking the footstool back. Tommy watched him walk to the bedroom and return a moment later with a suitcase. It was Rachel's suitcase. His head swiveled as his eyes followed Jake back past the couch, to the front door, and out.

Rachel stood and took one last look at Tommy, stuck her nose in the air and followed the big guy out, slamming the door behind her.

CHAPTER 50

Friday, August 19th, 2:17 p.m.

ANNIE DROVE SLOWLY down Rambling Road following her GPS. She saw 133 on her left, kept going for another fifty feet or so, and pulled over.

She threw her handbag over her shoulder, stepped from her car, and crossed the road, surveying the property in front of her. A whitewashed picket fence separated the property from the road. Twin stone pillars guarded the driveway entrance that was secured by a massive wrought iron gate designed to keep out intruding vehicles.

Set on perhaps five acres of land, ancient trees lined the long driveway running to the house making the dwelling barely visible from where she stood. A well-kept lawn, peppered with more trees, took up a large area in front. Bordered from the neighboring estates by a sea of trees and vegetation on either side, it appeared the huge properties on both sides of Rambling Road had once been carved out of an old forest, clearing only enough space for the buildings and front lawns.

Annie walked down the side of the road until she was out of sight of the house. She climbed the fence, swung her leg over, and dropped down, landing on a pile of dead leaves that had blown against the barricade.

She brushed herself off and continued on through the

forested area, keeping near enough to the tree line so she could see the house, while staying back out of sight in the dimness of the trees in case someone glanced her way.

After several minutes, she made it adjacent to the house. She had a clearer view from here. She crept a little closer to the tree line, keeping behind massive trunks and leafy bushes. Now she could see the full side of the mansion. There was a three-car garage directly ahead of her. Above, and behind the garage, were half a dozen windows, shining light into the house.

She studied the windows for some time. Finally satisfied there was no one in those rooms as far as she could tell, she took a chance and ran the short distance across the lawn to the garage.

She hugged the wall and eased along until she reached a small window in the side. She poked her head around and peered into the dim room.

She saw a red Mercedes convertible.

Her heart was pounding through her chest. She knew now, Hoffman had been the visitor to Vera Blackley's house, and unless he had another car, he was at home, prowling around his mansion somewhere.

But she had to get inside the garage. She had to know for sure if he was a murderer. There was no point in calling the police with what little circumstantial evidence she had.

She crept back along the outside wall to a small door at the side of the garage. She twisted the knob.

Locked.

She reached into her handbag, pulled out a small leather case, and flipped it open. The first real test of her brand new lock-picking tools. Hopefully, there was no alarm set in the garage. She didn't see any wires or other evidence of that around the door.

She had practiced a little when she first bought the tools,

but not nearly enough. She worked at the lock for ten minutes before she heard a pleasant tick, a click, and the knob turned. She held her breath and pushed the door open, ready to run. But there was no alarm.

She stepped inside and eased the door shut. There was another door on the inside wall of the garage, probably leading to the living area. The back wall was lined with metal shelving. It held containers of oil, gas cans, and a variety of small gardening equipment. A coiled-up garden hose was tossed in the corner. The other two parking slots were empty, and she stood still, staring at the Mercedes in the center space for a few moments.

She hadn't tried picking the lock on a car before. Would it be any different from a house lock?

She stepped to the back of the vehicle, her tools ready. There was no lock on the trunk. The latch must be inside the vehicle.

She went to the driver's side door. Again, she prayed there was no alarm, but nothing rang, buzzed, or screeched as she worked with the tools.

It took another few minutes to finally spring the lock, and she smiled as she pulled the door handle up. She snooped around inside the glove compartment and found a map, the manual, and a folder of maintenance invoices. She checked under the seats. Nothing. Nothing except dust.

She checked under the dashboard and found the lever to open the trunk. She heard a pop from the back of the vehicle as she gave it a tug.

She climbed back out, went to the rear, and lifted the lid. The trunk was empty.

What did she expect to find? Another body?

She dug out her keychain. There was a penlight fastened to the ring. She switched it on, and as the light glowed, she was glad she had changed the battery that morning.

She shone the light around, in the corners, and around the edges. Her eyes widened at the sight of a dark spot.

It looked like dried blood.

She flipped her handbag from her shoulder and pulled out a plastic bag. She removed a small bottle equipped with a fine mist atomizer, twisted the top off, and dropped in two tablets, one white, and one beige. She turned the top back on, gave the tablets a moment to dissolve, shook the bottle, and sprayed it over the spot.

An eerie blue glow lasted about thirty seconds before fading away. Her Luminol kit had worked. The dark spot was blood.

There was no doubt about it now. Hoffman was the killer.

She was feeling nervous and excited. It was one thing to suspect Hoffman, but now, being sure of it was terrifying. Her hands shook slightly as she reached into her handbag for her phone.

She heard a scrape and a click. It seemed to be coming from the side of the vehicle near the inner door to the house. Her head snapped up and her eyes popped.

It was Hoffman.

He had a sneer on his face, and the gun in his hand was pointing straight at her.

CHAPTER 51

Friday, August 19th, 2:30 p.m.

JAKE AND RACHEL walked back to where he had left his car by the park, and he swung by the bus station to drop her off. They had had a long talk in the kitchen and Jake had finally convinced her Tommy was no good. She had decided to leave him and go back to her family out west, where she had come from several years ago.

Jake gave her two hundred dollars and watched her lug her suitcase into the terminal, hoping he hadn't thrown his money away and she would make something of herself.

He knew Tommy Salamander was holding out on him. Tommy had been lying when he'd said he had taken a job from someone he didn't know. That was just too hard to believe. He wasn't going to get any more information out of him, but he had an idea.

He drove back to the street where Tommy lived, pulled over to the side, and looked across the road. Tommy's friends were back and hanging around the garage.

He coasted a little further, pulled a U-turn, parked the car, and jumped out. He walked back toward the hoodlums, being careful not to be seen.

He stepped off the sidewalk and strode toward them. Two of them were talking to each other and didn't see him. The other two scurried away. It didn't matter. Jake had his eye on one of them, a nerdy little guy who tried to look a lot tougher than he was.

"I want some information," Jake said.

They looked up at him uneasily. The nerd seemed to squeeze in a little tighter to the fence he was leaning against. Ugly was near him, sitting on the crumbling pavement, his back against the garage door. He sat up straight and glanced around as if looking for a way to escape.

Jake leaned down, grabbed a handful of Ugly's jacket, and lifted him off the ground. He swung him around and released his grip. Ugly landed a few feet away and scrambled to his feet. He stood still as if not knowing whether to run.

Jake looked at him. "Boo."

Ugly spun across the driveway and around the side of the building.

Jake turned back to the nerd. "What's your name?"

His voice quivered. "Jimmy." It sounded like a question.

"Well, Jimmy, it's nice to meet you. My name's Jake, and I'm not here to hurt you."

Jimmy looked as if he didn't know whether to believe him.

"Stand up, Jimmy."

Jimmy stood obediently, cowering back.

Jake cornered him between the garage and the fence. "You're Tommy's friend, right?"

Jimmy nodded meekly.

"Did you talk to him yesterday?"

Another nod.

"What about yesterday evening?"

"He wasn't around."

"Where was he?"

"He said he had a job to do."

"What kind of job?"

Jimmy shrugged.

"Did he say who hired him?"

Another shrug.

Jake grabbed Jimmy by the jacket, pushed him back firmly, and repeated, "Did he say who hired him?"

Jimmy looked around nervously. "I can't say anything. He'll kill me."

Jimmy's breath shot out as Jake pushed a little harder. "And I'll kill you if you don't."

Jimmy licked his dried lips. "You … you wouldn't do that."

Jake heaved and Jimmy's feet came off the ground about twelve inches. "How do you know?"

Jimmy wiggled and whined, "Put me down."

Jake did. Jimmy fell into a heap, landing back on his elbows. Jake knelt beside him and pushed him to the pavement. "Who hired him?"

"He … he just said he had an errand to do for his uncle."

"What kind of errand?"

"He … he said he had to pick up a package. I don't know what kind of package. Maybe some drugs. I don't know. Honest."

"Who's his uncle?"

"I don't know his name."

Jake studied him briefly and, holding him firmly with his left hand, he tightened his right into a massive fist. He showed it to Jimmy. "If you don't tell me, I'll break your nose."

Jimmy squeezed his eyes shut, turned his head, and brought his hands up as if to ward off the blow. "Please," he pleaded. "Don't hurt me. I don't know his name. I swear. If I knew, I would tell you."

Jake released his grip and stood up. "Get out of here," he said.

Jimmy's eyes shot open. He stared in disbelief a moment, then scrambled to his feet and scurried away.

Jake watched him run and then dug his iPhone out of the holder and called Annie's number.

No answer.

He let it ring a few times, frowned at the phone, and tried another number.

"Hello?"

"Chrissy, it's Jake. Have you talked to Annie today?"

"Not today."

"She's not answering her phone and I'm getting a little worried. Can you tell her to call me if you see her?"

"Sure."

"And Chrissy, can you watch Matty for a while in case neither one of us comes home in time?"

"Absolutely, no problem. I'll watch for him."

They hung up and Jake dropped his phone back in the holder.

Matty knew if he came home from school and no one was around, he should go next door. Chrissy was always there at that time, and she would watch him.

He knew Annie had gone to see Anderson Blackley a couple of hours ago, and perhaps she was still there, but he didn't know why she wouldn't be answering her phone.

But right now, he had to find out who Tommy Salamander's uncle was.

CHAPTER 52

Friday, August 19th, 2:52 p.m.

ANNIE STOOD FROZEN, staring at the gun Hoffman pointed at her, his finger tightening on the trigger.

She dropped behind the trunk and twisted around to the far side of the vehicle. She watched her cell phone leap from her hand, hit the concrete, and skid across the floor. If she went for it, she would be back into Hoffman's view. She would have to leave it.

"Stand up and come out," Hoffman called.

She heard him coming across the floor, around the car to where she was crouching. She scurried to the front of the vehicle just as he reached the side. A loud crack echoed off the walls of the room and a bullet whistled and smacked into the wall behind her.

She eased her head up for a moment. He had the gun ready and was moving to the front. She dropped down and looked around desperately for a weapon or some means of escape. She saw nothing useful, and she had but a couple of seconds to spare. He was between her and the outer door now, getting closer. She sprang to her feet, ran to the door leading into the house, and half fell up the single step into the landing.

Another shot sounded. It hit the wall near her head as she scrambled across the floor on all fours. She stumbled to her feet. She was in a large kitchen. She thought about looking for a knife but didn't have time. And a knife wasn't much good against a deadly gun.

She crossed the kitchen and dove through a doorway into a large living room as she heard his feet on the kitchen floor.

"You can't get away," he shouted. "If you stop and come back, I won't hurt you."

Annie knew that was a ridiculous promise. He had killed three people and she didn't want to be the fourth. She was sure Hoffman was the murderer, and didn't realize until she had seen the blood how much danger she had put herself into. She should have called Jake when she'd had the chance, or at least left a message telling him where she was.

She ran across the room toward another doorway. In a split-second, she saw that going to the right circled back to the kitchen, and the left went down a hallway, with a wide staircase to the second floor. She could be trapped up there, and circling back to the kitchen was dangerous. She took the unknown route down the hallway.

He wasn't far behind her, just coming into the living room. He knew his way around but she was running blind. A wrong decision and she would be trapped.

She made a quick choice and took the first open doorway into a large bedroom. She looked around frantically. In the closet, under the bed, or through the window?

Instead, she stood behind the door hoping he would pass. He didn't.

She heard him step into the room and stop. He was on the other side of the door but she couldn't see him. She stood motionless, her heart pounding as she listened to him breathe.

"I know you're in here," he called. "I'm not going to hurt you. I just want to talk to you and find out why you're in my house."

She watched his back as he came in further and crept through the door of a walk-in closet, his gun poised and ready, gripped in both hands.

When he came back out, he would be sure to see her. She had only one chance. She eased around the door and back into the hallway with a single objective: get out of here and get to a phone.

She was only familiar with one route, back to the kitchen, into the garage, and outside. But what about a phone? She had heard an uneasy snap when hers had hit the concrete floor. She didn't expect it would work. Should she look for a phone in the house or just go to the neighboring property?

She made a quick decision and headed for the garage.

CHAPTER 53

Friday, August 19th, 2:52 p.m.

JAKE DECIDED he would have to deal with Salamander later. It wouldn't be hard for the police to track him down and get the truth out of him once he had this thing figured out. He hurried across the street, climbed into the Firebird, and turned the key. The engine roared and the car leaped ahead. He took a left on Main and drove north, heading toward more familiar territory.

As he reached closer to home, he took a left, then a quick right, and pulled over to the side, directly in front of a row of townhouses. He jumped from the vehicle and went up the driveway to the door of number 633. He rang the doorbell and waited.

The door sprang open. "Hello, my good man. What brings you to my less-than-humble abode?"

Jake grinned and stepped in. "I need your help."

Jeremiah Everest and Jake had been good friends for many years. With not a lot of the same likes and dislikes, their paths hadn't crossed often, but they remained friends nonetheless. Jeremiah was aptly named "Geekly" by those who knew him best, a name he rather liked. Geekly had helped Jake and Annie a few times when they'd needed his expertise.

Jake slapped him on the back and followed him into a

room the builder had designed as the living room. Other than a small television and an easy chair, in this case, the room was put to better use. It was wall-to-wall technology, with makeshift shelving containing monitors, keyboards, mice, cables, and unknown things with dials and meters.

Pushed up against another wall, a desk was piled high with other curious pieces of computer equipment, rows of DVDs, software, stacks of manuals, and hard drives.

Geekly sat sideways at a smaller desk that contained two monitors and a keyboard. He kicked a chair toward Jake. "Have a seat and tell me what I can do for you."

Jake sat and pulled the chair in closer. "I need you to find someone for me."

"Piece of cake," Geekly said as he tucked his glasses back up onto his nose. "Who are you looking for?"

"His name is Tommy Salamander."

"Tommy. Probably registered in the birth records under the name of Thomas," Geekly said as he swung his chair around. He tapped a few keys. "I have two Thomas Salamanders. How old is this guy?"

"Probably midtwenties."

"There's only one, then. Thomas Salamander, born March tenth, 1987. That would make him twenty-six years old. Sound right?"

Jake nodded. "That sounds like him."

Geekly banged a few more keys. "Currently living at 12 Portal Street?" he asked as he looked at Jake.

Jake nodded. "Yup. Now I have to find out who his uncle is."

Geekly turned back to the keyboard. "Let's see here. His mother is Betty Salamander. She lives in the city."

"So Salamander would be her married name," Jake said. "What's her maiden name?"

Geekly continued to drum the keys. Finally, he turned to

Jake. "She was born Betty Hoffman."

"Hoffman," Jake shouted. He lowered his voice slightly and leaned in. "Does she have any siblings?"

"Let's see here." Tap tap tap. "One brother. Boris Hoffman."

Jake jumped to his feet. "Boris Hoffman. I don't believe it."

Geekly shrugged. "It's all here."

"Yeah, I mean, I know Hoffman. I just never suspected he was a murderer."

"You wanna fill me in a bit here?" Geekly asked.

Jake told him quickly about Hoffman and what he was now sure Hoffman had done.

"You should call the police," Geekly suggested.

"The problem is, I don't have any real evidence yet. Just the word of a homeless man who hates cops, and a lowlife who won't admit anything."

"So, what are you gonna do?"

Jake shook his head. "I'm not sure yet." He paced for a few seconds and then swiped his iPhone from its holster.

His call was answered on the first ring. "Anderson Blackley."

"Mr. Blackley, it's Jake Lincoln. Did my wife come and see you today?"

"Yes, she did. Just after one."

"Did she say where she was going? I'm unable to reach her."

"No, she never said."

"Okay, thanks."

"Wait," Blackley said. "There's one thing that might help. When I told her Vera had been seeing a psychiatrist some time ago, a Dr. Boris Hoffman, she seemed quite interested. She left in a hurry after that. She said she had some things to take care of right away."

"Thanks again."

Jake thought a moment and then spun around and looked at Geekly. "I think that crazy wife of mine went to see Hoffman." He ran toward the door. "I gotta go, Geekly. Thanks for your help."

"Yeah, yeah, any time," Geekly called as the front door slammed.

Jake ran to the car and powered it up. He threw the shifter in first, touched the gas, and left a few black marks behind.

He still had his iPhone in his hand. He called Philip Macy.

"Hello?"

"Philip, it's Jake. I think we have our man. Dr. Hoffman. Does that make any sense to you?"

"Dr. Hoffman?" Philip asked. "Are you sure?"

"I'd bet my iPhone on it."

Philip whistled. "It's starting to make a little bit of sense. Yeah, sure. He would have access to enough drugs to … kill Abby. And she would have let him into the house with no question, because she knew him." He was talking fast, excited. "Yeah, it makes a lot of sense now."

"And don't forget," Jake added, "he's the one who said your wife was delusional, and the police gave his statement a lot of weight."

"Wow. Exactly. He's the guy, Jake. I'm sure of it. Did you inform the police yet?"

"That's the problem. I can't prove any of this right now."

"So, now what?"

"I have to get over there right now. I think Annie went there this afternoon. She may be in trouble."

"Take me with you."

"What? No."

"Take me with you, Jake. He took my wife. I want to be there."

"Are you sure?"

"Absolutely. I'm in this a hundred percent." He paused. "I can meet you there if you want."

"I'll pick you up," Jake said. "See if you can find out where he lives and I'll be there in a couple of minutes."

"I'll be outside waiting for you. And I know exactly where he lives."

CHAPTER 54

Friday, August 19th, 3:21 p.m.

AS ANNIE SCOOTED from the bedroom, heading for the garage and freedom, she could hear Hoffman behind her again. He must have heard her, or perhaps stepped out of the walk-in closet in time to see her run.

She would have to dodge into the kitchen again. She was just going in circles, around and around. She needed a moment to think, but there wasn't time.

She swung into the kitchen out of his line of fire and stopped suddenly. Reaching up, she selected a large frying pan from a row of cookware hung on hooks from the ceiling. She swung around, hoisted the pan over her head, and waited.

"You can't get away," he called.

She heard him breathe. He was moving slowly, getting close. The tip of the gun appeared around the corner. Then a hand.

As she brought the pot down with all her strength, she heard a sickening thud as it connected with his wrist. The blow drove his hand down, but he held on to the gun. He cursed. The pot was now at her side, gripped in both hands. She stepped around the corner, swung up, and caught him full in the face. He stumbled with the blow, hit the wall with his shoulder, and went down.

He still had the gun, but another quick crack with the pan onto the back of his hand caused it to jump away and skitter against the wall.

She dropped the pan and dove for the weapon. He caught her by the shirtsleeve, but she retrieved the gun with her other hand, swung it around, and cracked him on the side of the head, wrenching her shirt from his grasp. It ripped, but she was free. She rolled away and sprang to a crouch, facing him, the gun in her hand aimed directly at his head.

He groaned and opened his eyes, frowning at her.

"Don't try anything," Annie said, "or I'll kill you." She stood and backed up a couple of steps. "Stand up."

He groaned again and rose slowly to his feet. "You won't shoot me," he said.

"You don't want to find out for sure, do you?"

He was silent, glaring at her.

The scuffle had put him between her and the kitchen. She wanted to get in there, get to a phone, and call the police. "Step back," she said. "Go into the kitchen and sit down at the table."

He scowled at her a moment and then stepped back, eyeing the gun.

"Another step."

He did.

"Now sit down."

He turned, pulled back a chair, and sat at the end of the table.

She looked around and spied the phone on the counter. She stepped sideways. The gun didn't waver as she swooped up the receiver.

"You don't want to do that," Hoffman said.

"And why is that?" she asked.

"Because you're an intruder in my house. You broke in here. I tried to defend myself and now you're holding me at gunpoint."

She hesitated.

"You will be in a lot of trouble," he said.

"You killed Abigail Macy."

"That's a wild theory."

He was right. She had no proof, just a theory. Except for the blood. "I found blood in the trunk of your car. Vera Blackley's blood," she said.

He laughed. "That's my blood. I cut my finger changing a tire." He held up his hand and showed her a scab on the side of his finger.

"A neighbor saw you parked at Vera Blackley's house."

He laughed again. "She was my patient, and I make the occasional house call. I went to see her a couple of times when she was feeling particularly down."

"What about Abigail Macy?" she asked.

He shook his head slowly. "It was very sad to hear about her committing suicide." He sighed. "Very sad, indeed."

She set the receiver back in its cradle. He was right. It was all circumstantial evidence, and if she couldn't back any of it up, then what kind of trouble had she gotten herself into? Maybe it really was his blood in the car.

She sat at the other end of the table, clenching the weapon tightly in her hand, and pointing it at his head.

CHAPTER 55

Friday, August 19th, 3:32 p.m.

JAKE FOLLOWED Philip Macy's directions to Rambling Road. As they drew closer to 133, he frowned and pointed. "There's Annie's car."

He spun onto the shoulder and came to a quick stop behind her vehicle, and they jumped out.

"I have to get something first," Jake said. He ran around to the rear of the Firebird and popped the trunk. He pulled a cardboard box forward and dug around, finally pulling out a baseball cap. He tucked it on his head and slammed the trunk.

"That's what's so important?" Philip asked. "A baseball cap?"

Jake grinned. "It's not just a baseball cap. There's a camera inside." He flipped it off his head and turned it over. Velcro ripped as he tugged at a flap hiding a tiny high-resolution video recorder. "There's the camera," he said, pointing to a barely noticeable spot on the front of the cap. He flipped it back on his head. "All I have to do is press the top of my head and the recording starts."

Philip was amazed at the gadget. "So, you think you're going to get a confession out of this guy?" he asked.

"I'll give it a shot," Jake said. "Let's go."

They ran across the road and stood at the end of the long

driveway. Jake was worried about being seen while approaching the house, but he didn't want to waste any time either. He was more worried Annie might be in some danger, and he had to take a risk.

"The way I see it," he said, thinking out loud, "if Hoffman is alone in the house, and even if Annie's in there with him, he's not going to be sitting there staring out the window."

"You're probably right, Jake, unless he's waiting for us."

Jake frowned. "If he's waiting, then let's let him know we're here. Either way, I'm going in," he said. He went a few steps to the right of the gate and approached the white picket fence.

Philip followed him as they climbed the railing and landed on the other side.

Jake pointed to the trees lining the driveway. "I think we can get most of the way there without being seen. If he's there."

They walked up the edge of the drive, keeping the large tree trunks between them and the house as much as possible. After a couple of minutes, they reached a large courtyard in front of the mansion and crouched down behind the last tree.

Jake eyed the house, examining the windows. Satisfied no one was watching, he said, "Let's go around the side. I need to see what's going on in there."

They strode quickly across the courtyard, around to the side of the house, and past the garage. Jake cautiously peeked in each window but saw no one. "Annie's in there somewhere," he said.

When they reached the back of the house, Jake poked his head around the corner. There was a massive deck attached to the back of the building, leading down to an Olympic-sized swimming pool. A variety of outdoor chairs, tables, and plants adorned the stone pathways and patios that covered a large area at the back of the house.

Jake pointed to a pair of sliding glass doors that led from the deck into the building. "I have to see in there," he said.

They crept across the edge of the house, through shrubs and rosebushes, and reached the deck. Jake turned to Philip. "Wait here," he said as he kept close to the building and pulled himself up over the railing, dropping quietly on the deck.

With his back scrubbing the wall, he eased over to the edge of the doors. He listened but heard nothing from inside. He would have to get one of those little spy mirror doodads if he got out of here alive. It would come in handy right now.

He touched the top of his cap and felt a click. No lights needed, camera on, time for action.

He crouched down as low as possible and peered into the room. He saw Annie sitting at a table, her back to him. Hoffman was at the other end. They appeared to be having a conversation.

He pulled back. This didn't make a lot of sense. He knew she was in danger and he had to act fast. He turned to Philip and whispered, "She's in there with Hoffman. I have to get in there."

Hoffman looked up as Jake moved to the door and tugged. It was locked. As Annie spun around, Jake's jaw dropped when he saw the gun she was holding.

Hoffman leaped from his chair, streaked across the kitchen, and disappeared. Annie stood up, aimed the gun in his direction, and began to follow.

Jake dove off the deck and hit the ground beside Philip. "Hoffman is running," he said as he sped across the back of the house. He didn't know whether Hoffman was going to leave the building, and if so, which exit he would take. But he had to catch him.

He rounded the corner, heading past the garage, toward the front of the residence. As he reached the front, he saw

Hoffman on the other side of the property, streaking toward the woods.

Hoffman had a long lead, but Jake vaulted over a short stone wall and chased after him. His quarry disappeared into the dimness of the forest, and when Jake reached the tree line, Hoffman had vanished. He stopped to listen. He could hear the snapping and crackling of twigs and leaves but it was hard to tell from which direction they came. He cocked his head and listened, but the sounds faded quickly and then died out.

Jake continued on slowly, stopping often to listen, but the only sound he heard was the hissing of the wind and the twittering of birds as they chattered among themselves.

CHAPTER 56

Friday, August 19th, 3:40 p.m.

AS HOFFMAN jumped from the table and ran, Annie swung around, aiming the Glock toward him. But before she had enough time to react, he was down the hall and had disappeared into one of the rooms.

She searched from room to room, finally entering what appeared to be a den or an office. There was a door leading out to the side of the house. It was wide open.

She ran outside just in time to see Hoffman tearing across the clearing, heading for the bush. Jake was some ways behind him. She turned and came back into the house, through the den to the kitchen. Philip was still outside the double doors leading to the patio. He had been watching the chase, and he turned as she unlocked the door and let him in.

"It's great to see you're okay," Philip said. "Jake and I were extremely worried."

Annie smiled. "I'm okay now. He had the gun on me, and we had a struggle, but I was able to get the gun and here I am."

"So now what?" Philip asked.

"I don't know. The problem is, even if Jake is able to catch Hoffman, we have no real proof he's the killer."

Philip nodded and then cocked his head. "Do you hear that?" he asked.

Annie listened. She could hear the faint sound of an engine. Maybe a lawnmower. Curious, she went into the living room and looked out the large front windows.

"It's somebody on a motorcycle," she called.

Philip came up behind her and looked out. "It's Tommy Salamander," he said. "Jake showed me his picture. I'd recognize that mean-looking scumbag anywhere."

Annie frowned. "Who's Tommy Salamander?"

Philip filled her in with as few words as possible as they watched the rider step from the bike. He was heading toward the front door.

"If he's the one who killed Samantha Riggs, then he's our proof," Annie said. "We have to grab him."

Philip looked uncertain. "That's, uh, not really something I'm very good at."

"It's our only chance. We have to get him." Annie thought quickly. "You answer the door when he comes and I'll come in from behind and corner him."

She ran from the room to the door leading to the garage, through the garage, and around to the front of the house. Salamander was just climbing the steps to the porch. She moved across the front and stood at the bottom of the steps behind him, holding the gun ready.

Salamander rang the doorbell and Philip opened the door. "Come in," he said.

"Who are you?"

Annie stepped up behind Salamander and shoved the gun in his back. "Don't move. Put your hands up."

Salamander spit out a string of curses and did as he was told.

Annie looked at Philip. "There's some rope in the garage. Run and get it."

As Philip turned and ran, Annie said, "Get down on your knees."

Salamander didn't move.

"Now," she said in a voice that meant business.

Salamander reluctantly went down on his knees.

Philip returned dragging a coil of yellow rope. He tied Salamander's hands securely behind his back as Annie held the gun to Salamander's head.

"Stand up," Annie said.

He stood.

She prodded him into the living room, the gun at his back. "On the couch," Annie told him.

He did as he was told and sat sullenly while Annie covered him with the gun.

"Philip, tie his feet. We don't want this guy to try anything."

Philip grinned and knelt down, tying Tommy's feet securely.

She sat on a footstool and held the gun, waiting for Jake to return.

Friday, August 19th, 3:44 p.m.

DR. BORIS HOFFMAN moved through the trees as quietly as possible. Jake was behind him somewhere and he wasn't sure what to do now. He had gotten himself into a real mess, but he was certain with the right lawyer, the circumstantial evidence they had against him would never stick. He cursed himself for not having his cell phone with him. He decided to go back to the house and see if he could sneak back in. If he could be the first one to call the police, perhaps that would be in his favor.

He swung around to the right and then circled over and forward again, staying in the thick trees that separated his property from the neighbor's. He had outwitted his pursuer, and now he was close enough he could see his house. There was a distance of a couple of hundred feet between him and the building, but he had to take a chance.

He frowned as he saw a motorcycle coming up the driveway. The idiot wasn't supposed to come until later. Now, he had to decide what to do. He dashed across the lawn, safely reaching the front corner of the house. Salamander was already climbing the steps to the front porch. He opened his mouth to call to him and instead he muttered a string of curses.

Annie was just coming across the front of the house. She had a gun in her hand. Hoffman watched helplessly as she stepped up behind Salamander and poked the gun in his back.

Now he had a real problem. If his stupid nephew had that letter with him, then he had to get it and destroy it.

He slipped along the side of the house to the same exit where he had left a few minutes ago. He opened the door quietly and stepped into his den. He could hear Tommy cursing in the other room. He crept carefully to his desk and swept up the phone receiver, dialed 9-1-1, and ducked under the desk.

"9-1-1. What is your emergency?"

"There are intruders in my house." He gave them his name and address.

"A car is on the way. Get out of the house if possible and the police will handle it."

No, he wasn't going to get out of the house. He had to get that note before the police came.

He tiptoed to the doorway, then into the hallway. Keeping low, he peered around the corner. He could see Annie sitting on a footstool, her back to him, holding the gun on Tommy.

He stepped quietly onto the antique Persian rug. He made no sound as he moved toward Annie. Tommy looked up as he approached and Annie caught his look and swung around. Hoffman jumped the last few feet and pounced on her. She was no match for him this time, and he wrestled the gun from her hand.

"Uncle, watch out," Tommy yelled. "There's another guy in the other room."

Hoffman lifted the gun and turned just as Philip Macy came in from the kitchen.

Hoffman jumped up and waved the gun. "Don't move," he said.

CHAPTER 57

Friday, August 19th, 3:45 p.m.

JAKE HAD GIVEN up the search for Hoffman. He was never going to be able to track him down among all these trees. He turned and jogged back the way he came.

As he ran from the dimness of the forest, he saw Hoffman running toward the house. What was he up to?

Jake increased his pace. It took him a couple of minutes to cover the distance to the side door of the mansion. He eased it open and peered inside. He saw a large office, but Hoffman wasn't in sight.

He stepped inside and crossed the room to a doorway that led into a hallway. He could hear voices. As he crept cautiously up the hall, he heard Hoffman say, "Don't move."

He peeked around the corner. Hoffman was standing with his back to him, a gun in his hand, aimed at Annie and Philip. Salamander was sitting on the couch all trussed up with yellow rope.

He stood back and thought. Salamander must have come to the house, Annie and Philip had captured him, and then Hoffman had come back and somehow got ahold of the gun.

Now what?

He peered around the corner carefully. Tommy couldn't see him unless he turned his head. Annie could see him if she glanced this way, but her eyes were intent on the wavering gun.

"Tommy, give me the note," Hoffman said.

Tommy dropped his chin, pointing to his breast pocket. "It's in my pocket. I can't reach it."

Hoffman stepped forward and dipped his fingers into Tommy's jacket pocket. He pulled out an envelope and slipped a piece of paper from it. He looked at it with satisfaction. "Ah, finally."

Jake frowned. What was in that note? He had no idea, but it seemed important to Hoffman. He had to do something.

Hoffman ripped the paper in two.

Jake stepped into the room. "Hoffman," he shouted.

Hoffman spun around and fired as Jake ducked behind a chair. The bullet sung as it smacked the wall above his head.

"You can't get away," Jake said.

Hoffman fired again. The bullet snapped helplessly into the ceiling as Annie dove into him. The gun hit the floor. The papers fluttered in the air.

Hoffman recovered and lunged for the weapon as Philip dove and swept it up. He lay on his side and held the gun unsteadily in one hand.

Hoffman stood up slowly, his eye on the gun.

Philip's hand shook, his eyes boiling with anger as he glared at the man who took his wife.

Hoffman gritted his teeth and rushed at Philip.

Philip fired and the bullet slammed into Hoffman's chest. Hoffman stopped, his mouth gaping open, his hand clutching his chest. He went down on his knees, his bulging eyes staring at the face of the man whose wife he had killed and who had now gotten his revenge.

EPILOGUE

Saturday, August 20th, 10:12 a.m.

ANNIE AND JAKE were getting some much-needed rest when the doorbell rang. It was Hank.

"I see you guys have been busy while I was away."

Jake laughed. "Come on in."

Hank followed Jake into the kitchen and dropped down at the table. Annie poured Hank a cup of coffee and slid it in front of him.

"I talked to Philip this morning," Jake said. "He's in pretty rough shape, but I think he's doing a bit better now that Hoffman has been caught."

"Abby's funeral is this afternoon," Annie said as she took a seat. "We're planning on going. Philip needs all the support he can get."

Hank took a sip of coffee and nodded. "I think I may drop by as well. He didn't get much police support and it might help to show we're behind him now."

"You were always behind him," Jake said.

"Yeah, I was. But it seems like I was the only one." Hank laughed. "The captain was a little timid with me this morning. I think this took him down a peg or two."

"Any news on Salamander?" Annie asked.

"By the time our guys got through with him," Hank said,

"he confessed everything. He'll be going away for a long time."

"And how's Hoffman doing?" Jake asked.

"He'll recover. He's lucky the bullet missed any vital organs."

"Do you think he'll confess?"

Hank shrugged and leaned back. "Doesn't matter. He's going to be given some free room and board as well, no doubt about that. I'm sure the letter Abby wrote is going to be the thing that puts him away. That, and the blood in his trunk. And of course, the video from that silly hat of yours. I don't think there's any jury that won't convict him on all three murder charges, especially with Salamander's testimony. The crown attorney offered Salamander a deal if he testifies against Hoffman."

"Oh, he will," Jake said. "He'll do anything to save his own skin."

"Speaking of saving skin," Annie put in. "My crazy husband almost got himself shot trying to save my skin."

Jake shrugged. "Better me than you. Besides, I knew if I could draw Hoffman's attention away, you guys might jump him. And you did. Perhaps you saved my skin."

"You might not be so lucky next time."

Jake grinned. "Yeah. Maybe not."

###

CPSIA information can be obtained
at www.ICGtesting.com
Printed in the USA
LVOW12s2317080916
503852LV00004B/166/P